A canoe approached the Allyns' landing. As the narrow craft drew closer, Elizabeth saw that it was paddled by a young shirt-sleeved man and that a much older man in a wide-brimmed black hat and grey coat sat in the bow.

If the old man was looking at the house, the young man certainly was not. He kept his eyes boldly fixed on her and when he smiled his teeth were startling white.

"Welcome to Part-of-Providence," Elizabeth said, remembering her manners.

"What did thee say?" the old man cried. "Part-of-Providence? What outlandish nonsense is that?"

"Now, Father," the younger man said soothingly. He turned to Elizabeth. "My father and I couldn't resist stopping off here to see the old place."

"Yes," the old man barked. "We wanted to look at *our* house—the house that was stolen from us!"

The Allyns of Alamance
is an original
Pocket Book edition.

Also by Carolyn MacDonald

Middlebend

Published by *Pocket Books*

 Are there paperbound books you want
but cannot find in your retail stores?

You can get any title in print in **POCKET BOOK** editions. Simply send retail price, local sales tax, if any, plus 25¢ to cover mailing and handling costs to:

MAIL SERVICE DEPARTMENT
POCKET BOOKS • A Division of Simon & Schuster, Inc.
1 West 39th Street • New York, New York 10018

Please send check or money order. We cannot be responsible for cash. *Catalogue sent free on request.*

Titles in this series are also available at discounts in quantity lots for industrial or sales-promotional use. For details write our Special Projects Agency: The Benjamin Company, Inc., 485 Madison Avenue, New York, N.Y. 10022.

The
Allyns
of
Alamance

by Carolyn MacDonald

PUBLISHED BY POCKET BOOKS NEW YORK

THE ALLYNS OF ALAMANCE

POCKET BOOK edition published August, 1971

This original POCKET BOOK edition is printed from
brand-new plates made from newly set, clear, easy-to-read type.
POCKET BOOK editions are published by POCKET BOOKS, a division of
Simon & Schuster, Inc., 630 Fifth Avenue, New York, N.Y. 10020.
Trademarks registered in the United States and other countries.

L

Chapter One

[1]

WHEN ELIZABETH Allyn got her first look at her new home on the Alamance, in the depths of North Carolina's Orange County, she gasped as though a fist had been driven into the pit of her stomach.

She knew then just how far she had come from her birthplace, Middlebend, the great and gracious plantation on the Chowan River. It was not the miles traveled, although there had been so many of those that she had sometimes despaired of ever leaving Nutbrown's saddle. More final were the unretraceable steps she had taken in departing a life in which the creature comforts and the social graces were taken for granted, and in which Allyn wealth and Allyn position had also been taken for granted.

On this dark, wet, chill December afternoon in 1764, three weeks before Christmas, she peered out from under the soggy brim of her canvas rain hat and heard her father say, "This must be the place."

"Aye, God help us all." her half brother, George, responded over his twin Philip's muttered curses against William Tryon, Lieutenant-Governor of the North Carolina Colony.

Elizabeth surveyed the wretched house, the jungle of briar- and sapling-choked fields. *I hate this place! I can't bear it! I'll die,* she said to herself.

So did she forget her thoughts of being the fifteen-year-old pillar of strength who would inspire her father, George, and Philip with her courage. So much for the frontier heroine who would fight off bears, panthers, and fierce Catawbas with pokers, axes, boiling water, and kitchen knives. Reining in her mare in the middle of reality, Elizabeth Allyn realized that she was a scared girl who wanted only to run someplace and hide.

She didn't belong here! She was no tough-as tawleather frontier woman "able to birth a brat at noon and chop wood for the supper fire." She was Elizabeth Allyn of Middlebend and all her life she had been pampered, trained to be a rich planter's lady, taught to read and write, and do sums and manage slaves. Nobody could expect her to change into a drudge just because William Tryon had exiled William Weyland Allyn to the end of nowhere. *It wasn't fair!*

But after a time she began to chide herself as a selfish chit. With new resolve, she forced herself out of the saddle, and sloshed along the muddy track to where Father and her brothers stood looking at their new home.

". . . smaller than I thought," Father was saying, "and in far worse disrepair."

George rubbed a hand over his square face. "At least we've got most of the winter ahead of us," he said. "We'll need the time to clear the fields."

"And build a house that's fit to live in," Philip added. "Surely that'll be first on your agenda."

George looked at the sagging ruin and shook his head slowly. "Nay, I'd say that's far down the list, brother. We can make do in that draughty place but the blacks can't stand the cold; they'd get the winter fever for sure if we put them in those old sheds. So first we'll have to build tight slave quarters and next we'll need stables and barns for the stock and—no, Philip, we won't be able to even start on a new house till next winter and maybe not then."

William Allyn's rigid stance suggested arrogance but his words when he spoke were full of self-pity.

"So this is what I brought us to because I did what I thought was right," he muttered. "Outcasts in a muddy swamp, we are, while cowardly scoundrels strut the streets of Edenton. And not a one who remembers what I did for him when he needed help."

Elizabeth winced at his despair and saw her half brothers flounder in surprise. During the long journey west it had been Father who had kept the others from giving in to useless regret, empty recrimination. He had been the one who had absolutely refused to play the sad game "if only" and always focused on the tasks that lay ahead.

"Now, sir," Philip began, uneasily, "you mustn't blame yourself."

"Nay, Father," George said huskily. "Things may not be as bad as they seem right now, the rain, the cold—wait till we build a fire and get some warm food in us."

"And wait till you see what Lis and I can do with this

house," Elizabeth said to her own surprise. "You won't believe it's the same place when we're finished."

Her father's haggard face swung toward her, his eyes empty, showing no response. She forced a smile to her stiff lips. "A mansion so fine that every ship that sails the Alamance will stop at our landing to marvel at it."

She didn't know what made her say it but she was pleased to hear the twins laugh out loud and to see her father's thin-lipped smile.

Little wonder. For of all the disappointments they had suffered that grim day, their first sight of the Alamance was the most shattering. After all they had heard of the Alamance, viewed close at hand it was no river at all; compared to the mighty Chowan they had left, it was a muddy trickle. They might call it the Alamance River back in Edenton—even Colonel Tryon had dignified it with that title—but hereabouts it was known as Great Alamance Creek. Elizabeth wondered at that "Great": if there was a Little Alamance it must be a tiny piddle, indeed.

It was not as though there were no real rivers in this part of the colony; they had had to cross half a dozen of them on their trek west, the Haw, the Saxapahaw, the Altamahaw and the others. With all those "haws," it didn't make much sense for easterners to call this "Alamance River Country."

She remembered the ultimatum that the elegant Lieutenant-Governor Tryon had delivered to her father in Middlebend's parlor. *For look you, sir, you have no alternative. On one hand, arrest, a mockery of a trial and the gibbet, your land seized, your children made paupers, if they don't suffer a worse fate, and all your enemies triumphant. On the other, removal to a fertile valley in a country that the geographer, Lawson, called "the flower of Carolina". . .*

The flower of Carolina? Elizabeth looked about her at the mud and dripping brambles, at the sluggish, roily creek, and wondered briefly whether it was Tryon or Lawson who had deliberately lied. But there was no time to ponder that, not if Father was to be kept from slipping back into his dangerous despondent state.

"If somebody will set a fire for me," she said brightly, "I'll see what I can do about supper. Dark will come early and if George has to set out at dawn to go back for the others, we have no time to stand here admiring the scenery."

After that, in spite of the leaky roof, the creatures that scurried in the loft and a bobcat's howling at midnight, things were never quite as bad as that first moment.

[2]

Thus did Elizabeth Allyn, so recently a privileged daughter of the Carolina colony's plantation aristocracy, reach the end of a torturous journey.

It had begun on June 14, 1764, some six months before when William Weyland Allyn, goaded into a fury by Rector Maule's heartless dickering over the baptism of his dying little son, Jeremy, reached for Maule's throat and tried to strangle him.

Maule did not die—although he never spoke again above a husky half whisper—but since that morning there had been nothing but misfortune for William Allyn and his family.

One catastrophe had followed another and the Allyns of Middlebend found themselves banished to a briar patch on Great Alamance Creek and grateful (or so William Tryon said they should be) that their father had not been hanged or beheaded for heresy.

That first night before exhaustion claimed her, Elizabeth lay on her pallet, praying for all of them but mostly for her mother. "Send her back to us, Lord," she whispered into her damp blankets. "Make her brave enough to defy her brothers and join Father again. For without her, I doubt he'll have the will to see this through."

She meant to mention the whole list of those for whom she pleaded God's grace, Becky, who lived in an even wilder place than this; Edward Dedshall who had pledged his word to come out and marry her as soon as he finished his law studies in Edenton; Edward's strange red-headed sister, Millie, who she supposed was her best friend; Louisa, Weyland Allyn's wife, and her new baby—and Weyland, too, of course, even though Philip had called him a traitor because he had stayed behind at Fairview, and . . . but the next thing she knew the dim, lemony sun was showing in the paneless windows. Slowly she forced her aching body up for the tasks that lay ahead.

While Elizabeth slept, William Weyland Allyn lay staring at the reflections of the fire on the ceiling. Sleep would not come for hours, no matter how saddle-sore his body or how heavy-laden his heart, and when it came it would be filled with such disturbing dreams that he would welcome the startled awakenings.

They're saying I fled like a coward, he thought, *but if it had been only I who suffered from my mad outburst I'd have stood and told them to do their worst. I gave in to Tryon only for the boys' sake, and Elizabeth's. And for Mary's sake, too.*

Ever since he had turned his back on Middlebend he had tried to convince himself that this was the truth but he had not yet been able to fully accept his own defense. After all, he had run to North Carolina from Virginia twenty years earlier in order to escape the persecution of the Church and the Royal Governor. Who would believe that he had not run to save his neck a second time?

Run to what? he asked himself, his wide eyes fixed on the flickering ceiling. *A peasant's existence in this muddy waste, trying to do it all over again, an empty hope on the face of it? To die, eventually, a broken and penniless old man, the laughingstock of these ignorant borderers who'll watch us fail and delight at the idea of the high and mighty William Weyland Allyn being brought to his knees?*

The arrogant William Weyland Allyn; aye, he had known that some thought of him that way—Ben Dedshall, for one, although he had kowtowed enough when Weyland had chosen his daughter, Louisa, for his wife—but most men of substance in the colony had respected him, admired him, and perhaps even liked him, when they sought his advice on matters political and agronomical.

And why shouldn't they? With his own hands and brains and will he had built the finest plantation in Chowan County. He had been the leader of the dauntless little band of Englishmen who had set down their roots there when it was still wild country, fighting off the Tuscaroras and river pirates and amassing fortunes from their tobacco and indigo yields. He had had the ear of Royal Governors and the agents of the Lord Proprietary, Baron Granville. When William Weyland Allyn spoke, they listened and nodded, all those ingrates who now shunned him lest they be linked with a priest-killer. Aye,

Maule might as well have died; the wrath of the church could not have been more virulent than it was now.

If Mary were only with me, he cried out silently. But if she had not deserted him in his hour of need, what then? Would life be more worth living if Mary Hughes Allyn lay beside him in this chill, smoky hut? No, for then his shame would be even harder to bear. Knowing that the young mother of Elizabeth and dead Jeremy slept warm and snug should ease his lot, not make it more bitter.

Elizabeth, poor child; would Edward Dedshall really come west to claim her for his wife, take her away from these hardships, as he had promised? Or would he show his Dedshall blood and go back on his pledged word?

If Edward proved to be a faithless swain he supposed Elizabeth would hate him for ruining her young life though he sometimes wondered if the child had any real regard for young Dedshall. She was a hard one to see through, that girl, nothing like her mother except in looks. More like him, if the truth were known. Well, she had better change her ways if she were like him: his standards had brought him to ruin.

Becky, now—but he was sworn never to think of Rebecca. Becky, Mary Richards Allyn's daughter, the beautiful, laughing girl who had held his heart in her two warm hands and then had crushed it to please that dog Harry Tarbell. When she had eloped with young Tarbell he had put her out of his life completely and he would never admit her again. He had had two daughters, now he had only one, and he could try to love this one as he once had loved the other.

He could be proud of his three sons. Before disaster struck, George had been known all over eastern Carolina for his innovations in planting and husbandry. Early in George's life, William Allyn learned not to shrug off an idea of his because it was unheard of; all but a very few of his daring experiments in agriculture, slave management, and stock-breeding had added to Middlebend's prosperity and renown.

Philip would surely have become a notable figure in the colony (and still might, Lord willing) had not the men who had turned against his father forced the boy's sponsor, Squire Reston, to dismiss him as his law clerk. God be thanked that William Tryon had really meant it when he promised to find another post for Phil in Childsborough; his son had already called on Squire Davis and the arrangement was set. It

wouldn't be Edenton but the boy had a fine mind, as well as
resilience and determination to succeed.

As for Weyland, the oldest, the son of Jessamyne Ardsley
Allyn, he would do all right in his steady, plodding way. His
brothers thought him a traitor for not coming into exile with
them, and William Allyn had trouble denying his own secret
disappointment at Weyland's decision to stay on the Chowan,
but common sense told him that his first son was right to
hold on to Fairview. If it pleased William Tryon to let Weyland stay on his plantation next to Middlebend with his red-
headed Louisa Dedshall Allyn and his three children, he
would have been a fool to sacrifice it for a noble gesture. And
Weyland was no fool: his father had brought him up not to be.

Philip had little hope of sleep when he first rolled himself
in his blankets on the rotting puncheon floor. He began to
think about Edenton's Green Ribbon Club, a supposedly
secret group of brash-mouthed law clerks and young would-be
politicos, and wonder if some of the things he had said at
those meetings were the real reason William Tryon had banished the family to this limbo on the Alamance.

There'll come a day, he swore to himself, *when North Car-
olinians will rise against Tryon and all those petty tyrants like
him. And leading them will be . . .* His thoughts were suddenly
lost in weariness. Philip dropped into sleep.

George began snoring as soon as he finished his brief
prayers. As he slept he might have dreamed: of Weyland's
redhaired wife or of his proud achievements in the life he'd
left behind at Middlebend, or even of tawny-skinned young
Yulee who was at the camp outside Childsborough with the
other slaves, or of some Edenton trull, or perhaps of his sister,
Rebecca, whose elopement with Harry Tarbell he might have
stopped if only he had taken her wild talk seriously.

Or perhaps he dreamed of nothing at all. Knowing the
back-breaking job ahead he may have closed his mind to such
frivolities.

[3]

Four days after their arrival on the Alamance, the Allyns
were joined by the first contingent of slaves. The others re-
mained in the charge of the overseer John Langhorn at the

fire-damaged grist mill outside Childsborough. The owner,
William Heinkle, had gladly rented Allyn the mill and outbuildings, since he had no plans to make any repairs until
spring and was happy to pick up a few guineas, plus the work
the slaves would do to make the place habitable.

William Weyland Allyn had brought eighty-two slaves with
him on the trek west after having given Weyland twenty-one
others, mostly young women and their small children, and
selling seventeen field hands to the traders who had flocked
to Middlebend like hungry buzzards as soon as word of the
move had spread. To assist them at the house on the Alamance
George brought Henry Langhorn, the overseer's gangling son,
old Lis, the tan-skinned Yulee, and fourteen black men. While
Elizabeth could have done very well without Yulee, the sight
of Lis, the woman who had raised her from a baby, provided
the lift her spirits needed.

"Don't look too close at what's to be done or you'll want
to go hide in the woods," she warned the old woman. "Did
you ever see such a rummage in your born days?"

Lis' rheumy eyes surveyed the squalor and Yulee wrinkled
her broad nose and sniffed. "You ain' spectin' to live heah, do
be?" she asked disdainfully. "Ain' fit fer a dawg let alone *my
folkses*, it ain't."

"Gel, hesh up," Lis snapped. "Liken dis don' suit, reckon
Ole Marster kin git yo some new folkses mighty quick." To
Elizabeth she said, "Ain' nuthin' so bad it kain't be fixed with
a li'l hot water and wukk, missy. You jus' leave it to Yulee and
me. Mebbe Marse Gawge, he bringin' down two-three othuhs
to help us, you askin' him, huh?"

Elizabeth shook her head. "No, he said he'd bring only
men to help him build the quarters and barns, at first, and
even when they're up he'll need whatever women he brings
down from Childborough to help clear the land of briars. For
awhile, you and Yulee will be the only house servants—and
me, of course."

Lis was visibly shocked. "Who say you bein' a servant,
missy? Marse Gawge, he just makin' jokes agin, is all."

The girl tried to make her laugh merry. " 'Tis no joke this
time, Lis. Things won't be like they were at Middlebend,
nothing at all. In time, they'll be even better but right now
it's root hog or die, Mister George says, for all of us."

Yulee sniffed again but was silenced by a swift look from

Lis. The old slave's eyes focused on the wooden bucket of water and the crude cane broom with which Elizabeth had been attacking the sagging floor, and jutted her chin. "No mattuh whut Marse Gawge say, you ain' gonner wukk lak ary nigguh, scrubbin' floors and tryin' to cook in 'at faarplace," she announced. "It ain' fitten, no way. Look at yo han's already, look at yo dress whar yo been honched down on yo knees. I tell you raat now, missy—"

If Yulee had not been there, Elizabeth might have tried to explain to Lis that her protests would serve only to add to Father's burden. But Yulee was there and almost openly sneering and so she had to interrupt Lis with a barked command.

"And I tell you right now—and you, too, Yulee—that I'm mistress of this place. I'll not be told what I can do and cannot do. You're the ones who'll be told that, and by me."

As Lis' jaw dropped she turned to the light-skinned wench and added, "As for you, if I get one more smirk or frown from you I'll have Mister George send you back to Childsborough —alone—and tell Mister Langhorn to sell you at the next market."

For a second she feared that Yulee would openly defy her (God only knew how far George would go in backing her against this wench who turned doe-eyed at the sight of him) but then the slave girl's eyes dropped and she dipped a curtsey. "Ain' mean t'smirk or frown, missy," she muttered. "Lis tell you Ah de ve'y hahdes' wukuh of alls back at Middlebend, liken Ah be heah, too."

"Hmph," the old woman grunted. "Ah don' recolleck you was all dat good at wukkin' but we find out fo suah befo' we gits dis place fit fer t'live in, huh?"

In the days that followed, Yulee made up for any former idleness with her dawn-to-dusk labors at the ramshackle new "manor house" on the Alamance. Elizabeth tried to think that she, in her new role as stern mistress, had brought on the transformation but she was pretty sure that it was Yulee's dread of being separated from "Marse Gawge" that made her such a zealous worker. She knew that she should not have such shameful thoughts but these uneasy suspicions were nothing new.

The job that the three women attempted seemed hopeless at times. George finally relented and sent Henry Langhorn

and two carpenter slaves to mend the floor and even young
Henry was appalled by his first glimpse of the interior.

"Phew, whoever was here before must've lived like pigs,"
he told Elizabeth. "Never saw such a hole. Y'r father sure
got swindled when Old Tryon swapped him evens, I'd say."

After nearly a fortnight of back-breaking toil, Elizabeth's
reply was frozen. "A hole, is it?" she asked. "You question
Mister Allyn's judgment, do you? I'm sure he'll be most in-
terested to hear your opinion, sir."

"Now, Betsy—Miss Elizabeth, you know I didn't mean
to—"

"It sounded to me that you meant it, criticism of *Mister
Allyn's* acumen, I mean. What else could you have meant?
Please do me the great favor of explaining your profound
remarks."

Henry's freckled face went fiery red, much as it used to
when she teased him as a child. "Aw, Betsy, I was only tryin'
to say I felt sorry f'r you, havin' to clean up this—"

"Sorry for me, pray?"

"No—I mean—well—aw, hell Betsy, you know."

"And cursing on top of everything else!" she said primly.

The boy who, at sixteen, stood nearly a head taller than
she, made another try, spluttered and flung himself off in
red-necked confusion. She watched him go, her weary anger
fading. Poor Henry. Less than a year had passed since the
day she had ridden Nutbrown down to the creek where
Henry sat, fishing for sea trout. A beautiful day with a soft,
salt-scented breeze coming up the creek from the Chowan,
a day made for dalliance—but she was sure, *positive*, that she
really had gotten something in her eye, something that stung
so much that she had dismounted to let Henry use her kerchief to take it out. Just what had happened after that wasn't
exactly clear, even now, but she had found herself in his
arms, feeding on his kisses, hoping he would never stop,
until Henry broke off the embrace.

There had been no more than a flickered, half embarrassed
exchange of glances since that day beside the creek. She
dimly wondered why there hadn't been more. Perhaps if
Father hadn't taken Jeremy to Rector Maule in Edenton, if
Edward Dedshall had not proved himself such a surprising
champion in the black days that followed, if William Tryon,
the handsome, haughty Lieutenant-Governor of the North

Carolina Colony, had not banished them all to this end-of-nowhere, if . . . there were so many *ifs* but that didn't change the fact that somehow Henry Langhorn was now the overseer's boy, a servant, and nothing more.

Thinking of Henry and that brief embrace on the creek bank reminded her of Millie Dedshall, Edward's thin, red-headed little sister. When she and Elizabeth had pledged their undying friendship, Millie had told of *her* first encounter with a boy, a royal frigate's midshipman who had jumped her back fence in Edenton to do far more than Henry had dared. Imagine anyone daring to loosen *her* ties and fondle *her* bosom. Just too scandalous, but Millie had grinned and predicted that when it happened to her she would neither scream nor swoon.

She wondered if Edward Dedshall would ever stop being a great gawk and seize her in his arms and . . . *To work, to work!*

Having the floor repaired helped and so did the hides that Henry's three-man gang pegged at the windows to keep out the worst of the chilling winds. Outside, the *chunkkk* of axes, the thrash and thud of falling pines and pinoaks, the rasp of saws, the rap of hammers driving in the oak pegs, provided a constant cacaphony.

The slave quarters went up with surprising speed. Everybody worked. Even Philip who freely admitted he didn't know one end of a sickle from the other rolled up his sleeves and worked side-by-side with the field hands, chopping away the stubborn second growth that covered the fields they hoped to start planting, come spring.

"You should be up in Childsborough, keeping on with your law," William Allyn fretted, almost every sundown when Philip staggered in, blistered, and sweat-soaked. "After Colonel Tryon went to the trouble of arranging that post, you'll seem ungrateful by y'r delay in attaching y'rself to the squire."

"Tryon's already been repaid tenfold for any trouble he went to," Philip replied darkly. "When we passed through Childsborough and I called on the squire, the old man nearly wrung my hand off. He said he was overjoyed to meet the new clerk that Colonel Tryon had promised him, after waiting all these months. I'll wager our esteemed Lieutenant-Governor extorted a handsome 'token of appreciation,' as he prefers to call 'em, for sending me to Davis. Or p'raps 'twas Fanning, the County Register, who did the extorting; they say he's Tryon's swagman in Orange County."

Big George, sprawled beside the fireplace sipping his evening cup of rum, barked with laughter. "Ho, I see our firebrand ain't been cooled any by our change of residence, Father—he's already picked a new target, this man Fanning."

William Weyland Allyn shook his head, "I pray to God he's cooled," he replied. "More trouble from the Green Ribbon Club or its like and we'll find ourselves in the Cherokee mountains." He sipped from his glass and added, "And that, I fear, w'ld be too much for me to bear."

"You have no reason to concern yourself," Philip said stiffly. "I'll hardly forget that Tryon made us all swear a new oath of fealty to the king and all his officers, great and small— even colonials—before he opened that great heart of his and bestowed on us this—this part of Providence."

Elizabeth saw her father's taut face cloud and spoke quickly. A supper of venison and mush was bad enough without making it worse with acrimony. "Part of Providence," she exclaimed. "There you are, George. You said the other day this place needed a name."

Her half brother started to laugh, then caught Elizabeth's eye. "Why that might do fine," he said. "I had rather fancied 'Richlands' because whatever else can be said of this Alamance estate, the land's so rich a peeled stick would sprout overnight, but Part of Providence? Why not?"

He tried the name for its feel on his tongue. "Part of Providence—what d'ye think, Father?"

William Allyn looked suspiciously from George to Elizabeth, seeking some indication of derision. When he read the silent appeal in his daughter's eyes, he nodded slowly. "Why, 'twill suit, if it's not intended to be irreverent. For, after all, it may have been the hand of Providence that set me down here 'stead of on the block or the gibbet."

"More than that," George said heartily, "before we're through here 'twill truly be a heav'nly place." He hoisted his cup of rum. "I pledge you all that before—what day's today, Phil? I've lost all count."

"Without looking it up on my calendar—wherever that is— I'd say today's—why, God in heaven, this must be Christmas Eve!"

So was the Allyn plantation on the Alamance named Part-of-Providence on Christmas Eve, 1764.

And on the following day, which William Allyn insisted must be a holiday (for all but Elizabeth, Lis, and Yulee who had the task of plucking, dressing, and roasting nine big turkeys that George shot at dawn for the occasion) John Langhorn came riding down from Childsborough with a surprise that made it the most memorable Christmas in Elizabeth's whole existence.

Hearing the hounds' clamor, Philip left the crowded table to see what was happening. His high, cracked shout brought Elizabeth and all the others to their feet.

"Becky! Oh, Becky, God bless ye for coming home!"

[4]

Elizabeth's first thought, as she was pushed through the doorway by George's thunderous rush, was that Philip had made a terrible mistake. The old woman in ragged linsey-woolsey and deerskin cloak who slid down from her bony nag into Philip's arms couldn't be Becky! Not Rebecca the beautiful, Rebecca the laughing golden girl who had been her confidant when she was growing up.

But Philip knew it was Becky and so did George. Then Elizabeth saw her smile. Even her missing teeth could not dim Becky's smile, so she scurried to embrace her long-lost sister.

"Oh, Becky, Becky," she sobbed. "Don't leave me again. Promise you won't—it'd break my heart." She wondered why she was weeping when she had never been so happy, never.

"Betsy, Betsy," she heard her half sister murmur, "lawks, how ye've growed." The warmth was still there, the love outpouring, even though this Becky smelled of woodsmoke and horse instead of lavender.

Then Elizabeth was gently pushed away as Rebecca turned to face the tall, spare figure who looked down at her from the porch. Silence descended. The dogs stopped their excited barking and even the slaves at their Christmas feast in the quarters were still. A cold wind passed high in the pines and

its thin whistle was the only sound. Finally, William Weyland
Allyn spoke.

"So ye've come back again, I see."

*Oh, Father, she's so tired and it's Christmas Day! Can't
you show her you love her and want her here with the rest
of us?*

Rebecca's voice had its own flinty edges. "Aye, if I'm welcome." The upthrust of her chin indicated that she did not
expect to beg.

"How did ye find us here?" her father asked after a pause.

Elizabeth's heart melted when she saw the familiar dimple
in Becky's weatherbeaten cheek. "Why, 'twould take a fortni't
to explain it all and I'm fair faintin' from the smell of that
good food—Mister Langhorn must be, too. Will ye ask us in?"

Her father's austere bow and the slight gesture his hand
made toward the door was more than she had hoped for. "Of
course," William Allyn said. He looked beyond Rebecca to
Langhorn, still in the saddle as though he, too, had been
uncertain of his reception. "Come down and join us, Mister
Langhorn." He paused. "I thank you for bringing Mistress—
Dame Tarbell to us on Christmas Day when you ought to be
with your own family."

Langhorn smiled. "Why, bless ye, sir, my woman was almost as anxious as Mistress Becky that I bring her to ye on
Christmas."

He dropped out of his saddle and tossed both horses' lines
to his son, Henry. "Feed 'em but not too much at once," he
ordered brusquely. "They done noble over that deer track ye
call a road."

Chapter Two

[1]

REBECCA'S STORY came out in bits and pieces over the
months that followed but on that Christmas Day of 1764 she
gave them most of the important and sometimes painful facts.

She told them that she had ridden into a settlement called

Cedar Valley, not far from Childsborough, following the Old
Trading Path from the savage mountains, on her way back
to Chowan County, and had been befriended by a borderer
family of Scots named Hoag.

"The nag I'd ridden from Bee Cove went lame and I was
at the end of my tether," she explained, the color beginning
to flow back into her gaunt face. "I'd walked more than I'd
ridden for three days so my footgear was in shreds. I'd used
up my food and I was coughin' fit to scare a panther. But
they took me in as though I was Lady Granville, herself."
Her light voice went solemn for a moment as she said,

"I'll never say my prayers again without puttin' the Hoags
at the top of my list."

She fell silent and they waited. When Rebecca found her
voice she used the familiar laughing tone that made light of
all her tribulations.

"I laid abed for three or four days and then, when I tried
to move on they made me stay longer even though they had
scurse enough to feed themselves. Mister Hoag searched about
till he found somebody willin' to trade even f'r my horse. He
said a little doctorin' w'ld make her sound again and I had to
believe him; I doubt he'd lie to 'scape the Devil, not Alan
Hoag.

"Then one Sunday they came back from church all in a
twitch. It seems their priest, or whatever Presbyterians call
'em, had heard that William Weyland Allyn and his family
had lately moved to these parts and were livin' on Alamance
Creek while their great host of slaves were camped at Childsborough."

Elizabeth could not repress a question. "Did'st hear this
pastor's name, Becky?"

The blue eyes found hers down the table. "Better than that.
He came to the Hoags' next day and talked with me. His
name's MacCutcheon and, aye"—her eyes moved to her
father—"he told me of Jeremy and somethin' of y'r troubles,
sir."

William Allyn bowed gravely. "He's a good man, Mac-
Cutcheon," he said. "I'm glad all's well with him."

Becky's mouth quirked. "How well things are with him is
open to some question. A more ragged priest I never met, not
even the missionaries in the mountains. But I agree with all

my heart; he *is* a good man. He wasted little time prayin' over me; instead, he got his people to fix me up with some good clothes and got one of 'em, a man named Duguid, to escort me to Childsborough to make sure I'd be safe—from what, I dinna ken, seein' it was a short ride and an easy one to the place where I found Langhorn. He left his family on Christmas, as ye know, and here I am."

She yawned and looked down at her plate, still piled with food although she had said she was ravenous. "Ye'll excuse me if I save this till later," she murmured. "I find my belly needs some time to get accustomed to such rich fare."

"You must be weary," her father said. "Do you wish to retire, ye'll be forgiven, Dame Tarbell."

George spoke quickly, possibly to take some of the chill off the way his father had spoken her name. "Aye, Becky, ye must have been through a devil of a time and from y'r looks ye need to sleep f'r a week. Ye can have Betsy's bed till we knock one together f'r ye, can't she, Betsy?"

"Of course," Elizabeth said. "She can have everything I've got."

"Now that our sister's come home you'll surely build a respectable house right away, won't you, George?" Philip put in. "You can't expect Rebecca to live in this pigsty."

"Hoity-toity, Philip, after some of the places I've been livin' in the last few years, this is a castle. George, whatever ye've planned, I'll not let ye change it a whit for me—even if ye would." Her full mouth went up at the corners. "Which I doubt, rememberin' the way ye rode roughshod over me when we were growin' up."

Elizabeth thrust away the pang of jealousy she had felt when Philip had proposed a new house for *Becky* after not giving a thought to *her* comfort. "Mayhap you can put on a new ell, George, or finish off the loft so Becky can have—"

"Nay, there'll be no prettyin' up the house till our first crop's in," George broke in harshly. "Now get off to bed with ye, Becky, before I change my mind and put ye to work even though 'tis Christmas Day."

Before his sister could argue, he turned to John Langhorn. "Ye'll spend the night, of course, John, so before it gets too dark let me show you what we've done so far with our fair savannah, eh? Betsy, show y'r sister to y'r room and come straight down again, d'ye hear? No plaguing her with questions. They c'n wait till later."

Elizabeth slipped out of her chair and went to Rebecca's side, holding out her hand. As they left the room she caught a glimpse of her father sitting at the head of the table, his grey eyes on his mug of toddy. In other days it would have been William Weyland Allyn who gave the directions, but now, more and more it was George who acted as head of the family.

The narrow stairs to the second floor had been patched and strengthened but they still creaked alarmingly as she led Becky up to her cold, little room under the eaves. She had a bed of sorts—a narrow wooden frame with rope laces, a pile of quilts brought down from Childsborough, and a bearskin throw.

"Pure heaven," Becky exclaimed when she saw it. "I hate to turn you out, little sister, but ye'll never know what a real bed can mean till ye've been without one as long as I have."

"You can have anything I've got, Becky," the girl said fervently. She tiptoed to the door and cocked an ear. Downstairs, they were all talking at once so she turned back and asked in a hushed voice, "Becky, tell me about—"

"Can't it wait till later?" Rebecca broke in, trying to smother a yawn. "God knows there's a deal of questions I have, too— about y'r mother and what happened 'twixt Father and that priest in Edenton—but I'm plumb wore out, I vow."

"Just this one question. Ian MacCutcheon—he's well?"

Rebecca's eyebrows went up. "Oho! What's this? Y'r voice fair trembled when ye asked after the ragged parson's health. Just what did happen at Jeremy's funeral—or have ye managed to see him since then?"

"Oh, hush your nonsense." Elizabeth felt her face flame. "I only saw him that once and I was so heartbroken then over Jeremy that I scarce remember what he looks like."

Her half sister lowered herself to the narrow bed with a groan and bent to pull her scarred shoes from her feet. Elizabeth hurried to her side, knelt, and pulled the shoes off, then helped Becky strip the thick, darned stockings down the long legs.

"Ahhh, thankee, Betts. 'Tis like I ain't been out of 'em f'r years." She leaned forward, pulled out a few horn pins and let her gray-streaked hair hang loose, shrouding her face. "As soon as I finish sleepin', I'll spend another fortni't or so washin'. Who knows, I may someday scrub myself clean again, eh?"

"Tell me about Ian MacCutcheon, do," Elizabeth urged impatiently.

Becky yawned again and dropped back on the bed. "What about him? He's poor as Job's turkey like all the rest of 'em up there. He speaks a language that ain't exactly Catawba but it surely ain't the king's English, either. He wears clothes I'd say were stolen from some scarecrow if he wasn't a Presbyterian priest and if they could spare old clothes to put on scarecrows." She saw Elizabeth's distress and spoke in a gentler tone. "Bless ye, child, I know naught about y'r preacher save he was uncommon kind to me, as they all were."

"Did he—did he mention my name?" *Fool, fool, of course he didn't!*

Rebecca's head stirred on the pillow with a nod. "Why, sure, he named all of ye when I asked after ye. He said— that's right, I remember now—he said he heard ye were married since he was at Middlebend." She looked at Elizabeth with curiosity. "He was wrong, wasn't he, Betsy? Ye weren't married and widowed, too, were ye? Or did Father drive y'r man away because he wasn't good enough f'r an Allyn?"

"No, no, of course not. I'm pledged to marry Edward Dedshall, Louisa's brother, but we're not married."

"Why ain't he here?" the woman on the bed murmured drowsily.

"He's finishing his law studies with Squire Reston in Edenton. As soon as he can, he's coming out here and. . . ." Elizabeth stopped talking as Rebecca's mouth sagged and a faint snore purred at the back of her throat.

Well, of all the rude, mannerless. . . . But she's worn out, poor Becky. She stood beside the bed looking down at the sleeping woman, remembering her as she had last seen her, beautiful and full of life, and wondered what story she would tell to explain the change. Rebecca's breasts were still full under the coarse gown but now they drooped as though they had nursed babies, yet she had not spoken of children any more than she had mentioned Harry Tarbell.

What had happened to Harry, the red-faced, sandy-thatched young man who had stolen Becky away from Mid-

dlebend? *Ye weren't married and widowed,* too, *were ye?* So
Harry must be dead but he must have really married Becky,
not just carried her off for—his pleasure. By the looks of
Becky, there hadn't been much pleasure in the five years since
she'd run off. But mayhap they had been happy years and
the haggardness apparent now was stamped there by the
tragedy that had robbed her of her dear Harry.

Elizabeth threw the bearskin over her half sister, resisting
the impulse to waken her so she could get out of those smelly
clothes. It was more important that she sleep now and, besides, she doubted that Becky's tiny pack contained a night-
dress and her own would never fit her since she was such a
skinny thing.

But beginning to fill out in the right places, she could not
help but notice lately. By the time Edward came for her. . . .

When she went downstairs again, George was gone with
John Langhorn and Henry. Lis and Yulee were out back at
the wash bench, scouring the dishes. Father sat at one side
of the fireplace, nursing a cup in his long hands. Phil was
slumped in a chair on the other side, his fingers laced over
his front, staring at the fire. He glanced at her as she headed
for the door to help the two slaves out back but Father did
not raise his head.

"Is she all right?" Philip asked in a low voice.

"Aye," she said cheerfully, "but she hardly got her shoes
off before she fell asleep. So don't ask me what she said—
'twas nothing."

Philip looked across the hearth at his father. "You'll let her
stay," he said. It was not neither a question nor a command
and Elizabeth held her breath, waiting for her father's response. Then she let her breath out in a sigh as William Weyland Allyn nodded.

"So long as she wants to," he said quietly. "I suppose that
when she's rested she'll go on to Harbor Oaks, the Tarbells'
place."

"Why would she want to go there?" Philip asked. He spoke
in a low voice as though Becky might overhear.

Allyn puffed on his churchwarden and said steadily, "Why,
because Harbor Oaks is a fine plantation, Philip; because
when a woman marries she leaves her own people and cleaves
to her husband's; because we have little that's homely to offer

her here, and because Dame Tarbell was always a woman who loved her little luxuries more than aught else."

"Stop calling her Dame Tarbell," Elizabeth said tartly. "It's Rebecca, Becky, and I should think you'd—" She pulled up short as her father's eyes fixed hers. Flustered, she stammered, "I mean, it—it was so long ago and she—she's been hurt so bad, Father. Cans't forgive her, on Christmas Day?"

"Don't you have duties that require your attention?" he asked. "If not, be good enough to retire someplace where you'll not interfere."

She wanted to protest but realized it would only make it harder on Rebecca, so she nodded, dipped a curtsey to the old man by the fire and murmured sweetly, "Yes, Father, of course I always have chores a-plenty waiting for me, as you must know, so if you'll excuse me, you and Philip. . . ." She snatched a cloak from a peg and left. The trouble with ill-fitting doors on thick leather hinges was that they couldn't be slammed. Not that she would have dared.

Outside, she went to the wash bench where Lis worked alone, cleaning up the few remaining dishes. "I done sent Yulee down to the quartuhs," the old woman explained before Elizabeth could ask. "She so twitchin' t'git down dar and tell'em 'bout Mizz Becky she warn't no good heah, nohow, and, besides, it's Chris'mus Day."

As the girl stepped in to help her, Lis pushed her aside. "Naw, naw, ain' but a few and you stay with Mizz Becky, chile."

"She's resting. She fell asleep before I could ask her a single thing about what happened."

"Ain' been good, none of it, looks lak." Lis heaved a ponderous sigh. "Fur diff'runt heah f'm what 'twas when she lef', too, fur diff'runt." Then without warning, the old black woman raised her head and laughed. "Jes' thinkin' 'bout dat ole fool, Mornin'star, back yonduh," she explained. "Set he'se'f up fer de goodest conjuh man in Ca'lina, he did. Had de nigguhs doin' mos' of he wukk fer t'gits good fawtune f'm de signs. Buck name Joe-Dan, he give old Mornin'star he share of white sugah gift las' Chris'mus iffen Mornin'star tell'm whar he be *dis* Chris'mus. So Mornin'star say he be at Middlebend, acco'se, on'y he be a house servant 'stead of a field hand."

She laughed again. "So now Joe-Dan, he sold away to

Gawgia and Mornin'star, he even wuss off—he breakin' he wuthless back fer Marse Weyland at Fairview."

"Why, Lis," Elizabeth protested, "Mister Weyland's no slave-driver."

"No, missy, he ain' no bad marstuh but same time, he ain' no Marse Gawge, neithuh. Marse Gawge, he put up wid Mornin'star's foolishmints 'cause he figguh a plantation's bound to have a conjuh man 'mongst the hands, sure as a midwife. But Marse Weyland, he tell de hands dey gotter find dey own signs in de catfish innards and Mornin'star, he been choppin' faarwood twill he back feel lak it broke evvuh sence he went to Fairview." She laughed again. " 'Twouldn't surprise me none iffen he out dere swingin' he axe on Chris'mus Day."

Elizabeth picked up a plate and wiped it dry. "You're making this up," she accused. "It's just what you hope happened to Morningstar because you two never got along."

Lis chuckled as she handed the girl another dish. "Ain' makin' up nothin'. Ah knows."

"But how could you know? We've had not a single word from back there since we left."

"Ah knows," Lis said stubbornly. Elizabeth almost believed her. The blacks' mysterious lines of communication had surprised her more than once so she was not ready to dismiss Lis's claim lightly. Instead she said, "Well, if you know so much, tell me, what's Mister Edward doing this fine Christmas Day?"

"How sh'ld Ah know?" Lis grumbled, scowling. "Marse Edward's 'way back dar in Edenton."

"But Morningstar's 'way back there in Fairview. What's the difference?"

"Ah still knows folkses in Fairview," the old woman explained with calm dignity. "On'y folkses Ah evvuh seed in Edenton war de quality."

Elizabeth picked up a pewter mug. "Then I don't suppose you know anything about Mister MacCutcheon, either," she said idly.

"Co'se not, Ah ain' no witchwomans, chile." She ran her hand around the bottom of the wooden tub. "Ah'll say one thing 'bout de preachermans, though, an' you won' lak it. It's best you remembers day an' night you is gone marry Marse Edward 'stead of thinkin' how handsome Marse MacCutcheon

look when you dress him in yo' mind with silk britches and
set a powduh'd wig on he haid."

"I've never done any such things," Elizabeth cried. "Of all
the silly things I've ever heard! I met him just that once so
why in the world would I even give him a thought?"

"You jes' did, didn't you?"

"Only because Miss Becky said he helped her find us here.
I was surprised that he even remembered being at Middlebend."

She stepped forward as the old black woman strained to
lift the heavy tub. Pushing Lis aside, she grasped the worn
rope handles and tilted the tub into the waste trough that ran
down to the creek. Mud leaped from the soggy ground, clotted the hem of her gown, and splattered her shoes, but she
paid no heed; even on this most festive day of the year she
had not opened the box where lay her Middlebend finery.

"Ain' fitten you do dat," Lis said automatically: she had
about given up trying to keep her mistress in her proper
place. "Ah tells you 'nothuh thing you won' lak," she went
on in a lowered voice. "Lessen you stan' up fo' yo rights, you
liken t'find yo'se'f 'nothuh house servant 'round heah while
Mizz Becky, she taken ovvuh as mist'ess of dis place."

"Lis!"

The old woman pushed out her lower lip. "Kain't he'p it,"
she said. "Yo're mah chile twell Mizz Mary come back an' I
ain' gone stand silent while *she* walk in an' tek away what's
yours by rights. An' she'll do it, too. She'll get her brothuhs
eatin' outta her han' befo' you kin wring a chicken an' Ole
Marstuh, he ain' gone stan' off long, no mattuh how hahd a
face he turn on her now."

"Lis, that's a horrid thing to say," Elizabeth managed in a
smothered voice. "Poor Becky's just got here and you say—
why, she *can* be mistress here if she wants to. It'd be the
happiest thing that ever happened to me if Father forgave
her and—and put her in charge of everything.

"That's a terrible way to welcome her home," she went on.
"I'll forget what you said because—because it's Christmas
but don't ever let me hear you say such a thing again."

"No, Mizz 'Lizabeth," Lis said, without contrition. "I'se
sorry, 'deed Ah is. Iffen yo mama was heah she tellin' you de
same thing but ain't fitten fo' ole Lis to talk about mah folkses

dataway, even on Chris'mus." She hung a rag towel over a peg and shuffled off, humming tunelessly.

Elizabeth watched her go, still stung by the reminder that her mother was not there. Till now she had succeeded in keeping all thoughts of her mother out of her mind but now her mother's image rose before her and the tears misted her eyes without warning.

Mother, will I ever see you again? Do you love me so little that you can stay in Virginia and forget I ever lived?

[2]

Rather than go back inside with her sorrow, Elizabeth huddled into her warm cape and set off down the creekbank. George had speculated that the path she followed was an old Indian trail.

In the fantasies Elizabeth had concocted about the life she would lead in the Alamance country, she had always cast herself as a heroine who won everybody's admiration with her cool bravery in the face of savage Indian raids. The journey west from the Chowan had punctured these fine dreams, not because Elizabeth was less brave but because the Indians were less fierce. A great deal less fierce—wretched beggars, in fact.

After all the stories she had heard, Elizabeth's first glimpse of real, live Indians was a jarring let-down. Philip had explained that they were "tame" Indians, derelicts from small tribes that had been decimated by war and the pox. The stronger tribes, he said, had moved to the western mountains where they still chopped off white settlers' heads and burned their cabins whenever the bloody whim seized them.

After their arrival on the Alamance, George had met a small hunting party while hacking a path toward their western boundary line but that had been the Allyns' only encounter with Indians. Not even one canoe had passed up or down the Alamance although there was no reason why the stream should not serve as a waterway to the Haw River and thence up to the trading post at Childsborough.

"I tried to find out something about the Injuns hereabouts," George had reported after his one encounter, "but all I got were grunts and headshakes and a lot of hand motions that looked like they were beggin' f'r somethin', I never found out what. After a lot of this foolery, off they went with the deer they'd killed slung from a pole they carried on their shoulders."

"Did they wear feathers and painted faces?" Elizabeth asked.

"One or two of 'em had feathers stuck in their hair but they weren't painted. They were a seedy lot, though better lookin' than those we saw on the way here."

"Too bad they didn't understand you," William Allyn had put in. "If they had, mayhap we'd find out what the name Alamance means, for it surely must be an Indian word for something."

"I thought I told you," Philip said, "when I stopped in to see Squire Davis at Childsborough I asked him what the name meant. Or p'raps he brought it up himself; I can't remember which way it was. He's a talkative old gentleman and it seemed he hated to let me go, so fearful was he that I wouldn't be back, I guess, so he kept bringing up things to talk about and keeping me there with him."

"Never mind the squire's loquacity," his father said. "What about the name, Alamance?"

Philip wrinkled his forehead. "As I recall, he said it came from the Saxapahaw or Sissipahaw word 'alemons.' He said it meant 'swift water' and since I hadn't yet seen the mighty Alamance I didn't laugh in his face."

"Philip, I find it most disturbing for you to regard Squire Davis as some humorous bumpkin," William Weyland Allyn said severely. "You must remember that—"

"Oh, I do, I do," Philip said. "He's a friendly old gentleman and if his law library ain't exactly equal to the Inns of Court, why, then I'll make up for my lack of reading with my own inborn brilliance, eh?"

Elizabeth spoke quickly, before her father could become too nettled. "Saxapahaw?" she asked. "Were they part of the Tuscaroras that you drove away from Middlebend?"

Allyn's frown relaxed. No matter how often he told his younger daughter that he had played a very minor role in the Tuscarora War, Elizabeth had always insisted that he was captain of all the North Carolina troops. "Nay, daughter," he replied. "Far from being part of the Tuscarora band, the Saxapahaws were the settlers' allies, as I remember. And because of that the Tuscaroras killed the Saxapahaws, down

to the last man, before making their great exodus north to join
the tribes that were warring 'gainst us on the side of the
French at that time."

"Which proves that turnin' one's coat 'gainst one's own
kind never pays, eh?" George asked.

"Not exactly. For as I heard it, the Sissipahaws stoutly refused to aid the borderers 'gainst their Tuscarora brothers—
and so the Tuscaroras wiped them out, too, whilst they were
about it."

Philip laughed. "In that case, I guess the only point that's
proven here, *ipse dixit*, is that it's bad luck to be an Indian
who lives in the same vicinity when the Tuscaroras go to war."

Now, on this Christmas Day, when she had no reason to
fear Indians, Elizabeth let her thoughts turn to her mother
and the strange misadventure, that had robbed the family
of Mary Hughes Allyn at a time when she was needed most.

She had sailed from Edenton on the *Gryphon* while Rector
Daniel Maule still hung between life and death and while
Father was under his pledge to Governor Dobbs to appear
before either a church or crown court when summoned. Since
that dire day when little Jeremy had died and her husband
had nearly strangled the priest who demanded an extortionate
price for baptizing him, Mary Allyn had kept to her room,
blaming herself for insisting that her little son be taken to
Edenton for baptismal, as sick as he was.

Elizabeth had had to take over the running of Middlebend
and, indeed, the family had secretly despaired of Mary Allyn's
mind, so it was little wonder that they had hailed the change
that had come with the letter from Virginia. When she told
them that her father, Thomas Hughes, Esquire, of Rose Hill
on the Rappahannock, had sent word that he wanted to see
her once more before he died and that she must go to him,
she seemed almost like her old self.

Elizabeth had been shocked by her mother's blithe disregard of her husband's situation. But when she had spoken
of it, her mother had said he was better off without her there
to be a millstone about his neck, always sobbing and expecting the worst. Besides, she said, she would be back long
before the trial, she was only going to Virginia, not the end
of the earth. Finally she suggested that Elizabeth ask her

father if he, himself, had not strongly advised her to make the trip.

So off she had gone, with Lis and Nappy Langhorn, the overseer's half grown daughter, to look after her. The last Elizabeth had seen of her mother was when she had boarded the Middlebend sloop, *Primrose*, at the plantation landing for the voyage down the Chowan to Edenton. Mary Allyn had not turned to wave as she bent to enter *Primrose's* little cabin; her farewell had been said earlier, on the dock, when she had hugged her and whispered, "It's for the best, always remember that." And then: "May God bless you, sweetling, forever and ever."

I should have gone with her, Elizabeth thought now, recalling the scene.

She turned off the path, her tears hot, then turning cold on her cheeks. She brushed a hand across her eyes, found a flat rock, and sat down. She let herself weep for a while then straightened, sniffed back her tears and used the hem of the old cloak to dry her face. As if to help her regain control, a muskrat bobbed above the creek's surface near the other shore, wedged its way cross-current toward her and then, when she moved, dove in a swirl of water.

Perhaps she would tell George what she had seen and have him trap enough for a fine, warm robe. But, if he did that he'd give the skins to Becky, not her. Becky was after all his real sister.

Now that Becky was back there would be no more of George's little kindnesses. And Philip—why, he had looked at his sister with the eyes of a man in love! She might as well bid Philip farewell for always. No, it was as Lis had said, from now on she would be nothing but a drudge.

She felt the tears coming to her eyes and then loudly remonstrated herself. "Betsy Allyn, you're a sniveling fool, sitting out here in the cold, weeping on Christmas Day!"

Her words sent a rabbit bouncing out of its hiding place almost at her feet and when her heart dropped back to her chest she felt better. Again, her thoughts returned to her mother.

Mary Hughes Allyn had been gone almost a month before Father had received his first word of her desertion. In Edenton on another matter (Elizabeth suspected it had been the sealing of the marriage contract between herself and Edward

Dedshall) he had been told by the harbor master that a small coaster's captain had brought a message sent from Walter Hughes, her mother's brother, saying that Mother would stay in Virginia "until her health improved."

Of course William Weyland Allyn's first impulse had been to sail for the Rappahannock to find out what was happening. His sons had dissuaded him by reminding him, first, that he was pledged to keep himself available for summons on the Maule affair and, secondly, that he was under interdiction in Virginia where his enemies might still thirst for his blood. In fact, as they debated the situation, the men of the family agreed that Mother's father was probably dead and that her brothers had staged the whole affair at the urging of Virginia colonial and church authorities who wanted Allyn brought to trial there for past offenses, real or trothless.

Nappy and Lis had finally come back to Edenton by coach, but they were unable to shed much light on the affair. They had been met by Walter Hughes at the quay in Norfolk and immediately separated from their mistress. After more than a fortnight's stay in a mean waterfront hostelry, they had been put aboard the New Berne coach by a brusque stranger for the trip back to Middlebend.

Elizabeth had been present when William Tryon had promised to use his offices to wrest Mary Hughes Allyn from her brothers' hands. But she also had witnessed Father's cold response to the Lieutenant Governor's proposal. Even in such a dire extremity, William Weyland Allyn could abide no outside interference with an Allyn family problem.

Perhaps, she told herself, when Edward came out to claim her and they were married, he would take her to Virginia. The Dedshalls were under no interdiction at Williamsburg and the ogre, Walter Hughes, would hardly dare harm Dame Elizabeth Dedshall, daughter-in-law of Lord Carteret, Baron Granville's bailiff at Edenton.

She nibbled on a twig and saw herself stepping from a canopied barge onto the Rose Hill landing, Edward at her side. In her vision, he became seven feet tall, wide-shouldered and somehow clad in a cuirass with plumed helmet. His appearance would be enough to cow even the haughtiest Hughes brother.

"Mother," she heard herself say imperiously, "have your box brought here instanter—or better yet burn everything a Hughes has touched. Come with us and never fear; the king's navy lies just 'round the bend with forty thousand brave men ready to assault this evil bastion should these vile catiffs try to stop you."

"Aye, madam," Edward said in the deep, rolling voice of command, "and when you're safe away I mean to call out every vile catiff mixed up in this plot and run them through the liver, one at a time or all together, it matters not a whit for I'm the best swordsman in the colonies and I. . . ."

No good. She had overstepped the bounds of her own imagination, as sometimes happened. If she had left Edward aboard the canopied barge it might have worked, but no, she had been greedy and had clad her beanpole swain in a cuirass and given him a deep voice and made him utter heroics that he could no more manage than a pig could fly.

"But he was a hero once, remember that," she told herself aloud.

Aye, even Philip, who had despised poor Edward, was impressed by her beloved's intentions if not by his success, the one time he had shown his true colors. It was when William Tryon had invaded Middlebend with two bargeloads of soldiers and sailors, choosing a time when Father and Philip were in Edenton. It had been up to her to meet the great villain at the landing, George being miles away at the furtherest boundary of the plantation, and she had done this bravely, she hoped, even though she had been close to wetting herself with her fright.

But she was thinking of Edward's heroism: Father and Philip were hove to in the *Primrose* in a thick fog when Edward came along, trying to skull a broken-masted skiff with his one remaining oar. Edward had known naught about sailing, and yet he had set sail for Middlebend to rescue her from Colonel Tryon. Even the monster, Tryon, himself, had been overwhelmed by the thought.

When they were married. . . .

Elizabeth wished she could believe that she was going to become Edward Dedshall's wife. She, who usually was so adept at making-believe, could not—*she just could not!*—imagine herself in Edward Dedshall's arms, in his bed, suffering Edward Dedshall to perform on *her* the incredible act of love.

Well, perhaps not incredible because she had spent all of

her years on a big plantation where the most careful guard could not keep her from glimpsing animals and barnyard fowls at their mating. And once she had accidentally happened upon a wench and her man in a roadside ditch, oblivious to aught but their own fever. So she knew what would be expected of her when Edward married her. She would not flinch—indeed, if her response to Henry Langhorn's kisses meant anything, she might pant and gasp as much as the wench had.

But she doubted it, no matter what Becky had told her before she ran away with Harry Tarbell. Perhaps she was cold-spirited—but no, she had Henry to prove she wasn't. But with *Edward!* Ah, she hoped there would be some magic transformation when he claimed his rights because, after all, he deserved better than a cold wife.

She told herself, these were fine thoughts for a maid on Christmas Day!

She got up, walked to the creek bank and threw the twig she had been chewing into the water. She stood there a moment, watching it revolve slowly in a little eddy, then glide off and disappear around a bend. She wondered where the twig would go if it managed to float free, escaping entanglements. She found that she actually knew little of the waterways thereabouts. The Alamance flowed southeastward into the Haw River and the Haw—perhaps it joined the Chowan somewhere in the distance. Mayhap some miracle would carry the twig into Edenton Bay and it would somehow give a message to Edward Dedshall, reminding him that he was betrothed to a girl who pined for him every minute of the day. And he would come buckety-buckety over the Old Trading Path and pound at the door of Part-of-Providence some midnight, crying that he would no longer be denied, he must have her now, instanter. And then she would. . . .

[3]

While Elizabeth indulged in reverie on the creek bank, her half sister, Rebecca, turned restlessly on her bed, muttering in her sleep until with a strangled moan, she came wide awake.

For a moment she huddled there, her eyes searching for a

familiar object. The bed, the slant of the roof, the nicker of horses and the distant murmur of voices—they were all wrong. It was almost as though she were back at Middlebend but she knew she wasn't. Those beautiful dreams of her former home had never included smells and sounds as real as this.

She was—she was—she sank back into the quilts with a sigh of relief. She wasn't back at Bee Cove nor in MacLynn's cabin; she was an Allyn again, returned to her family, welcomed lovingly by everyone but Father who was, at least, allowing her to remain by his silence. And this was more than she had dared hope for, even though the ragged Scots preacher, MacCutcheon, had predicted that William Weyland Allyn's tribulation would have tempered the old man's stiff-necked ways.

She raised herself on an elbow and cocked an ear toward the open doorway. There was the rumble of men's hushed voices, probably Father and her brothers discussing her fate, and a dull clink of a jug touching a cup's rim. She had no idea how long she had slept, whether she should go down for supper (for her belly was complaining about all that good food she had pushed aside at the Christmas table) or if Betsy might need her help in fixing the meal.

Better make yourself useful, Becky-girl, she told herself. *Show the old man you've changed from the giddypate you were when he last knew you.*

But, ah, the bed was so soft and she had been so long without one under her! She rolled back, burrowing into the pillow, seeking sleep again. But whatever dream-demon had awakened her had robbed her of all chance to doze again. Awakening had meant getting up instanter for so many years that now, when she had a chance to rest, the old habits still took charge.

She muttered a word under her breath and rolled over on her back. One arm flung across her forehead, she looked up at the night that was blackening the eaves. At least she would take a few minutes to ready the story that the people downstairs were waiting for. It had to be full enough to satisfy the old man's searching suspicions and yet leave out enough to keep Phil and George and Betsy, especially that pure child, from despising her for a drab.

It was not going to be easy. The whole story would be impossible for the Allyns of Middlebend to understand. They would never believe that that which was considered a stern rule for plantation ladies on the Chowan was regarded as elegant nonsense in the Nolichucky Valley, 'midst the towering hills to the west. Even George, who she knew was randy enough when he was out of the family's sight, could not forgive her for some of the things she had done although they had been taken as a matter of course—or at least survival— out there.

Nobody except perhaps Elizabeth's mother, if she were here—could forgive her the recklessness that had made her and Harry flee like a pair of thieves in the first place. That part of it would have to be left unsaid. There was no way anybody could *prove* that she was carrying the beginnings of a baby when she ran away. Just as nobody whose word counted a whit could ever *prove* that she and Harry had made love like a pair of rabbits, wherever and whenever they got a chance, for nearly a year before their luck ran out and they had to run for it.

"Let me go to my father and beg his forgiveness," she had asked Harry when the truth could no longer be wished away.

"He'd put a ball through my head," he cried. "Or if he didn't, Philip would, or George."

Ah, Harry, so handsome, so rantum-scantum, always the one to put his horses to the breakneck jump while others rode around it, Harry the wizard at love-making, the one who could always find a laugh—where was his courage and his wit that day? Gone, and in their place a terror that somehow reflected blame on *her* for letting this happen.

"Nay, they love me too much to harm you, sweetling," she had argued. "I'll tell them—I'll tell them I coaxed you into it. Too much wine, moonshine, one feckless moment. Now both of us are properly contrite. We want only to patch up this misadventure as best we can."

But Harry was shaking his sandy head. "One feckless moment, when every black on Middlebend knows we went at it twenty times a night?" he jeered.

"Only Kundo and Lis, mayhap one or two others," she countered, "and who w'ld listen? Besides, the servants all think more of me than anybody else in the family. Save Lis; she's fair daft about Betsy. But for that reason she wouldn't blab on me for fear she'd break her darlin's heart."

Rebecca brought her arm down and rolled on her side. She

had expected her lover to leap at the chance of throwing off the shabby secrecy, of making their love a public bond in the sight of God and man, especially one man, William Weyland Allyn of Middlebend. But instead he had proved craven, wriggling like a hooked fish, turning this way and that until finally her eyes were opened to the fact that what he really wanted to do—*would* do when his fear grew great enough— was to ride off alone, abandoning her to face their shame.

The shock of her discovery still jarred her after all this time. She rolled back onto her other side and cursed under her breath. She damned Harry, wherever he or his ghost tilted demijohns, real or phantom, but even more she damned herself for the way she had clung to him.

"I tell ye 'twould mean my disinheritance," he had whined when she told him they must elope to Winton Landing.

"Disinherited? For marrying an *Allyn*?" She could not believe she had heard right.

He nodded, turning sullen. "Ye needn't think y'r family's acceptable just because ye're rich and Middlebend's so big. My father came from Virginia too, remember, and when he's in his cups he calls y'r father a renegade, if ye must know."

Rebecca remembered her flaring anger. Fat, besotted Prescott Tarbell calling Father names? Why, if Father hadn't rescued him from the usurers, Harbor Oaks would belong to somebody else. Which it probaby would in time, anyway, seeing the way Prescott Tarbell was selling off land to meet his debts.

Becky had wanted to lash out at Harry but she was helpless. To save her own skin—aye, and the brat in her belly—she had to swallow the insult to the Allyn name and fawn and wheedle and kiss Harry's arse so he'd take her with him when he fled.

"All right, but not to Winton Landing," he had finally agreed. "They'll expect us to go there. George and Philip would be upon us before we got halfway. We'll head out in another direction."

"Anything you say, darlin' Harry," she had told him. "Anything you say. You're wisest so just tell me what you'd have me do."

For the next few days, Becky lived with the fear that Harry would desert her but he had met her where he'd promised, astride his father's best stallion and leading another good mount for her. Prophetically, it was a windy, rainy night and although she had turned to look back at Middlebend when they reached a break in the trees, she had not been able to see a single glimmer of light.

Because she was supposed to be spending a few days at Weyland's plantation, they hoped to have at least twenty-four hours' time before it was discovered that she was gone. Becky laughed now in the darkness. She should have known better than to think her father would come hallooing on their trail, letting the world know that his daughter had disgraced him. Looking back on it, she knew that she and Harry could have safely *walked* to Winton Landing as far as any pursuit was concerned. Whatever her brothers might have wanted to do to "rescue" her had been forbidden. Her name had been stricken from the family record on the spot and William Weyland Allyn had wiped all trace of his beloved daughter from his mind and his heart.

His referring to her as *Dame Tarbell* was evidence of that.

Her nose itched and she scrubbed it with a knuckle. Someone was thinking of her, eh, or was she going to kiss a fool? No, no more of sweet Becky Allyn's kisses for any man, even if there were a man in this land who would want to kiss such a harridan. The Red MacLynns were back in the coves along the Nolichucky. Here on the Alamance, a man doubtless required that the woman he cuddled would have a soft skin and a clean smell.

She gave up the thought of going back to sleep, sat up and hugged her knees under the bearskin that Betsy had thrown over her. She scratched another itch on her flank and idly hoped it was only an itch; 'twould seem an ungrateful thing to bring bugs into dear Betsy's bed.

The grateful, penitent sinner—that was the part she had to play if she hoped to win the old man back. *Aye, Father, you were right and I was wrong and if you'll let me, I'll spend the rest of my life making up for all the hurt I've caused you.* That was the tune to sing and she had to guard against letting the pride and the temper show.

Quickly she rehearsed the story of the humbled prodigal before she went downstairs.

She and Harry had been married at Cottones Cross Roads on the Halifax Trail by a clergyman named Middlemas. She could give them chapter and verse about that because it had been at Cottones Cross Roads that she had come closest to

really being married. She got Harry as far as the miserable
little chapel where Middlemas waited with the marriage paper
but her gentle lover was too drunk and quarrelsome for even
the priest with his three-shilling paper to stomach. She had
tried desperately to convince Harry but all her coaxing and
complaining had gotten her was a clout beside the ear. And
when he had screamed and called her a whore, the villagers
had driven them out of town, pelting *her*, not Harry, with
mudballs.

So had her wedding day ended. And the dear little babes
who had been born of this great love? The child who had
been to blame for all her woes had not lived a full day, a puny,
blue-faced mite and what more could be expected of the son
of such a father? True, Harry had actually seemed grief-
stricken (or perhaps it had been just another excuse to stay
drunk) and had insisted that the little grave be prayed over
by Boyette, the trader who owned a prayer book and could
read, but she knew that the babe's death was a merciful thing
compared to what his life would have been with them.

But for those who waited for her story, her son, *William*,
was born a full year after she left Middlebend and—and was
killed in the same Indian raid that took the life of poor, brave
Harry. She had better make it *two* children taken from her
by the fierce savages, William (if she dared she'd make it
William Weyland but the old man might find it too much to
swallow) and a dear little girl named Jessamyne. Both slain
by the bloody Catawbas, their tiny bodies thrown into the
blazing pyre of the Bee Cove cabin to join their dear father.
How had she escaped? Why, as bad luck would have it, when
the Indians struck she had been visiting a family in the next
cove, an old couple named MacLynn. She had been sent there
by Harry with some necessaries that they lacked, dear old
souls.

After the massacre she had stayed with the MacLynns until
the old woman died. Then she had returned to Bee Cove to
try to eke out a lonely existence from the rocky soil. Old
MacLynn had begged her to stay with him but everyone
would understand why, because of the proprieties, she could
not even though he must have been close to eighty.

Lying in the growing darkness, she had an instant's vision
of Red MacLynn, the great brute, the tireless stallion, as he
belabored her, teeth bared, nostrils flared, full of a fire that

made her forget what a cruel animal he really was. She had hated him except at times like that but he had given her a roof over her head and food for her belly and whiskey, too, when there was enough for both of them. Besides, he had owned certain rights to the use of her. Dear Harry had put his name to a contract that had hired her out to Red MacLynn as his "housekeeper" for four golden guineas before he had disappeared.

She must never breathe a word about Red MacLynn when she went downstairs. Nor could she give a hint of the humiliations and beatings that she had suffered at Harry's hands when he had found he could not shake loose from her, no matter how hard he tried. Luckily, most of the men to whom she had been loaned by Harry from time to time were dead and those who were still alive weren't likely to come looking for her here. She and Harry had used a dozen names in their wanderings but never the name of Allyn or Tarbell. Somehow she had kept from besmirching her family name even though Harry had had no qualms about misusing the names of his friends and relatives when begging, or as he called it, borrowing.

MacLynn had known who she was but MacLynn was dead. She left him vomiting his lifeblood, his own knife stuck in his gut, so there was no chance of him rearing up out of the past to spoil everything. Even in the unlikely event that Harry was still alive, he wouldn't dare show himself. The last time she had seen him, she had sworn that her brothers would track him down to avenge her. It had been an empty threat but poor, befuddled Harry Tarbell believed it. He would die, hopefully had died, looking over his shoulder, hearing Philip's and George's hoofbeats behind him.

As far as she knew, there were only two persons who could expose her and both of those were black slaves. She knew that old Lis was there but she had not seen Kundo at the house, although he may have been feasting with the others in the quarters or still be up at Childsborough. Kundo would never betray the secret of her wantonness back at Middlebend —for, as she remembered him, he had barely spoken a word to a white master or mistress. About Lis she was not so certain. The crone adored Elizabeth and, as she had once told Harry, might keep her silence to save her darling from the truth. But then again, a privileged old body slave like Lis would risk the lash if she thought her mistress's place was being usurped.

So, above all, she must make Betsy her closest, stoutest ally. That would seem a simple task, indeed, seeing how much her half sister loved her and remembering how open-hearted and trusting she was in all things.

Not that she intended to harm the child. No, she was finished with harming anyone, just as she was through with men, forever. But if Lis despised her because she had found her playing the two-backed beast with Harry Tarbell, it behooved her to make Elizabeth love her so much that she'd not believe Lis, not on the old woman's deathbed.

She groped about on the floor of the dark room until she found the horn pins she had pulled from her hair. She fixed her thick mop in some kind of order, then found her stockings and her shabby shoes and put them on. Just before she stood up she threw back her shoulders, raised her chin, and practiced her smile, keeping the left side of her upper lip drawn down in order to hide the damage that her beloved Harry had done to her teeth with his playful love-taps.

What lay ahead might seem an ordeal to most women but she had had good training in lying and here the prize was survival, comfort, even luxury if George could perform a few of his miracles with the crops and animals. So how could she fail? Why, with her wits sharpened and sustained by plenty of food and warm shelter, and with love replacing fear and hate in her life, she'd have them all eating out of her hand in a month.

[4]

They talked long past their usual bedtime that Christmas Night, talked until the tallow candles guttered in their holders and even Elizabeth's wide eyes drooped.

It was a sad tale that Rebecca told and her half sister's heart ached for her, particularly when Becky reached a point where she said quietly, "By y'r leave, I'll skip that part f'r now. P'raps later, when it's not so fresh in my mind."

Those dear children, little William and the baby, Jessamyne, how she would have loved to have held them in her arms. How terrible to die like that, at the hands of howling, painted savages, their brave father tortured before their eyes before he, too, was slain.

"Leastwise, that was how my good neighbors thought it must have happened after they poked through the ashes," Becky said. Her voice was freighted with sorrow but it was steady, never breaking. "I couldn't bring myself to join them."

"Did y'r neighbors mount a chase after the scurvy dogs?" George rumbled.

Rebecca shook her head. "Nay, brother, 'twould have been a waste of time and mayhap 'twould cost more lives. Ye don't know those mountains. The Catawbas can spring like a panther, make their kill and lose themselves back in the hills, all in a trice. If ye try to follow them, ye'll wind up in their ambush, more often than not. Better to bury y'r dead and forget all thoughts of revenge."

William Weyland Allyn said slowly, "Strange that we got no word of this back east." It was one of the few times he broke his stony-faced silence.

Rebecca shrugged. "I trow there's more things happen out there that're never heard of than are. We were on our own once we passed through McKinney's Gap. They warned us 'twas Indian land beyond the Gap and the Crown disowned all who passed through. Whatever happened to us was our own doin', good or bad."

"But why did you go?" Philip cried. "If you were warned about what could happen, why didn't you turn back?"

Elizabeth watched her half sister's full mouth twist in a wry grimace. "Ye didn't know my husband as well as ye might have thought ye did, Philip. Once he got the bit in his teeth there was no stoppin' him. It was always beyond the next ridge that our fortune was waitin' f'r us. Beyond the next line of mountains we'd find land so rich that even he c'ld live a life of ease without turnin' a spade. Or there were gold or furs or rubies scattered over the ground, ours f'r the pickin' up. The way he saw it, the Crown wanted to keep us out lest we pick up riches there that belonged to the king."

She shook her head and before anyone else could speak she went on "I know, I know, he never got around to explainin' why the king didn't send somebody in there to do the pickin' up f'r him if it was so simple. You see, he couldn't be bothered with little matters such as that."

"Has Prescott Tarbell been told about Harry?" George asked.

Another shrug, "I dinna ken f'r sure, George."

Elizabeth could hold herself in no longer. "You've said that two or three times, Becky, 'I dinna ken.' It's Scottish for 'I don't know', isn't it?"

"Aye, Betsy. I got in the habit of sayin' it 'cause most of them in the hills were Scots. Don't they abound here, too? At Cedar Valley ye'd think there was no other breed in all of Carolina, I vow."

"There's a-plenty of 'em, and Germans and Quakers and God knows what-all," George said. "But as ye've noticed, we ain't exactly hemmed in by neighbors and aside from that preacher, MacCutcheon, I doubt that Betsy's met a single dour Scot, have ye, Betsy?"

She shook her head, grateful that the deep shadows hid the ridiculous blush that had risen to her face at the mere mention of Ian MacCutcheon's name.

"Do you think we ought to send a message to Harbor Bluffs?" Phil asked.

"Why, I s'pose so," his sister replied half-heartedly. "Though from what my husband said, his father didn't care whether he lived or died after he married me." She looked down at her workworn hands, twisting in her lap. " 'Tis hard to say but—well, Mister Tarbell accused Harry of marryin' beneath his station."

"*Beneath his station!* That rakehell?" Philip burst out. He caught himself and quickly added, "I don't mean to demean the man now that he's dead—and died bravely, too—but there never was a day when a Tarbell could look down on an Allyn and you know it. Why, if Father hadn't come to his rescue, Prescott Tarbell would've lost—"

"Enough, Philip," William Allyn put in sharply. He swung his face toward his daughter and said, "If that was the Tarbells' opinion, I doubt you'll get any warm welcome at Harbor Bluffs now, since my trouble. Was it your intention to go back to your husband's people, Rebecca?"

Elizabeth brightened. Father had called her *Rebecca* instead of *Dame Tarbell*.

Becky was still examining her hands. "I thought of it," she said after a pause, "but 'twas not set in my mind. 'Strooth, I didn't really know where I'd find a place to stay out my days. I thought—well, I feared my headstrong ways had shut Middlebend's door 'gainst me forever." Her eyes came up to meet her father's. "Have y'r own troubles made ye more forgivin' so's ye'll let me stay here?"

Philip, George, and Elizabeth all joined in saying that she mustn't think of leaving, but Becky waited for William Weyland Allyn's answer, never taking her eyes from the hawk-beaked face. It seemed to Elizabeth that her father took an unconscionable time to reply but the answer when it came flooded her with joy.

"Aye, daughter," he said. "By your own story you've done enough penance for your wilfulness and as you said, perhaps my trials have made me less stiff-necked than I was. So make this your home, Rebecca, so long as you like." A second's pause. "And though you grieved us all, I can speak for the family when I bid you warm welcome home."

If she had been Becky, Elizabeth told herself, she would have rushed into Father's arms. But Becky was far wiser than she; she proved this by nodding gravely and simply saying, "I thankee with all my heart, Father, and I'll do my best to make it up to you f'r my disobedience."

Rebecca took the bed while Elizabeth made do with a shuck pallet on the floor. But before she finally consented to the arrangement, she made Elizabeth agree that they would take turns with the bed, once she had overcome the worst of her aches and pains. The returned prodigal insisted on getting up at dawn with the others, too, and helping with the early chores although everyone, even Father, urged her to wait until she had put some flesh on her bones before pitching in so strenuously.

"I'm as strong as a horse, no matter how I look," she said cheerfully. "As f'r prettyin' my face, I fear that's past doin' without the touch of some fairy's wand."

When Langhorn saddled up to return to the camp at Childsborough, Philip decided that he would go with him so that he could take up his studies with Squire Davis. It was a last-minute decision and one that pleased his father greatly, although he greeted Philip's announcement with only a hint of a smile.

"I'm not runnin' ye off, am I?" Becky asked with a laugh.

"You know you're not. It's just that I'm more in the way here than ever now that the family's got another pair of able hands to take the place of my two bungling ones." Philip sobered suddenly. "No, I find myself atwitch to get back to my calling, Becky, even though Childsborough's not Edenton and backwoods law is likely to be pretty tepid tea compared with what I'm used to."

"Law should never be tepid," William Weyland Allyn said with a show of his old decisiveness. "Each case means the whole world to the litigants, even if it concerns only a single foot of land in a boundary dispute."

"Speakin' of which," George put in, "see if ye can make up that County Register's mind to give us an exact plat of this property, will ye, Philip? With you on the ground, mayhap ye can goad him into doin' what should've been done when we first got here."

"Aye, and make sure the former owner's quitclaim is entered in the records," Father added. "Colonel Tryon said 'twas all arranged so there should be no trouble over it but I'd feel easier if I was sure it was all set down properly. We surely don't want Hosban showing up some day and claiming title."

"I'd brain him if he tried, after all our work," George said grimly. "But Father's right, Philip. There's some mystery about Hosban and this whole land deal and it's up to you to clear the air."

"I'll send back word the minute I get the facts," Philip promised. He kissed Rebecca and Elizabeth on the cheek, shook hands with his brother and his father, mounted his sleek gray, and went up the narrow, twisting road with Langhorn, reining in at the first bend to wave back at them.

The first chance she got to speak with Elizabeth alone, Rebecca asked, "What did George mean, there's a mystery about this place? Ain't it ours? Didn't Father trade Middlebend f'r it when Tryon told him 'twas take this or stand trial f'r near murder?"

"You know about that, then?"

"I got some of the story from y'r friend, MacCutcheon, and others. Ye may think ye're buried in the wilderness but ye know this country—or ye will; the least morsel of gossip is chewed over till it's worn out. But I heard naught of anybody named Hosban or a word about a mystery."

Elizabeth filled Becky in on what she knew, which admittedly was not too much. This land now called Part-of-Providence had once belonged to a family named Hosban but for some reason, William Tryon had been able to offer it to William Weyland Allyn as a condition of his ultimatum. On the way out to the Alamance, Allyn had made inquiries about the place for which they were bound but had learned nothing until they reached the little settlement of Long Creek Ford.

"I thought some others knew but wouldn't tell us anything," Elizabeth confided. "They were an unfriendly lot, those settlers along the trace. I vow, sometimes I thought I could see hate in their eyes when they looked at us, as though we were a conquering army come to rule over them."

"I can imagine." Becky laughed. "Here come the high 'n' mighty Allyns atop their fine horses, with a regiment of slaves trailin' after 'em. And Father looks down his long nose at some henscratch farmer and asks questions in a way that'd rile the simplest Simon. Unfriendly, were they? If Father did the askin', what c'ld ye expect? Why didn't ye leave it up to George? He speaks their language."

Elizabeth knew that was true, but at the time they were all trying to rebuild Father's self-confidence, deliberately or not. Middlebend's loss had stricken him and if he had not led the way on Chanticleer and asked the questions he would have shrunk even more within himself. But she said, "Oh, Becky, it wasn't that way at all! Father was most gracious and—"

"Gracious! Ye don't earn the borderers' friendship by bein' gracious. Most of 'em are out here 'cause they couldn't stomach their gracious lords wherever they came from. But what about Hosban and the mystery?" Elizabeth went on with her story.

At Long Creek Ford a man named Caldwell had finally volunteered a scrap of information, and that, as he was careful to explain, only because he understood that William Weyland Allyn had originally come from Virginia. "They run me out of there, too," he had said.

Caldwell was a thin, knobby man with a ferocious squint. He had cast his peculiar eyes along the string of waggons, the blacks squatting beside them, the horses, and the small cattle herd, and said, "I wish ye and y'r family good fortune where ye're goin', Allyn, but I warn ye, they have no love f'r the gentry there, or so I've heard."

It was George who said, "The name of gentry's not f'r us, my friend. Bad fortune's gnawed us to the bone, if ye but knew."

Another look at the halted caravan and Caldwell turned to

spit into the brush beside him. "Ye may call y'rselves paupers but I'd say ye'll be the richest ones on the Alamance,
hands down."

"Do you know that country well?" Father had asked.

"As well as anybody that don't live there, I guess."

"Then maybe you know of the plantation we're taking over.
'Twas owned by a family named Hosban, Herman Hosban."

The man nodded. "I've heard of him but they say—did ye
buy from Hosban himself, perchance?"

"No, the County Register at Childsborough arranged everything. Fanning's his name."

Caldwell spat again before he said, "Oh, aye, we all know
that name hereabouts and ye'll get to know it better, no doubt
o' that. When ye reach Childsborough ye can ask Edmund
Fanning what kind of a pig ye have in y'r poke—and then
save y'r jumpin' f'r joy till ye see the place with y'r own eyes."

Rebecca, who was ripping the seams of one of Elizabeth's
dresses so it could be made over to fit her, chuckled. "Good
advice, I'd say. And this Fanning, did he warn ye of what ye
were gettin' into, Betsy?"

Well not exactly, Elizabeth went on, because when they
reached Childsborough they learned that the County Register,
Mister Edmund Fanning, was off on a journey, but his clerk
had told them that the Hosban plantation was one of the finest to be found anywhere. Squire Allyn, he assured them, was
bound to be most pleased with his great bargain.

"If it's such a fine place, why did Hosban sell it?" George
asked bluntly.

After hemming and hawing a bit, the clerk had admitted
that he could not rightly say, possibly a sudden disaffection
for plantation life. "A Quaker, you know," he had added, as
though that explained everything.

Elizabeth, who was helping Becky with her sewing, bit off
a thread and said, "But no matter how rundown it was—"

"Rundown it is, don't ye mean?"

"You should have seen it when we got here. It may not
show but this house is ten times better than it was. Lis and I
have worked our—"

"I know, I know. I didn't mean to scant y'r fine work, baby
sister."

"Well, Lis and Yulee did most of it," Elizabeth said generously. "Yulee fair amazed me. You know how slack she could be at Middlebend—or did we have her before you left?"

"Oh, aye, she was there but scarce more than a pickanin', then." A pause. "I don't doubt my randy brother, George, had his eye on her even then."

"Oh, Becky, don't say such a thing," Elizabeth protested.

"Pish-tush! If ye're to be marrit to Edward Dedshall it's time ye found out that men, even good men like George, needs must have a wench to try themselves on when they get to be a certain age." She stuck her thumb with a needle and muttered a genial oath. "And some ne'er get over the need f'r variety, so to speak." She glanced over at Elizabeth and smiled. "But I wouldn't worry about this happenin' to Edward Dedshall—I remember him as a solemn, straitlaced boy, the few times I saw him. No Yulees f'r y'r darlin' Edward, I'll be bound. Mayhap y'r only trouble might be gettin' him to pay ye enough attention to suit y'r needs, eh?"

Knowing that her face was a bright crimson, Elizabeth bent her head. "I was telling you what George said about the land." she said firmly. "He said it beat him why the Hosbans let this place run down so, since it was the finest growing soil he'd ever seen."

Becky grunted. "That's George f'r ye. He c'ld live in a cave and never miss a single comfort if there was rich land to go with it." She sewed in silence for a few minutes, then asked, "D'ye think we c'ld coax him to leave off his land clearin' long enough to build another room f'r us, Betsy? Not meanin' to complain, but that cubbyhole of yours ain't big enough f'r the two of us to draw a full breath in."

"P'raps he will if you ask him," Elizabeth replied dubiously, "but by the way he frets when bad weather keeps the hands in the quarters, it will take some doing."

"Leave it to me," Rebecca said. "I used to have good luck gettin' him to do me favors without him knowin' he did."

But for once, Rebecca had overestimated her own powers of persuasion, for although she obliquely nudged George a hundred times with her comments about the discomfort of the little room under the eaves, he never took the bait. As more housing was built on the Alamance the camp at Childsborough was emptied of Allyn slaves. And with the arrival of additional labor barns and sheds went up. Later a forge, a granary, an abattoir, indigo vats, and even a small distillery were thrown up. Yet not a stick of wood was added to the "manor house" nor where there any repairs made that were not absolutely essential.

Only once did Becky come close to overstepping the mark. That was when she finally asked George straight out when he was going to do something about building her more comfortable quarters.

"Why, when we can all stop and take a deep breath and look to ourselves," her brother replied. "That'll be in the fall, from the looks of things, seein' we had an open winter and were able to do better than we hoped at the start."

"D'ye expect me to live like a pig till next fall?" she cried, forgetting her characteristic caution. "Why, y'r wench, Yulee, has a better—" Too late, she caught herself: she should have remembered that George, although slow to anger, had a monstrous temper when roused. "I mean, it ain't fair to Betsy and y'r father to expect them to suffer while you put the blacks first," she finished lamely.

Elizabeth held her breath, watching the color flow into George's windburned face. When he spoke, his lips were barely open. "If ye can't bear the way ye're treated here or if Yulee vexes ye too much, remember, dear sister o' mine, ye c'n always ride down the trace to Harry Tarbell's fine house and knock on that door."

"Nay, George, I didn't mean to offend ye," Rebecca said quickly. "I but—ah, forget I said it. I sh'ld know ye do what ye do f'r the best of all of us."

"I try to," George said, nodding. "Till now, everybody's done what's had to be done and gone without what's missin' without any whinin', as Allyns should. Ye used to be an Allyn, Becky; did y'r sweet life with darlin' Harry change ye so much?"

They stared at each other, until Elizabeth could bear it no longer. "Hush, both of you," she commanded. "George, Becky's tired, worn out, and you're overly touchy about having to do first things first. Of *course* we know you'll be build us a fine house, as soon as you can. Won't you, George?"

George broke off his glare and looked at her, his taut face relaxing. "Aye," he said beginning to smile, "and the first thing I'll do is build you a room big enough to hold a ball in, Betsy. For God knows' ye've earned it these past months and with ne'er a balk or whimper."

"And what would I need a grand room like that for?" she asked with a laugh. "You forget that soon a gentleman named Edward Dedshall will come a-riding to Part-of-Providence to claim me for his beautiful bride."

George ran a hand over his cued brown hair. "'Strooth," he admitted, "that had slipped my mind." His smile faded. "If ye're bound to marry him, why, I s'pose ye must, but I c'n tell ye now that he ain't half good enough f'r ye. I mean to tell him so when he comes f'r ye, too."

"Now, George, don't scare the poor lad away," Becky said. "There ain't exactly a rush of young gentlemen passin' here these days so I'd say Betsy had better take young Dedshall, good or bad, or she might end up an old maid."

Elizabeth laughed with the others but she knew that George was wondering the same thing that she was: would Edward Dedshall really come out to the Alamance to marry her or had his ardor cooled? Of course it was a long, rough way between Edenton and the Alamance but surely one letter could have gotten through. Did he still love her or had she been jilted *in absentia?* There had been a time when one tiny, obstreperous part of her mind had told her that Edward wouldn't dare jilt her because of what George and Philip might do to him if he did but that was when he was still at Middlebend; perhaps now, distance had lent Edward the courage to risk her brothers' anger.

[5]

The Allyns would not know it for some time but on that same April afternoon in 1765, William Tryon, lieutenant-governor of the North Carolina Colony, was pacing the parlor of a fine house in New Berne Town, waiting for a most important piece of news.

He was a striking figure in his black coat, black *moiré* vest, black silk breeches, and shoes with buckles of pure spoon silver. He wore no dress sword on this occasion although he seldom was without one, and the queue of his powdered wig was tied with a sober black ribbon. Those who had watched him descend from his coach at the door of the house had muttered that he had come fully prepared, but even if he had overheard these comments, Lieutenant-Colonel William Tryon, late of His Majesty's First Foot, would not have cared a whit.

He did not pace the parlor long before his game leg forced him to seek one of the spindly carved chairs that crowded the room. The whole place was overcrowded but he understood that the fair Justina Dobbs had been collecting colonial furniture to take with her when she and her septuagenarian husband sailed for England. There she had planned to enjoy life as Lady Dobbs (for surely a grateful king would knight the old man for his long and thankless service as governor of North Carolina) in the grand estate that Arthur Dobbs would be able to buy with the fortune he had by one means or another amassed in the colonies.

Tryon pulled out his snuffbox and daintily applied a pinch to each nostril, sneezed, and whisked a lace-trimmed kerchief past his thin hawk's beak. He wondered idly what Justina would do with all this furniture, now that her old husband was gasping his last upstairs. She had better sell it for what she could get because her husband's family would leave her without a shilling when they got through wrangling over the estate. Tryon knew, although he doubted that the widow-to-be did, that the Dobbs family had engaged a New Berne attorney to look after their interests the day they had learned the old man was ill and that they were prepared to question the validity of his marriage if Justina forced them to it.

Considering the venality of the county registers, clerks, and even the priest who had performed the absurd ceremony that had married a fifteen-year-old girl to a man well over seventy, this should be easy to do.

Tryon thrust out his leg and waited for the throbbing to subside. He was always quick to explain that his occasional limp was *not* the result of a war wound but a stupid bit of horsemanship during a hunt. This was not because of modesty but because he felt his record as a soldier was so unquestioned that he liked to surprise people with his uncommon honesty about his bad leg.

He glanced at the clock on the mantelpiece and found that it was stopped at quarter past nine. No matter, he was prepared to stay there as long as necessary, all night if need be. When he left this house he intended to be governor of the colony and Arthur Dobbs could take all the time dying that he needed.

One thing was sure, never would there be a smoother transition from one governor to the next. Ever since he had landed at Wilmington he had made preparations for the day when he would succeed to the position. He knew which of his enemies he would have to silence immediately and which could be allowed some time to fret and fume before he crushed them under his heel. The thieves like Ben Dedshall, the Lord Proprietary's bailiff at Edenton, he could deal with in a day or so, the others within a month. He had trusted agents scattered from New Berne to Old Brunswick to the western frontier and they had noted every word that had been spoken against William Tryon, even in the most secret quarters. His lockboxes contained thick dossiers on colonists who probably never suspected that their affairs had been thoroughly investigated and when the time came he would confront them with the proof of their past sins and give them the choice of supporting him or risking transportation to England as criminals.

As for the Assembly, that yapping pack needed muzzling instanter and, if they didn't come to heel he would take great pleasure in ruling them out of existence. Did they think he wouldn't dare? Ah, let them test him, then, and find out what sort of man he was, far different from the dying dodderer upstairs.

Those rascals in the Alamance country had better behave themselves, too, and stop badgering his agent, Edmund Fanning. He had hoped to tame that unruly crowd of peasants by providing them with gentlemanly leaders like William Weyland Allyn but that might take more time than the unmannerly rebels, the so-called "Regulators," would permit him. If so, they needn't think he'd hesitate to use bullets and bayonets on them. Perhaps he'd use arms even if it weren't absolutely necessary; that would show the rest of the colony that he was a man of action.

Now as to the northern hundreds . . .

He got to his feet as the sound of sobbing came from the head of the stairs in the hall outside. He walked to the parlor door and stood there, watching Justina Dobbs as she moved down the stairs, leaning heavily on a body slave. She was weeping brokenly and he was surprised that her grief seemed genuine; Justina, the child-wife, might actually have been fond of the old fool, after all.

When the widow reached the bottom, she found William

Tryon waiting for her. He took her limp hand and bowed low over it. Such a tiny hand, so young, so sweetly fleshed—how could such a morsel tie herself to the old bumbler? Ah, money, of course, and the position of First Lady of the Carolina Colony, and she probably had kept a lover somewhere about, even though his sharpest-eyed agents had never found out his name.

"Madam," he murmured in his deep, rich voice, "try to be consoled by the fact that all North Carolina shares your great loss. He was a fine man, good and wise, and it will be a long time before this colony benefits from his like again."

Justina Dobbs took the kerchief from her swollen face and managed a feeble thanks. "He took my heart with him, dear man," she said. "Oh, Colonel Tryon, what shall I do without him?"

Very well, I should think, once your eye lights on another rich dotard—this one without a rapacious family, I trust. "Ah, madam, what will any of us do without him to lead us?" he murmured aloud. "And though I know it must break your heart to think of leaving him, even though his great spirit has slipped away, my wife bids you to do us the honor of staying with us whilst the grievous arrangements are being made."

Justina's eyes widened and she looked about her, almost in fear. "D'you mean I must leave here, now that you're governor?" she asked, her voice trembling.

"A thousand nayes to that, madam," he said. "You must stay here as long as you wish—for all your days if that be your desire."

She lost her dread and began to weep again. "You're so kind, Colonel," she sniffled. "Exceeding kind, upon my soul."

He gestured and murmured in self-deprecation but silently, he laughed within himself. Oh, aye, Justina could stay here as long as she could afford to. He wanted no part of this draughty barn. Now that he was governor he intended to raise the taxes so that he could build a governor's palace that would be the finest structure in this whole country. It was one of the first items on his agenda.

Chapter Three

[1]

*A*LTHOUGH WILLIAM TRYON hoped to catch all the men on his blacklist by surprise, he reckoned without Ben Dedshall's natural survival instinct. The Lord Proprietary's bailiff at Edenton had come a long way from his birthplace in the rabbit warrens of London's Ramsgate but in his rise to wealth and influence he had never overcome his inborn distrust of success or of the men on whom his prosperity depended.

Dedshall's sources of information might not have been as extensive as Tryon's but they were sound. A good many of his informants were persons who had been Ben's accomplices in various tax irregularities and they well knew that if Dedshall's ship were scuttled, they would go down with the bailiff. They had every bit as much at stake as the short, pudgy, agent, and so their snooping was absolutely reliable.

As long as old Arthur Dobbs clung to life, Ben knew that he was safe from William Tryon. But he knew, too, that the minute Dobbs breathed his last, Tryon would come after him at a gallop, armed with the Royal Governor's seal. Therefore, the round little bailiff almost cheerfully paid a handsome fee for frequent reports from Dobbs' bedside. These were supplied by the physician who tended the dying governor, a man who hated Tryon and who was saddled by an awesome load of gambling debts.

William Tryon had strong suspicions about Dobbs' doctor but the lieutenant-governor found himself unable to replace him with his own man. He reasoned that if he did this and Dobbs promptly died, his enemies would loose a flood of ugly rumors that would take too much time to put down. Tryon knew he would have enough opposition from Milord Granville and the Commissioners of Plantations and Trade without whispers of murder, so he let Dobbs' boozy friend stay on to the end, though closely watched—or so he thought. Actually, the man assigned to watch the red-nosed medico was in Ben's pay, too, so the doctor was able to give Dedshall

53

the latest word of the old governor's condition right up to the last.

"He'll die f'r sure within three days," was the last report, given Ben at a rendezvous on the outskirts of New Berne Town. "The piss is minglin' with his blood and he's yellow as saffron. We can't keep him alive much longer, even with doubled blood-lettin'."

Dedshall handed over his last bribe and cantered back to Edenton where he gathered together his five children. Quickly, he told them that they must prepare to leave.

"Leave?" squawked twenty-five-year-old Ethelind. "Why, f'r mercy's sake?"

Redheaded Millie, a wise and cynical fifteen, sneered, "'Cause old Dobbs is dead and Tryon's comin' after Pa, ye dolt. Anybody c'n see that."

"He's dead?" Edward asked. "Are you certain, Father? The latest word I got at the courthouse was that the governor is making a miraculous recovery. His physicians expect him to be able to resume his official duties in a fortnight."

"Oh, aye," Dedshall said sourly, "I've no doubt that's what Tryon wants us to believe. No, Dobbs ain't dead but he will be tomorrer or the next day, and when he does I want all of us to be out of Sir Bloody Guts' reach."

"But I can't possibly leave," Edward protested. "Squire Reston is depending on me to present arguments in a most important litigation that's calendared for next week. Besides, if Colonel Tryon really dares take any action 'gainst you, Father, you can be sure Squire Reston and I will protect you."

"It'll be *Governor* Tryon," Dedshall snarled, "and y'r protection won't be worth a fart in the wind. So pack only what ye must—none of y'r female junk, Ethel; I'll just dump it 'side the road, I warn ye—and be ready to leave this very night."

The two young Dedshalls, David and Francis, eleven and twelve, whooped and pranced at the prospect of an adventure. "Any more of y'r wild shenanigans and I'll leave ye f'r the governor's sojers to deal with," the bailiff growled. "Edward, tell the coachman to have all ready to leave at midnight, at the latest."

"What about my wench, Jessie?" Ethelind demanded. "Ye don't expect me to live like a savage just because ye've run afoul of William Tryon, do ye?"

"By God, ye'll be lucky to live at all if ye don't stop y'r

squallin'," Dedshall said grimly. "If Tryon's spies hear ye on the street it's gaol f'r all of us."

"But I can't be expected to dress m'self and do my own hair," Ethelind complained. "Jessie won't take up hardly no room at all and I vow, I'd ruther be hung than have to live like a pig."

"Ho, listen to Her Highness," Millie jeered. "She's had her own wench f'r less'n a month but to hear her, ye'd think she was born quality."

"Shut up, ye little minx, or I'll tell Pa who ye've been meetin' down at the back gate nights when ye thought nobody was lookin'."

"Silence, all of ye," the fat bailiff said. Sweat trickled down his cheeks and his wig had slipped over one eye. Despairingly, he looked at his oldest son. "Edward, f'r Christ's sweet sake, can't ye do somethin' besides stand there like a dumbstruck stork? There's God's own amount of work to be done and y'r law trainin' sh'ld have made ye able to at least help me burn my dangerous papers before we skedaddle. And shut y'r mouth—ye look like a droolin' idjit."

Edward closed his slack mouth, swallowed convulsively, and let his jaw drop again. He was stupefied by the knowledge that his father meant it when he said they were in danger of prison. Worse than anything else, perhaps, was the fact that he, who was so proud of his high connections, had been kept in the dark about how badly the Dedshalls would fare when William Tryon became governor. He had known his father was no great friend of Tryon but this—it was impossible to grasp! "I—but—if ye really mean we must flee, where will we go?" he finally stammered.

"Go? Go? How do I know? Anywhere but here, that's f'r sure. We might try f'r Virginny but Tryon's almost sure to have the roads blocked in that direction. West, I s'pose. There's a deal of wilderness out there where even that monster might have trouble trackin' me down."

"If ye knew this was comin', why didn't ye make some preparations f'r it?" Ethelind whined. "We c'ld have sailed to England and—"

"Aye, and asked the King to put us up at Windsor, eh? I did have everything all arranged but it went awry, if ye must know. Then that old fool had to go and catch a colic before I c'ld make new plans."

"We c'n go to the Alamance, Pa," Millie piped up, "The Allyns will give us sanctuary, I know they will. Elizabeth's my dearest friend and she said if we had to run f'r it we sh'ld come straight to her, she'd hide us. She promised. Besides, Edward's betrothed to her so how c'ld they turn us away?"

"Aye," Edward said feebly, "what's wrong with that?"

Ethelind snapped, "If ye think I'm goin' out there to live like a Injun, ye're wrong, the lot of ye."

"Hi!" young David said. "Injuns! Massacrees! Whooo whooo whooo!"

"And I hope they chop off y'r head, first thing," his spinster sister said unkindly. "'Twould finally quiet y'r yap."

"'Twill be you they'll go fer," Francis shrieked delightedly. "Eddie Forster says Injuns go fer the wimmen and tear their clothes off and roger 'em till their eyes pop out."

Ethelind wailed, "Pa, can't ye shut 'em up?"

"Quiet!" the beleaguered bailiff roared. "Quiet, before I do what any sensible man w'ld do, which is ride off and leave ye all to fend f'r y'rselves."

"You can't do that," Edward cried. "You got us into this trouble, now get us out!"

Millie jeered, "There speaks the great hero! I wish Elizabeth Allyn c'ld hear ye now. I warrant she'd fair swoon with pride."

"You, too, Millie," her father said. "Ye'll mind y'r manners to y'r elders. As f'r suggestin' we head f'r the Alamance, it ain't the worse idee I've heard. Tryon's man out there is Edmund Fanning and I've always got along all right with him. Meanin' he owes me a debt or two. And as ye say, Will'm Allyn did seal a sort of marriage contract with me though it's been some time ago and I ain't heard no more about it. Mayhap he's changed his mind since, and wants out of the arrangement."

"Ho, if ye think that, ye don't half know what stuff real gentlemen are made of," Millie scoffed. "If Mister Allyn gave his word to anything, he'd ruther cut off his hand than go back on it. I know that much."

Dedshall peered at his strange little daughter, so much wiser than her years. "P'raps ye're right," he said slowly, a thumb scratching his chin. He turned to look at Edward. "Ye ain't heard from the Allyns and kept it from me, have ye?"

Edward's sallow face colored faintly. "Nay, but—well, if ye must know, I've recently been addressing myself to Mistress Fanny—"

"Ye'll unaddress y'rself, then," his father said curtly. He turned back and said, "It's decided, then; we'll try f'r the Alamance. And ye'd all better pray that Will'm Tryon don't find out we're gone afore we've put many a long mile behind us."

"D'ye really mean ye're goin' to leave this fine house behind and all that's in it?" Ethelind half-sobbed. "The new ell and all? Just when the highborn folks was gettin' ready to finally accept my invitations and offer me some of theirs? I won't have it, I won't!"

Ben Dedshall's voice softened. "Ah, gel, don't take on so. We had all these good years here and now they're over and done, finished. Thank heav'n that y'r ma died thinkin' they'd last f'rever." His harassed face brightened a bit as he added, "Besides, who says Ben Dedshall can't find new good times f'r ye on the Alamance, hey?"

[2]

Elizabeth was in the front yard that May day with Henry Langhorn and Rus, Lis' youngest child, when the dugout canoe came pushing up the Alamance.

Fine spring weather had advanced George's plans ahead of schedule so that he had finally given in to his sister's urging by ordering Rus and Henry to help the girls do some planting in front of the house.

There would be no fine lawn such as at Middlebend; there was no time for that. Elizabeth and Becky had been warned that they had to do the job within six days. "And ye needn't think ye c'n wheedle me into givin' ye another week. This is the last time I give in to y'r naggin', I vow. 'Twixt the new bedrooms, the kitchen and y'r laundry house, ye've got half my field hands tied up with y'r fancies now."

For Rebecca had finally succeeded in flattering and chiding poor George to the point where he had consented to making some improvements in the main house before his first crops were in. She had done it all so cleverly that her brother was only half aware that the decision to start work on the sagging ruin was not entirely his own. Elizabeth had silently marveled at the way her half sister twisted George around her finger, just as she sometimes wondered how William Weyland Allyn was able to resist her blandishments.

She finally realized that Becky was two women in one, the teasing, quick-witted, warm coquette when she was with George and the prim, proper, almost priggish, widow-woman when she was in Father's presence. When her father was not there, she was almost her old self, full of laughter and nearly as beautiful as she had been before she left Middlebend. No longer the beaten creature who had sat sagging in her saddle on Christmas morning, Becky now seemed to have more energy than anybody else, except George.

Her taking over direction of the few house slaves that were needed in their new home was a relief to Elizabeth, no matter how old Lis might scowl and mutter. "After all the fine work ye've done, I don't want anybody to think ye're bein' set down, Betsy," her half sister had said.

"What a thing to say," she had replied with a laugh. "If only you knew how I've hoped you'd take over. I'd have begged you to long before this but you needed more rest."

"Pooh, I'm tougher than taw-leather and always was. Back at Middlebend, they were bound to set me on a silken cushion and feed me clotted cream like a proper Allyn leddy." She pushed back a tendril of her gray-streaked hair and laughed. "Not that I argued 'gainst it—far from it."

Then she sobered and asked, "D'ye think the blacks will sulk over my takin' charge, Betsy?"

"No, of course not. They'll work more willingly for you than they ever did for me; you know that."

"No, I don't know that, 'specially when it comes to Lis. She's never had much love fr me and now she'll prob'ly throw a cat fit over me pushin' ye out of y'r rightful place." Her full mouth slanted wrily. "Which I'm doin', I s'pose, but I'll go stark mad if I have to sit in a corner and remember what's happened to me. Work's my only hope of forgettin', though I don't s'pose Lis c'ld ever understand that."

"Don't worry about Lis. She's old and it's time she did some sitting in a corner, herself. I'll make her understand, Becky. She'll listen to me."

But of course the old woman could not accept Elizabeth's explanation of the need for the change. She had not openly protested, but her grunt and the reproachful look in her rheumy eyes before she shuffled off to the slave quarters had been statement enough. If her Mist'ess 'Lizabeth was not going to be in charge of the household, this usurper could not expect her to serve as the stewardess whose sharp eyes and tongue had kept the Allyn house slaves hopping for so many years.

Elizabeth sent for her old nurse to help her every time she could concoct a reason but once the made-up task was finished, Lis disappeared into her cabin again, never stirring forth, no matter how fine the weather outside.

"Maybe she'd stop acting this way if you talked to her," Elizabeth said to Rebecca.

"She'll get over it in time," Becky said lightly. "But till she does, don't be surprised by anything she says against me, baby sister."

"Lis? You wrong her, thinking she'd do that. She's old and crochety but she'd never say a word against you or any other Allyn."

"But I'm a Tarbell, remember?" Rebecca laughed at her half sister's expression and hurried on. "Na, na, I was only jokin'. Be off with ye to y'r greenyard. Young Langhorn's been moonin' out there f'r the past half hour, doin' everything but pluck a lute and sing a ballad askin' f'r ye to come out to him."

"Oh, Becky, don't be silly. I'll bet Henry's all in a huff at being taken off men's work to help me."

"He's uncommon handy at hidin' it, then," Becky said dryly and Elizabeth fled before her damnable blush could rise in her face.

For weeks, she had been marking flowering plants and trees close to the house, young dogwood and Judas trees that were small enough to transplant, wild forsythia, morning glory, vetch, honeysuckle and such, and so there was no time lost getting her new gardens planted once the scrub had been hacked out. Rus was a tall, desceptively thin black who worked tirelessly without saying a single word except in answer to a direct question. Except for the fact that he was exactly her age Elizabeth did not know anything more about him. He looked something like Kundo, the massive black who had been left behind to man the sloop, *Primrose*, for Weyland but Rus was so slight of build that it was hard to imagine him being Kundo's son. She had never asked Lis; inquiring into a slave's parentage was something a young lady simply did not do.

Two hound puppies, Fey and Feckless, had been making nuisances of themselves all morning, getting in the way, dig-

ging up newly planted bushes and swarming over Elizabeth
in spite of her brandished stick. It was they who first gave
notice of the approaching dugout.

"Be burnt f'r a heathen if yonder ain't a traveler," Henry
said, straightening. "Two of 'em. I'd best go f'r y'r father." He
shook his head at his own suggestion. "But ye'd be left alone
then and—Rus, run tell Old Marster and Marse George they's
strangers comin'."

"For pity's sake, don't act as though 'twere an Indian
massacre party," Elizabeth scoffed. "They look harmless
enough and—Rus, can't you hush these silly dogs?"

With a few firm words from Rus the hounds obediently
squatted and watched the canoe's approach, tongues lolling.
As the narrow craft drew closer, Elizabeth saw that it was
being paddled by a young shirtsleeved man. A much older
man in a wide-brimmed black hat and gray coat sat in the
bow.

The old man was looking toward the house, but the young
man in the white, open-throated shirt kept his eyes fixed so
boldly on her that he nearly sailed the canoe past the landing.
Elizabeth tried not to stare back but it was hard: he had
blond, almost yellow, hair that hung to his shoulders and his
face was as bronzed as George's. When he smiled his teeth
were startlingly white, and his eyes were the bluest she had
ever seen in a man's head.

She remembered her manners just in time; another minute
and one of the two would have been forced to greet her first.
"Welcome to Part-of-Providence," she said with a half curtsey.
"If you'll come ashore I'll send for my father, Squire Allyn,
and he'll welcome you properly."

She turned to signal Rus to go for Father and found that
the black boy had already left, taking the two puppies with
him.

"What did'st thee say?" a harsh voice cried. "Part-of-Providence? What outlandish nonsense is that?"

"Now, Father," the younger man said soothingly. He steered
the canoe in with an expert twist of his paddle and as the prow
bumped the shore he lithely leapt ashore. Leaning over to
grasp the gunwale he turned to smile at Elizabeth, over his
shoulder. "A good day to thee, Mistress Allyn," he said. "My
name is Robert Hosban and this is my father, Herman Hosban,
and we both thank thee for thy welcome."

Thee, thy, what kind of talk was this? She peered at the man as he straightened, wondering why he was laughing at her, but there was no derision in those remarkable eyes. Hosban—why, that was the name of the family who had owned this rundown place before it had been given to Father. Were these two here to lay claim to Part-of-Providence after all the Allyns' back-breaking work?

Her face must have reflected her thoughts because Robert Hosban said, "My father and I are on our way to see friends at the Gum Creek Ford and couldn't resist stopping off to see the old place."

"Stolen from us," his father barked, his scowl as black as his hat.

"This young lady did none of the stealing," the son chided. "Mind, thee promised there'd be no raking over dead coals if we stopped here."

"Stolen from you?" Elizabeth said, "Why, sir, this land was given my father in exchange for our home on the Chowan."

"Sh'ld have made inquiry about rightful title before takin' it," the old man snapped. Herman Hosban was a gnome of a man with a hooked nose and a jutting chin. Elizabeth thought he looked older than her father but his bright eyes, his snappish speech, and his constant wriggling gave evidence of his boundless energy.

"Make inquiry?" Elizabeth asked. She knew she was overmatched here and, besides, it was not a lady's place to dispute a gentleman's word but she had to answer that. "Sir, my father was assured by Colonel Tryon that—"

"Hah!" the old man broke in rudely. "If y'r father trusted William Tryon, he must be a fool."

"Father!" the son said sharply, but too late.

"I don't know y'r name or y'r errand, old man," George boomed behind her, "but any crooked old stick who calls William Weyland Allyn a fool ain't welcome here. So be on y'r way, both of ye, before I dump ye in the river."

The big man in the white shirt lost his smile but kept his temper.

"My father has a sharp tongue, friend, but he meant no disrespect to thy father, believe me." Robert Hosban said. "If any man may have reason to speak harshly of another, my father has the right to rail against Governor Tryon and his

officers"—the smile reappeared faintly—"although I agree that
it ill becomes him as a Quaker."

"Don't make excuses f'r me," the old man growled. "I'll do
my own talkin'." Slowly, carefully, he got to his feet. Fearfully,
as though the dugout might surge into midstream he stepped
ashore, then straightened to face a scowling George Allyn. A
short, bandy-legged man, Herman Hosban had to tilt back
his head to address George.

"I apologize f'r my rudeness, friend," he said, "but not f'r
my contention that His Excellency, Sir Bloody Guts Tryon,
ain't to be trusted. Nor his henchman, Fanning, nor—ah, there
be a pack of 'em, all thieves, usurers, criminals of the same
stripe. If that offends thee, friend, then my son and I will take
ourselves off, and gladly."

"Never mind William Tryon," George said gruffly. "I walked
up to hear ye callin' my father a fool."

"Why, as to that, I trusted Tryon's henchman so I must be
a fool, myself—aye, a bigger fool than any of thee 'cause I'm
left without an inch of land while thou hast Swarthmore Hall."

"Swarthmore Hall?" George echoed.

" 'Twas what we named this place, after Judge Fell's estate
near Ulverstone—but that's of no interest to thee, I trow."
The bird-bright eyes flickered here and there. "Thee've done
a deal of work on the old place since Robert and I last saw it."
He turned to Elizabeth. "Ar't planting pretties in the yard?
My goodwife had beds of phlox, marigolds, and larkspur when
we lived here. She'll be glad to know her yard's in good hands
again." She started to murmur a response, but the old man
cut her off.

"Awaitin' our return to our rightful home."

"Now, hold hard, old man," George roared. "Ye can't come
sailin' in here layin' claim to this land because ye once had it
and lost it—by y'r own stupidity or shiftlessness, from the
looks of it when we took over."

As Herman Hosban spluttered with rage, Elizabeth tried
to smooth things over. "What a thing to say to a guest," she
scolded. "My brother didn't mean it, sirs—'tis just that he's
surprised. We both are, as you can imagine. My father will be
here soon and whilst we wait for him, will you not come up to
the house and refresh yourselves?"

Receiving no response, she swung toward her half brother.
"Father's been sent for, hasn't he?" When George nodded

grudgingly, she turned back to the Quakers beside their dug-out canoe. "He'll be passing glad to see you, gentlemen—why, you're the first visitors we've had here, the very first to be offered *Allyn hospitality.*"

She bore down on the last two words, hoping they would remind George of his manners. "Aye, polin' that clumsy craft must've made ye hot and thirsty, by the looks of it," George said, regaining some of his composure.

"Made it m'self," old Hosban retorted. "Has't ever tried to hollow out a pirogue usin' live coals and a hatchet? No? I thought not, else thee'd not speak so lightly of somethin' thee c'ld never fashion in a thousand years."

Before George had a chance to explode, Elizabeth cried, "Why I think it's a *lovely* boat, Mister Hosban! And now, if you'll follow me, gentlemen . . . but mind the steps; they've not been fixed yet."

"There are a hundred and one things that've not been fixed yet," George said sourly. "Every time I turn around there's somethin' else that has to be done. Tryon's been in North Carolina but a little over a year. If you blame him for oustin' you from this place how do you explain everything falling into such ruin overnight?"

"Oh, that can wait till Father's here," Elizabeth chattered. "I'm sure he'll want to know all about this place so to save you from telling it twice—mind the steps, please."

They followed her up the sagging steps onto the creaky porch. She told herself that they really should have built a new front porch—but living, as they did, in the wilderness where there were no visitors, nobody had given it a thought.

Well, at least the front door was fairly respectable even though it hung on leather hinges and the two missing fanlight panes were still stuffed with rags. She had wondered about that fine door. It was the only part of the house that showed evidence of quality workmanship. The rest of the building had been hand-hewn and not by the most skilled craftsmen, either.

As if in answer to her thoughts, old Hosban said, "I brought that door from Philadelphia when I first came to this colony. It had shiny hinges then but they proved to be not brass at all but some base metal tricked out to cheat the buyer of his hard-earned money." He wagged his head. "The deceit of those Philadelphia sharpsters is beyond understandin'," he added.

"I've always thought it a lovely door," Elizabeth declared
in a syrupy voice as she pushed it open. "Becky," she called.
"We have visitors, our first at Part-of-Providence."

"Swarthmore Hall," Herman Hosban muttered, then almost
smiled as Rebecca came into the front room and dropped him
a curtsey.

And no wonder, Elizabeth thought with admiration. Becky
had been working since dawn, scouring the new raw planks
in the newly-built sections with vinegar and rubbing them
down with tallow and beeswax to give them color and grain.
But in spite of her labors, she looked as though she had just
bathed and napped, and risen in time to greet the guests
whom she had been expecting for days.

Just being in the same room with her efficient, comely half
sister made Elizabeth feel grimy and awkward. She thanked
heaven that there was no mirror over the fireplace mantel as
there had been at Middlebend: if she caught sight of herself
in her gardening clothes she would surely sink through the
floor.

Still, she managed to say quite cheerfully, "Rebecca, this
is Mister Herman Hosban and Mister Robert Hosban. Gentlemen, this is my sister, the Widow Tarbell."

The old man gave a jerky nod but made no move to remove
his hat. "Herman Hosban is the name, young woman," he said
grumpily. "We don't hold with titles."

Robert did his best to take the edge off his father's ungrac-
ious greeting. "We must beg your pardon for appearing at
your doorstep like this, Dame Tarbell. From the looks of
things, you're all very busy. We'll not stay, but my father had
to see the old place—we've heard that you've done wonders
with a place that I fear you found in a sadly ruined condition."

"Why, ye must stay, sirs," Becky protested. "We have too
few visitors to let you leave without a sup and a bite." She
turned to give a low command to a slave who was just out of
sight in the kitchen. Turning back, she gestured to the chairs
and settees. "Please make y'rselves comfortable, do. Friend
Hosban, did I hear this used to be y'r place? Then I pray ye
don't consider us interlopers, do ye?"

Elizabeth marveled silently. By voicing the old man's re-
sentment in a smiling question, Becky had made it impossible
for Hosban to hold to his view without appearing churlish.

Without answering, the old man went to the settee by the

hearth and lowered himself with a groan. "The chimney don't draw as good as it used to," he announced with relish. "Should draw better'n that. Somebody's been tamperin' with it. Wasn't no need to. I built that chimney with my own hands and it always drawed perfect."

George had left his precious fields to spend two full days repairing that chimney. Now, his face reddened under the old man's criticism. But instead of retorting he gnawed his lip and Elizabeth blessed him for it.

Her eyes met Robert Hosban's and the big, fair-haired Quaker gave her a quizzical glance before he asked, "Thee've passed the winter without sickness, I trust?" When Elizabeth assured him that there had been no illness to speak of, he hurried on before his father could inject any more caustic remarks.

"There's been a deal of fever in Cane Creek and Childsborough, though not so bad as some winters. I saw thy brother, Philip, just the other day and when I told him we might pass Swarth—thy place here, he bade me bring thee his fondest remembrances."

"How's he doin' up there?" George asked. "Has he turned the law courts upside down yet?"

Robert chuckled and started a reply but the old man by the fireplace interrupted. "That's what's needed, young Allyn, men with enough spine to turn the law courts upside down and those rascal officers with 'em. Upside down in a ducking pond—that would rid the county of some of the worst snakes. Though I doubt not that such men as Fanning and Jamieson and Jelke c'n breathe under water like water vipers." He glared at George, his hatchet chin thrust out belligerently. "Do'st thou hold with that crowd, young man? If thou do'st, we can't accept thy hospitality, not even a sup of cider."

"Nay, friend Hosban, we know naught of such matters," Becky said smoothly, as Yulee entered with a laden tray. "So do thee tell me what thy preference might be in thy refreshment. They say this Barbadoes is better than most."

Rum, for a strait-laced old Quaker? He'll walk out in a rage. But Herman Hosban nodded and said a drop of rum might be just the thing. His son followed suit and when George saw that their "drop" consisted of half a mug he seemed a bit more kindly disposed toward the pair. He had a deep suspicion of beer, cider, and malmsey drinkers and had always been down-right uncivil to teetotalers.

Now he filled his own cup with Barbadoes and addressed the younger Quaker in a voice that was almost genial. "Where did ye say ye're bound in ye'r dugout?"

"Pirogue is a better word," Hosban said, barely lifting his mouth from the cup.

"Pirogue then," George shrugged. "Where are ye bound— or am I pryin' to ask?"

"Nay, friend," Robert said easily. " 'Tis no secret, at least there's no reason why thee shouldn't know. We have friends in the Gum Creek settlement upstream and we came by boat up the Alamance out of a wish to see our old homestead."

"And because we thought it likely that Edmund Fanning might set an ambush f'r us on the Gum Creek Trail," Herman Hosban added bluntly. In answer to George and Elizabeth's shocked expressions he cried, "Think thee that that's unlikely in this honest and just colony of North Carolina, friends?" He squinted at Becky and added, "Ah, there's one who thinks it c'ld be so, am I right, Widder Tarbell?"

Becky kept her eyes on her cup as she poured another dollop of sack. "I've just come from the wild western hills, friend," she said in a low voice. "I know naught of politics, neither hereabouts nor where I've been."

The old man persisted. "But even out there in the wilds, didn't the thievin' tax collectors and forgin' registrars make thy life miserable?" When the young woman shook her head, anxious to steer the talk away from the Nolichucky country, the old man said, "Thee needn't fear to speak the truth here, child. Th'art on the Alamance now and soon—soon the Reg-ulators will rise and take this fair land from William Tryon and his creatures and we'll claim it for our own!"

[3]

"Father, watch thy tongue, I beseech thee!" young Hosban said, as the latch on the narrow side door beside the great stone fireplace lifted and William Weyland Allyn stepped into the room.

His looming presence reduced the room to silence until

he removed his tricorn hat to salute the two strangers who rose to acknowledge his entrance.

"Welcome, gentlemen," he said in his deep, rolling voice. "I beg your pardon for not being here sooner to receive you but I was overseeing a tree-felling crew deep in the woods and young Rus had trouble finding me."

He walked to the center of the room, stripping his riding gloves from his hands, his bootheels clacking on the puncheon floor. Because the day was warm, he wore a light linen coat, full skirted and falling almost to his knees. His breeches were workaday and so were his boots but his falling band was crisp and snowy, as always, and his wig, although unpowdered, was carefully arranged.

By the time the Hosbans visited Part-of-Providence, William Allyn had overcome most of his early dejection. He was not the William Weyland Allyn of old, far from it, but he had regained enough of his aristocratic composure to awe the two Quakers, at least for a few moments. But Herman Hosban recovered quickly. "Pardon granted," he grumbled. "Thee must be William Weyland Allyn I've heard so much of, eh?"

Allyn nodded and smiled, his dark eyes examining the little cockerel. "And you're Mister Hosban, I take it, the gentleman who once owned this place. I'm most grateful for your visit, sir. I've wanted to talk to you and settle certain questions in my mind."

"Aye, I've no doubt thee did," Hosban said dryly. "The first question I can settle, by y'r leave, is that Swarthmore Hall is still rightfully mine, no matter what Edmund Fanning or William Tryon or His Majesty, George the Third, may have told thee."

Elizabeth held her breath, waiting for the lightning to flash and the thunder to roll. She relaxed when she saw that her father seemed to be giving the remarkable statement thoughtful consideration. After a moment of silence, he turned to Rebecca. "Is there a drop of cider left in the springhouse, daughter? Or mayhap some small beer? I'm parched beyond a taste for wine or spirits, at the moment."

Without thinking Elizabeth said, "I'll get it, Father." After she left the room she swore at herself for being so quick to volunteer for the errand. She would miss all the best part of the conversation.

The springhouse was cool and fragrant with the smell of

cheese and butter, sausages and other smoked meats, and vats
of pickled food and such, but she did not tarry to enjoy the
aroma. Frantically, she pulled the stone jugs out of the spring-
hole by their anchored tethers, yanking the stoppers from three
bottles of buttermilk before she found one full of cider.

After scrambling up the path, she stood outside the back
door to catch her breath and to pat her hair. She wondered
fleetingly if she looked as disheveled as she felt. After a few
moments, she walked sedately into the parlor to hand the cider
jug to Becky.

" . . . by the blackest lie ever set down in the Book of
Judgment, friend," Hosban was crying. " 'Tis a wonder the
villain's hand didn't shrivel when he put his name to it."

William Allyn had taken a seat on the settee across the
hearth from the old man, drying his high forehead with a
lawn kerchief. His acquiline face showed deep concern but no
anger. He took the cup that Becky handed him, murmured
his thanks, and spoke to Hosban.

"But did you seek redress for your grievances in the courts,
may I ask?"

Herman Hosban came close to spitting on the floor in his
disgust. " 'Tis easy to see thou art new in these parts, friend
Allyn. The courts are in the hands of the same villains that
have made such a mockery of justice in every other office. I
tell thee our only chance f'r redress lies in our darin' to throw
the thieves out and set up our own government."

"But that's rebellion," George said. "D'ye think Tryon will
sit idly by, twiddlin' his thumbs in New Berne Town, whilst
ye take up arms 'gainst him and the king?"

"Nay, not the King," Robert said quickly. "That's got to be
understood at the start. We're loyal subjects of the king—
'tis only his corrupt colonial officers we'll rise against, particularly Fanning and his crowd in Childsborough."

George said wryly, "Which one of ye has the king's ear so
he'll know this?" He drained his cup and thrust it toward his
sister for a refill. "Nay, gentlemen, I know little about politics
nor do I want to, but I'll wager that by the time word of y'r
protests gets to Windsor Castle, Tryon will have made ye out
a pack of bloodthirsty savages worse than the Tuscaroras."
He nodded his thanks to Rebecca for the freshened cup and
added,

"But by that time, the governor will have stamped ye flatter than new wheat in a hailstorm, usin' troops and cannons to destroy ye."

"He dare not!" Herman cried. "Draw the sword 'gainst his own people? 'Twould be his ruination. Besides, even if he durst try to mount a force against us he'd have to call on colonial militia and they're our brothers. They suffer from tax oppression and corruption in high office just as we do, don't they?"

Both George and his father seemed about to speak but apparently each thought better of it. Elizabeth wondered if they wanted to express her own doubt that the plantation gentry who served as officers in the militia would balk at riding out against an uprising of yoemen along the western frontier.

She knew nothing about the militia except what Philip had told her. He had belonged to an Edenton troop for awhile but had quit with the excuse that the balls, routs, and alehouse pipe parties encroached too much on his law studies. Under William Allyn's questioning he had admitted that some of the troop's randans were too rich for his blood.

"Great God, we have a prig in our midst," George hooted when he heard this remark, but he had not really been sneering because George despised the young dandies of Edenton, himself.

She wondered how the men who commanded those eastern militia companies would respond, if William Tryon should tell them that a crowd of henscratch farmers had risen against His Majesty, George III.

She could almost hear them. Yoicks, halloo, gone awaaaaay! Hunting down ragged yoemen would be more of a lark to them than drawing a covert with the Chowan Hunt. Or perhaps she did them an injustice. Some of these same young gentlemen must have been involved with Phil in the Green Ribbon Club that Tryon had accused of plotting sedition.

Still, if she were Herman Hosban she'd not depend too much on the Edenton militia troop to fling their arms wide and embrace the Alamance rebels.

"Aye, that may well be so," she heard her father say. Then he continued. "Not to interrupt your discourse, sir, but can'st tell my son and me why this plantation is so isolated, why your fine house and this good land was let fall into such a sad state? You're the first travelers we've seen on this river and the trace has felt no hoof or wagon wheel save our own. Prithee, why is this?"

"Tell him, son," the old Quaker said. "The story's too painfull f'r me to risk rememberin'," He huddled on the settee, and handed his cup to Rebecca for another drink.

Robert Hosban seemed to Elizabeth more like what a peace-loving Quaker ought to be. His speech was low-voiced, throughtful and at times touched with humor in spite of the terrible story he had to tell.

According to the younger Hosban, the family's troubles began soon after they finished building their home and the outbuildings and putting in their first crops. "We were in a position much like thine, though not so well provided as thee must be, having no slaves, of course."

Why of course? Elizabeth asked silently.

"Then out of the blue came a notice from Fanning, the County Register. It seemed that the surveyors had made a bit of a mistake, a matter of an acre or two. They asked my father to present himself in Childsborough so the error could be fixed."

"Aye, 'twas there I made my first mistake, answerin' the dog's summons," the older Hosban muttered. " 'Twas his own surveyor who'd made the supposed mistake; I sh'ld've made *him* come to me."

Robert shook his long-haired blond head. " 'Twould not have mattered whether thee went to him or he came to thee," he said quietly. "The scheme was already made up."

"What scheme was that?" George asked.

Well, Robert explained, when he and his father had ridden to the Register's office in Childsborough they had found that the "bit of a mistake" involved more than half the tract they called Swarthmore Hall after the estate of Judge Fell, a Quaker sympathizer during Cromwell's time.

"We were told that our title was worthless but that a new, correct deed to the tract would be drawn up forthwith so that all our work would not have gone for naught." Robert managed a faint smile. "Of course there would be a small fee for the Register's new survey and the drawing-up of the papers. The fee was as far beyond our reach as the furthest star, a fact that the honorable County Register knew full well."

George made an exclamation under his breath. "What did ye do then, accuse him to his face of extortion?"

Hosban shook his handsome head. "Nay, friend, remember we were new here. We couldn't believe that it was extortion. We thought Fanning's surveyors had made an honest mistake and while the cost of setting the mistake to rights was high, we had no doubt that an equitable solution could be arrived at. We carefully explained our position, the pittance we had left after supplying our farm, the modest sums that were due us from the sale of our goods back in Pennsylvania, our hopes of earning a good return on our first crop, and so forth. We suggested that if Fanning could cut his fees in half, say, and give us a few years to pay, we'd be able to meet these unexpected obligations."

"Hah," Hermon Hosban snorted, and said nothing more.

The son glanced at the father, and shook his head ruefully. "Of course he said no," he went on. "I say of course because 'twas never Edmund Fanning's intent to merely swindle us out of this trumped-up fee. Nay, when he first sent for us he'd already put his name to another deed for our land and accepted a fat pouch of guineas to bind the bargain."

"Why—why, that was embezzlement," William Weyland Allyn exclaimed.

"Friend, embezzlement and all other like crimes come as easy to Edmund Fanning as breathin'," the older Quaker said. "But thee hath yet to hear the worst of it. Go on, Robert."

After the confrontation in Childsborough and after having been warned that they must meet this exhorbitant charge within the month, the Hosbans sought the services of an attorney.

"Nay, 'twasn't Squire Davis," Robert said before the question could be asked. "I understand thy son is reading law with him and as far as I know, he's a man of integrity."

"All of a pack," his father growled, but then subsided.

"This lawyer's name was—ah, what's to be gained by naming him?" young Hosban said with a shrug. "If a rumor was to get around that we'd reproached him he'd run baying to the judge for a writ of slander." The faint smile appeared again. "And in our position, we can do without that," he added.

William Allyn's face stiffened slightly. "If you fear that I'd not keep this conversation in full confidence, sir. . . ."

"Nay, 'tisn't that at all, friend Allyn," the Quaker said quickly, "and if I offended thee with my clumsiness, I ask your pardon. Nay, 'tis just that over the years we Hosbans have become unduly careful, mayhap, because we know that Fanning and his cronies mean to have our neck on the least excuse."

"We'll live t'see 'em all dance on air," his father said stoutly. "Or driven out of this country, at the very least."

"Not hanged, Father. We don't wish that fate for any man." The younger Hosban's voice was gently reproving.

George grumbled, "Well, if 'twas me and this man did what ye said, tried to cheat me out of the land I'd cleared and planted, I'd call hangin' too good f'r the bastard—beggin' y'r pardon, Becky, Betsy."

"But thou art no Quaker," the other said softly. "We try to be men of peace and forgiveness, no matter how hard it is at times."

"What of these Regulators ye spoke of?" the younger Allyn asked. "Ye barely mentioned 'em but they didn't sound to me like any meek crowd of peacemakers."

His father said, "Later, by your leave, George. I'd hear more of this unprincipled business with the County Register. You say you engaged an attorney—did he enter demurrers for you?"

"He listened to our story with great interest and sympathy, clucking his tongue and shaking his head at decent intervals, and when we were done he told us that although it grieved him deeply, he'd be unable to take our case. He pleaded a press of clients. To hear him tell it, they were battering down the door to get at him."

George took a swallow of rum and said, "I s'pose every other legaler ye went to had the same sad tale, eh?"

Herman Hosban spoke from the settee. "Thee catches on quick, friend. Aye, they're all of a stripe and all so beholden to Fanning and his venal judges that not one durst say aye if the others say nay."

Elizabeth's father spoke quietly but confidently. "I can promise you this, gentlemen, that when my son, Philip, finishes his reading with Squire Davis and is admitted to practice, there will be at least one lawyer who'll dare say aye or nay on the merits of the case offered him. You have my word on't."

The younger Hosban said, "Good. There's a screaming need for such a man. The sooner he's admitted, the better, I say."

"But the question is," his father put in sourly, "will the Fanning crowd let thy son practice his profession, Allyn? There have been other honest lawyers—or as honest as any lawyer can be, beggin' y'r pardon—there've been others who've tried to crack the Fanning ring and have been turned away. Most of 'em were hounded out of these parts by the unscrupulous dogs."

"My son won't be intimidated," Allyn said. "Besides, his place under Squire Davis was arranged by Governor Tryon, himself." He met the Quaker's stare steadily. "I'm certain that I don't have to assure you that there were no strings attached," he said frostily. "My son's not Tryon's man nor anyone else's save his own."

After a brief silence, Robert resumed his story. "To get on with our tale of woe, we made inquiries about town and learned the true state of affairs, that Fanning meant to rob us of our rightful property no matter what we might try to do to stop him. He had to snatch Swarthmore Hall from us, you see; the man to whom he'd fraudulently sold our land was coming west to claim his new estate."

On their return to the Alamance, the Hosbans had rallied their few neighbors and enlisted the support of other Quakers in the county. Meanwhile, they had sent a protest off to Governor Dobbs at New Berne, demanding the investigation of the skullduggery in Childsborough.

"What did the governor say to that?" Allyn asked.

Hosban shrugged. "We doubt he ever got the petition," he replied. "Our courier could never get to see the governor and though his secretary pledged his word that he would bring it to Dobbs' attention. . . ." He shrugged again as if to ask the worth of a governor's secretary's pledge.

"This was before Tryon came here?" George asked.

"A full two years before he graced us with his presence. But this colony's ills didn't begin with William Tryon's arrival on these shores, no matter what people believe. Nay, there were venal colonial officers in North Carolina long before Tryon ever thought of becoming our little king. Fanning did exceeding well for himself long before Tryon. Unless he's unseated from his high horse now, I daresay he'll keep on getting richer after Tryon's gone."

"Dead and gone," his father amended bitterly.

"What did Fanning do, oust you and y'r friends from this place when ye made y'r stand?" George asked, to cover the silence.

Both men nodded. "He sent a small army of sheriff's men to seize us and our friends and all our belongin's," the older man explained. "Carried us all off, men, women, and children, to Childsborough chained like desperate criminals. Claimed we attacked the officers with clubs and stones and even pistols when they came to enforce the law. And I swear this to thee, Allyn, not a one of us offered the least resistance —why, 'tis against our deepest convictions."

He paused and almost smiled. "I must confess there was one unfortunate happening," he said. "My good wife forgot herself when one of Fanning's brutes tried to lay hold of her and bounced a skillet off his pate." The shadowy smile blossomed into a real grin. "It made a pretty noise although of course my good wife was properly repentent of her unseemly lapse, after it was over."

Good for her, Elizabeth thought. *If I'd been there. . . .*

"Were you in gaol long?" George asked.

"Just long enough for everything we owned, livestock, furniture, even our clothes, to mysteriously disappear from Swarthmore Hall." Robert replied. "Then we were taken before one of Fanning's judges. The man was so drunk that I spent the entire hearing wondering how he managed to keep from falling off the bench. He managed to tell us that we were to be set free by virtue of Edmund Fanning's unbounded generosity but were under strict bond not to venture within three statute miles of any boundary of Swarthmore Hall."

"Aye," his father said, "if Fanning found out we were here now he'd have us jugged f'r disobeying the court's dictum— and thee, too, no doubt, Allyn, f'r offerin' us y'r hospitality."

Elizabeth saw her father's frown. The girl could tell that he was dismayed by the idea of having these two persecuted Quakers under his roof if the law had forbidden them to be there. *Ah, Father,* she thought, *you don't mean that this tyrant, Fanning, can intimidate you?*

George finished his drink, wiped his hand across his mouth, and said, "Ye still haven't explained the reason f'r this place bein' such a ruin when we came here—and why it's been avoided like the plague since."

The two visitors exchanged a silent glance, and there was a long pause before Robert took up the story again. "Why, as to that, it's summat of a mystery, friend George, and a bloody mystery, at that. Less than a fortnight after the new owners, a family of Virginia slaveowners named Moore, took possession, a fur trader named Haskell stopped off here on his way down the creek to the Haw and found them all murdered, every one."

"*Murdered!*" The stark word was sounded by all four Allyns in a single voice.

The Hoskans nodded. "Aye," the son said, "Moore, his wife, their three young children, and the wife's spinster sister. All six most foully slain by brutes who"—he flicked a glance at Elizabeth—"cruelly mistreated the women and the young daughter before they ended their misery." He looked around at the appalled faces. "I'm sorry to have to tell thee this but— well, it's what happened."

"Did they ever catch the murderers?" Becky managed.

A headshake. "Nay. The slaves had vanished so some thought they were to blame. But others argued that Moore was a kindly master—if a man can be said to be kindly to his human chattel—and they had no reason to do such a terrible thing. These latter held to the view that a band of renegades did the foul deed and took the slaves with them, to sell them in South Carolina or Georgia where I understand few questions are asked, as long as the black is sound of wind and limb."

"What about Indians?" William Allyn asked.

"Nay, 'tweren't no Injuns' work," Herman Hosban answered. He looked down at his cup. "My son didn't mention a third opinion that was whispered about at the time," he said cautiously. "A few of us thought it passin' strange that the murderers did no damage to the house nor stole a single head of livestock, only the blacks who might bear witness 'gainst 'em if by some miracle a court would let a slave testify. For don't ye see? When 'twas all over and done, Edmund Fanning had this land back in his hands again, with all those horses and oxen and milch cows to pay him f'r his trouble in reclaimin' the place f'r the colony."

"Ye don't mean to charge the man with murder, do ye?" George asked huskily.

"Nay, I lay no charges 'gainst anyone," Hosban replied. "I but point out that he was the only one who gained through the whole string of misadventures." He laughed mirthlessly.

"He stood to gain a deal more, mayhap, if word hadn't spread that this place was accursed. There were so many stories of witches and warlocks revelin' here and so many people who dropped out of sight f'r one reason or another that there was not a man in these parts but wouldn't travel ten miles out of his way to 'scape layin' eyes on it."

The old man rattled his cup to gain Becky's attention. "Poor Edmund Fanning found he had a valuable tract on his hands but that he couldn't drain another penny from it, try as he might." He paused. "Till his protector, William Tryon, jerked the strings that drew thee out here, friend Allyn."

[4]

There was a strained silence during which Elizabeth looked around the room with round eyes. This house, perhaps this very room, had been the scene of brutal murder and unspeakable rape? The hardy folk of this border country so feared the witches and warlocks they said still haunted the place that they traveled miles to keep from passing by, lest they be grabbed by the ghosts? Were *all* the night sounds she had heard in the loft really rats and mice and squirrels? Had *all* those night cries come from owls and bobcats?

She shivered as she remembered all the night visits she had made to the privy without a second thought, when all the time there may have been. . . .

Her tremulous thoughts were jarred by Rebecca's free-flowing laughter. " 'Struth, Father," she chuckled, "if weren't too silly, I'd swear this man thinks he can scare us Allyns off this land with wild stories of ghosts and goblins."

As Herman Hosban emitted an outraged squawk, Becky held up a hand. "Oh, I know thee didn't mean any such thing. Ye said at the start thee'd heard of William Weyland Allyn so thee must know 'twould be a waste of time to—"

"I didn't come here to be called a humbug," old Hosban broke in. "Thy father and thy brother wanted to know why this place had been avoided and I told 'em. Accusin' me of some deceitful intent scurse recommends thee as a proper modest woman, Widow Tarbell, and—"

"Now, hold hard," George grated. "My sister only said what we all thought. Such talk of ghosts and goblins are meant f'r children, not f'r grown men. Don't tell me *you* believe any of this nonsense, do ye?"

"What I believe and what I don't is my own concern," the old man retorted angrily. He stomped across the floor to the door. There he turned, his face black with anger. "To set the record straight—though thee don't deserve any explanation— my son and I came here to bid thee join the honest folk here- abouts in our war 'gainst persecution."

"A Quaker, recruitin' sojers f'r a war?" George jibed.

"Gentlemen, gentlemen," William Weyland Allyn cried. "Rebecca, I'll ask you to apologize to Mister Hosban for your implications—quite thoughtlessly spoken, I'm sure."

"She needn't 'pologize t'me," Herman snapped. "I need no lord o' the manor condescension from a pack of haughty slaveholders."

"Father," Robert Hosban implored, "hold thy temper, do! The young lady meant no insult—she only laughed at the idea of witches holding covens here, as we both do, thou knowest full well."

"She said I made up the story so they'd leave Swarthmore Hall in a fright," the bandy-legged man said stubbornly. "Thee dids't hear her as well as I."

Rebecca spoke in a smooth, warm voice. "Why, if that's what it sounded like, I mixed my words, friend Hosban." She dropped a low curtsey, bending so that the Quakers could not help but see her two firm white breasts. As Becky straightened, she smiled and said,

"Now ye must sit at our table for supper and lodge here tonight, else I'll be chided f'r my rude behavior." She kept her eyes on the furious old man, the appeal in her gaze making her almost as beautiful as she had been before all her hardship. "Please, sir, do'st forgive me?"

Oh, clever clever Becky! She had laughed away the black taint of murder and ghosties and when her derision had angered the Quakers, she had proceeded to charm her way back into their favor. That fleeting glimpse of her white body had been no accident and yet it had been so artfully done that no one could say she overstepped the bounds of propriety.

Her kind of witchery worked faster on Robert Hosban than on his father but both men were obviously subdued. Robert answered Rebecca's curtsey with a bow and said,

"We only meant to drop by and meet the new owners of this place, Widow Tarbell, and so we'd not put thee to all the trouble of—"

"Nonsense," William Allyn interrupted. "We have too few guests to let you escape so soon. Do sit you down again, Mister Hosban, and perhaps you, sir"—with a nod toward Robert—"would like to ride over the place with George and see what we've done and are trying to do with, ah, this place you were so cruelly robbed of."

"I'd like that," Robert said quickly. "Whilst we're gone, Father, please give friend Allyn the latest news at Childsborough—but avoid the skittish subjects, I beseech thee."

George managed to put on a good face in serving as young Hosban's guide. But Elizabeth knew that George resented having a cloud cast over the plantation that he was beginning to love almost as much as he had loved Middlebend. After he and Robert left the house, William Allyn settled back in a chair beside the elder Quaker. Having replenished their cups, Elizabeth went to the kitchen to help with supper. The yard planting would have to wait: she refused to leave the house and risk missing something.

When Becky came in, Elizabeth whispered, "Thank heavens you had the sense to laugh at that story. Another minute and I might have believed it, myself."

Rebecca threw a warning look at Hauny and Yulee, in a far corner of the kitchen. "Fool," Elizabeth said to herself, "another second and you'd have blurted the word 'ghost' and then—big trouble!" There still might be, if the kitchen slaves had been eavesdropping and had heard talk of murder and witches. If they had, the story would spread over Part-of-Providence like a grass fire under a gale, embroidered beyond belief with each retelling.

She had heard of this happening on other plantations. When Horace Iglehart of Maple Hill had shot himself after his wife drowned in a squall, one of the house servants had claimed to see his ghost walking on the gallery at dusk. Immediately, word spread that the house was haunted and soon the ghost was seen everywhere on the plantation, riding a white horse by the river, standing beside the sawmill door, even strolling through the tobacco barns. The result was that Jake and Morgan Iglehart hadn't been able to get a decent day's work out of a single one of their field hands no matter how hard they tried.

A lot of the Maple Hill slaves tried repeatedly to run away no matter how they were punished. It got so bad that finally the young men had to sell off the whole lot at a great loss and bring in a new crew from Virginia who knew nothing of the "Ha'nt of Maple Hill."

Now, Elizabeth wondered if their hopes for Part-of-Providence were to be dashed by panic among the slaves. Her eyes sought some assurance from Rebecca but she seemed oblivious to the awful danger. Her voice was matter-of-fact as she called, "Yulee, Hauny, where's Ella?"

Yulee answered first. "She sick, Mistess. She gone back her cabin fo a spell."

"Does yo need her bad, I go git her," Hauny offered. "But she pow'ful cramped, Mizz Rebecca."

Becky shook her head. "No, we don't need her—not right away, at least. You go back to what you were doing, Hauny. Yulee, come into the buttery with Mistress Elizabeth and me."

Elizabeth followed Becky into the small room off the kitchen, the supply wench just behind her. Once inside, Rebecca turned to Yulee and asked in a low voice, "How much did ye hear of what was said in the other room just now, girl?"

Yulee's eyes grew larger than life, their whites gleaming in the semidarkness. "Me, I dint heah nuthin', Mizz 'Becca," she replied in a low, scared, voice. "Ain' mah place to lissen when de quality speaks. Ah don' know what they talkin' 'bout, nohow, Mizz 'Becca."

"Don't lie to me," Becky said with hushed ferocity. "Y'r eyes gave you away just now."

"No, missy, I dint heah nuthin', I sw'ar I dint."

Rebecca paused and then her voice grew heavy with menace. "All right, but I warn ye, Yulee; if one word of what was said gets to anybody—*anybody*, black or white—I'll have ye whipped and sold away from here so fast y'r head will swim. And don't think Marse George will lift a finger to stop it. I promise ye, he'll be the first to lay on the cat. D'ye understand?"

"Mizz 'Becca, Ah don' know why you sayin' this to pore Yulee. Ah sw'ar Ah ain' heard nuthin' and I woon't tell nobody effen Ah did, which Ah dint." The huge black eyes moved to Elizabeth. "Miss 'Lizabeth, you tell Mizz 'Becca Ah been a good guhl, ain' nevvuh made no trouble, no way."

Elizabeth said firmly, "You'd better listen to Miss Rebecca, Yulee. If you didn't hear anything, there's nothing you can tell anybody. If you did listen—well, what Miss Rebecca said is true; you'll be whipped and sold away if you repeat it."

"No, missy, no, don' sell me away! Ah sw'ars iffen if it do be tole, won't be tole by me, Ah sw'ar!"

"We'll have ways of knowin'," Becky said grimly. "Now get back to y'r tasks and don't dare to snivel in front of Hauny and get her to askin' questions, too. When she asks ye what we were talkin' about, tell her—tell her I scolded ye f'r bein' late yesterday mornin'."

"I tole you about that, Mizz 'Becca."

"I know ye did and I don't believe a word of it. Now get back to work and remember—I'll have my eye on ye from now on."

"D'you think she'll blab?" Elizabeth asked when Yulee left.

Rebecca shook her head. "I ain't even sure she heard anything but if she did, I don't think she'll spread the bad word. She's smarter'n most of 'em, mebbe smart enough to brave ghosties rather than lose darlin' George. I'll have a word with him, too. If Yulee needs a bigger scare throwed into her, he's the one who c'n do it."

Becky started to leave the buttery, saying, "Now we've got to make sure these two fine guests of ours don't spread any more yawp about ghosts at the table or anywhere else where black ears might hear." She paused and added, "Which prob'ly was the reason they stopped here in the first place."

Following her half sister out into the hall, Elizabeth murmured, "I can't believe they'd do anything like that on purpose, Becky."

"Ye can't, eh? Well, I can, with no strain at all. Quakers think all slaveholders hide cloven hooves beneath their boots and horns under their perukes. Seein' that this precious pair think we're holdin' title to land that's rightfully theirs, they must hate us more than usual. So it wouldn't make me swoon with shock to find out they came here intendin' to ruin us with a slave panic started by a pack of lies about murder and ghosts."

"But there must be some reason why nobody uses the trace or the creek past our place."

"D'ye think Phil wouldn't have heard about this murder if there was aught to it? And in Cedar Valley they swallowed and spit up more rumors than they could keep down, from as far away as London, but never a word did I hear of this massacre that's supposed to have happened right next door to 'em, so to speak. It don't sound right to me, Betsy."

Elizabeth considered Becky's words. "Nor me," she admitted. "But—well, perhaps I can see where the old man might do such a thing, but his son, Robert—"

"Ho, ye've got much to learn, child. The prettier the man, the more he's to be suspicioned, take my word f'r it." Rebecca paused in taking some pieces of special china down from their shelves. "And he is a pretty one, that Robert Hosban, ain't he?" she asked. Her voice lost its hard edge. In fact, Elizabeth noted with astonishment, it was almost dreamy.

Whether William Allyn somehow convinced Herman Hosban that any more talk of ghosts could be ruinous, or George explained the danger to Robert during their tour of Part-of-Providence, or Becky used her wiles to charm both Quakers into silence, Elizabeth never knew, but for whatever reason, not a word of haunted houses was passed after that.

Elizabeth often wondered just how much the blacks heard of their owners' conversations. Some of their neighbors back on the Chowan had acted as though their house slaves were deaf and dumb; they said *anything* in front of their blacks and sometimes talked about a slave in his hearing as though he were miles away. The Allyns tried to keep all personalities out of their conversation when a black was within earshot. While this rule was often broken, especially during the heat of a squabble between the younger members of the family in the days when they were growing up, Elizabeth, for one, was always conscious of the fact that a slave could hear and see as well as anybody else.

Lis, for instance, could not only understand what was being said but usually knew what lay behind the spoken word. Trying to keep a secret from Lis had been almost impossible when she was a child; the old slave could ferret out the truth every time, no matter how clever she thought herself in hiding it. As for Yulee, Elizabeth knew little about the light-skinned wench except that she only had to explain a task to her once whereas it took three or four times with the others before they got it right. Once in awhile she had caught a look in Yulee's eye which hinted that in spite of her gullah talk and occasional deliberate stupidity, the wench understood a lot more of what was going on than she wanted to be given credit for.

Kundo, the giant deckhand who had been left behind at Weyland's plantation, Fairview, was another slave who had sometimes given her this same impression. Kundo had not spoken a dozen words in her hearing but there had been times when she had seen him squatting on the foredeck of the sloop, responding to a joke told in the sternsheets as fast as the quickest witted white man.

But these were the exceptions Elizabeth told herself. Most slaves were willing, cheerful, loyal, but lacked wit. An example was Ella, the kitchen wench: when she came into the kitchen, Mother, Lis, and Elizabeth had told her how important it was for her to pick all the pieces of shell from crabmeat before fixing cakes. Each time they had crabcakes, Ella was given the task of picking out the bits of shell and each time she had picked the meat fine. Then one day somebody forgot to tell Ella about removing the shells, and even though she had performed the task a dozen times before, the crabcakes had come to the table bristling with bits of shell.

"Nobody done tole me," Ella had wailed when Lis descended on her, sparks shooting from her eyes, and so of course she had not been punished.

The trouble was they couldn't *think*—or perhaps that was the blessing the Good Lord had bestowed on them. For sometimes when the blue devils claimed her and all the world was grim and gray, Elizabeth found herself wondering how it could be right for her to have so much and Rus, for example, to have nothing, nothing at all except his ragged hand-me-down britches and a kind master and a life of hard work that stretched ahead, on and on, day after day. Then she had explained away her doubts by remembering what her elders said—that blacks were born, lived, and died in a world all their own, and for a white to try to judge their happiness or lack of it by his own standards was pure folly.

Even Father admitted he knew almost nothing of what went on in a Negro's woolly head but this much was sure: they had no memory for either joy or sorrow, they never looked beyond the end of that one day, there was no love between them, as their masters knew love, and, all in all, their lot was better than many of their owners' because they had no worries, no defeated ambitions, no fears beyond the moment's superstition and, most of all, they had a childlike faith in an afterlife in which they would all be white and rich and never have to lift a finger at work again.

Once she had overheard her father explaining it to Philip.

"Let the Quakers and those others who say that slavery is inhumane explain why, if this be so, every black in the colonies hasn't run away? You know as well as I do 'twould be impossible to keep them if they all made a run for it. No, the unarguable fact is that they're created to be slaves and they're content with their lot. They're suited for no other place in our enlightened civilization and the Lord has given them their understanding of this fact."

And then there was mention of the sons of Ham and how they had been cursed to dwell as slaves forever. That was Holy Writ so who could argue against it? As for Father's simple explanation that slaves must be happy or they would all run away, Elizabeth thought she must be an unnatural daughter for remembering the few times that a slave from Middlebend or a neighboring plantation had tried to escape and been caught and dragged back to suffer the whip or sometimes to have his ear notched.

"Discipline," Father would say. "They need it, they must have it, if they don't get it they'll go wild."

Why she should be thinking of these things at table that night, she did not know. Perhaps it was because she was hoping that these two Quakers would not rile George with any talk against slaveowners. As it turned out, both Hosbans minded their manners and kept the conversation away from ha'nts and slaves and only made passing reference to the Regulators, although George kept after them to tell him more.

" 'Tis a band we've formed to work f'r justice in this country," Herman Hosban explained, almost reluctantly. "We're all men with modest holdin's. I doubt you gentry would find aught of interest in it."

"D'ye mean us Allyns would be barred because we have too grand a place? But ye said this property was once yours, so why d'ye call us gentry when you were not?"

Robert explained quietly that although it was true that they had held title to this land, they had not cleared a third of what the Allyns had put in cultivation in the short time they had been there nor had they intended to for a long time to come.

"Then why did ye need so many acres?" George asked.

"Now, son, it's not our place to inquire into the gentlemen's reasons," William Weyland put in.

" 'Tis no secret," the older Quaker barked. "I meant the land f'r my children and my grandchildren. Just as thy forefather did, Allyn, when they first started buildin' the family's fortune."

Father bowed down the table to the fierce old man. "Most certain, friend Hosban. A gentleman's concerns are ever fixed on the wellbeing of his line."

"Thee beant callin' me a gentleman, be thee?" Allyn started to say something more but the Quaker held up a hand. "Na, na, 'twould require even more than this fair land of North Carolina can offer to make a gentleman of me or mine. Besides, we Friends hold that all titles be vanity. Why, even Edmund Fanning calls himself a gentleman and so does this newcomer, Dedshall, who everybody knows was—"

"Who?" The word was shouted by all four Allyns at once.

Both Hosbans looked startled. "Why—why, I b'lieve the name's Dedshall," Herman managed when he recovered his voice. "He *says* he's from Virginia but he talks like a Bowditch scamp and he's been recognized by one of our Regulators as one of Granville's tax collectors in the eastern hundreds. They say he stole more taxes than ever saw Granville's purse and further that—"

"Your pardon," William Weyland Allyn broke in, "but I'd best tell you that my oldest son is married to a Dedshall and my youngest daughter"—with a nod toward the numbed Elizabeth—"is betrothed to Mister Edward Dedshall of Edenton."

There was a stark silence and then Robert Hosban said manfully, "Then I'm sure my father must have the name wrong."

But old Hosban refused to be silenced, even though Elizabeth prayed he would take his son's hint and shut up. "No," he said, "I'm certain sure I have the name right. Dedshall, Ben Dedshall, and, aye, he's from Edenton."

It can't be! Or mayhap Edward didn't come west with his father. But even so, Mister Dedshall would have sent word to us unless—unless the marriage contract's been torn up and I'm not betrothed at all.

[5]

After the first feeling of amazement ebbed, Elizabeth had
a sense of relief. But this feeling was quickly supplanted by
one of indignation. Who was that great gawk, Edward Dedshall, to think he could jilt the daughter of William Weyland
Allyn? *He* had been the one to press his unwanted attentions
upon her, barely waiting until little Jeremy was buried. And
what a splendid proposal Edward Dedshall had made her!
Why, it had been more of a threat than a lover's plea.

When she had warned him that Father would likely set
the hounds on him if he asked him for her hand at that black
hour, Edward had replied, *If you'd see your father cleared of*
the crimes he's charged with, even saved from the gallows if
old Maule dies, which is likelier than not, then you'll think
twice about letting any hounds be set on Edward Dedshall.

She remembered every word he'd said; they were stamped
on her memory for all time. And she had sat there like a nit-
wit, letting him insult her and her family instead of calling
George or Philip or *somebody* to have him thrown off the
place.

But then Edward had tempered his rude outburst with a
lawyer's arguments that had seemed so *reasonable*. Her
father needed allies in high places if he expected to escape
total ruin. Several men of position who should have been
loyal to William Weyland Allyn for past favors had already
indicated where they stood by staying away from Jeremy's
funeral. But if the Lord Proprietary, Baron Granville, could
be swayed to Father's side by Milord's trusted bailiff, Benjamin Dedshall, then the whole outlook would be changed. And
how could Ben Dedshall refuse to do this if his oldest son
were betrothed to William Allyn's daughter?

True, the Dedshalls and the Allyns were already linked by
Louisa Dedshall's marriage to Weyland Allyn but according
to Edward, this was not enough to enlist Ben's full support.
Louisa had always been a most rebellious daughter, not in
the least sympathetic to her father, and since her marriage
she had stayed close to Fairview, only rarely inviting her
family to visit. Elizabeth knew that her half brother, Weyland,
had not helped matters; he loved Louisa with all the passion
his phlegmatic soul was capable of but Ben Dedshall's con-

niving disgusted him and the bailiff's posturing bored him and Weyland was never one to hide his true feelings.

So, the evening of Jeremy's burial, Elizabeth accepted Edward's proposal, in the belief that it was the only way to save her father from the gallows. Later, she discovered that her father and Ben Dedshall had been making preliminary moves toward a marriage contract between Edward and herself before the Maule incident turned their world upside down.

If there had been another swain, she might not have accepted Edward but the truth was that there had been no cavalcade of young gentlemen beating a track to Middlebend in pursuit of her hand. The reflection in her glass revealed that she had no great physical virtues except for a rather astonishing bosom. And although she had been schooled to read, write, do sums, sew, play the dulcimer, cook and ride and manage household slaves, she was no shining prize over whom beaux would fight duels. So if it was required that she marry and birth a litter of children, she supposed it might as well be Edward Dedshall.

Later, her attitude toward Edward had changed from sufferance to something close to love when he came to her side after Tryon's invasion. Or if not love, then certainly pride; at least one man had found her desirable enough to jump into a skiff in a storm to come to her rescue. Edward Dedshall might not look like much and he might favor double-jointed words where simple ones would do, and he might be so pallid as a lover that he never kissed her, but, by God, he had recklessly risked his life for her and for that he could be excused everything else.

And now this! The—the scurvy dog!

"How long has he been in Childsborough, do you know?" Father was asking. His voice was low-pitched, conversational, as though Benjamin Dedshall's appearance in these parts was interesting but not important.

"Not f'r long," Herman Hosban said. His tone was uncharacteristically subdued. "I've not talked with the man, myself. Indeed, I doubt that he's met anyone outside Fanning's little clique. They keep to themselves, ye know—they have to, else—hm—nay, as I said, I've not met him."

George rumbled, "Is the whole family in Childsborough or just Ben, d'ye know?"

The elder Hosban looked across the table at his son, seek-

ing assistance. He plainly wanted his son to take over and
get them out of this awkward spot.

"Why, I believe *some* of his family came out with him,"
the big Quaker said carefully. "I know even less than my
father about the true facts of the matter but I did hear they
stayed for some time at Bartram's Forge, east of Childsborough, before coming on."

George put the next question before his father could cut
him off. "D'ye s'pose my brother, Philip, knows that the Dedshalls are right there in the same town with him?"

"I can't say. Perhaps not, for while Childsborough ain't the
biggest town in the colonies, 'tis curiously split in little groups
that don't mingle much. As my father said, the courthouse
crowd stays to itself and, ah, my understanding is that Dedshall—well, it's hard to explain."

He turned toward William Weyland Allyn at the head of
the table. "You asked about the Regulators. They're not the
villains that some would name them, not by any means. We've
been branded traitorous rebels by Governor Tryon but we're
not, believe me. Our only quarrel is with the corruption and
venality in colonial offices and the denial of a voice in the
conduct of our own affairs. Ever since this country was opened
up we've been overtaxed, brazenly swindled, and persecuted
when we protested the injustices heaped upon us. If thee'd
only talk to some of our members, sir, I believe thee'd not only
drop any suspicions thee might have of them as lawless malcontents but sympathize with our cause, morally or even
actively."

Devil take your Regulators—what about Edward Dedshall?
Elizabeth thought.

But Father seemed eager to accept the turn of the conversation, even though George, hunched over his plate, looked
as if he wanted only to learn the details of the Dedshall's
arrival. Elizabeth could feel Rebecca's eyes glancing from
one to the other. She must be bursting with curiosity but she
was playing the gracious hostess again.

"Aye, friend Allyn," Hosban said heartily. "Why not come
along with us to Gum Creek Ford? There's a man or two up
there that c'n tell thee some things that'll join thee solidly
with us to the very end, I pledge thee."

The man at the head of the table smiled as he shook his
head. "I thank you for the invitation, gentlemen, but I can't

go with you. Although my son manages this place, I still have some small duties that require my presence here."

"Ye make y'r own part sound too insignificant," George protested. "We'd be lost without y'r direction, sir—ask anybody on this plantation if ye don't believe me."

Dear George! Was there ever a man so thoughtful? And to think that he laughs at what he calls his field hand manners.

"My son flatters me," William Allyn said, the pride brightening his acquiline features. "But apart from my work here, there's another reason why I can't accept your invitation, friend Hosban. You see, when Colonel—Governor Tryon arranged for our removal to the Alamance, he ordered me to swear a new oath of fealty. It wasn't necessary, of course, but the fact remains I did swear it and so did all other members of my family, saving Dame Tarbell who was not present. And by the terms of that oath I'm sworn to show no opposition, spoken or active, to any officer of the king, from the highest rank to the lowest, from the Chancellor to—why, I suppose to the newest clerk in County Register Fanning's office."

He cast his calm smile at the dumbfounded old Quaker down the table. "So you see that even though I'm sure I'd be convinced of the true cut and just aims of your Regulators, I could be considered an enemy in your camp should I go with you. And on my own part, I'd be risking a breach of trust should I listen to any remarks that Governor Tryon or any of his officers might consider seditious."

Herman Hosban struggled to find words.

"But—but d'ye mean to say that no matter what crimes are committed by Tryon's thieves and cutthroats ye'll remain silent? Why, ye're as bound and muzzled as any Scot after Culloden—aye, worse, for there's many of them that are callin' the Culloden Oath a tyrant's imposition and therefore null and void."

"An oath is an oath," William Weyland Allyn said quietly, adamantly.

"And I say that no man, not even thee, friend Allyn, can sit idly by whilst his fellows are risin' up in righteous protest 'gainst cruel injustice."

Allyn deliberately raised his cup to his lips, sipped and set it down again. His voice was low, pleasant, almost serene when he answered. "I'm an old man who's done his share of protesting, joined causes, even killed in the name of justice, law and order. I'm nearing the end of a long road, not in the place I'd have chosen to be had the choice been left to me but in a country that's pleasant enough and will be still more comfortable before I'm finished here.

"I intend to spend the years left me in peace, fully savoring the satisfactions of my situation—something I neglected to do back at Middlebend, whence we came."

A faint smile touched the thin lips. "And so you see I'm done with protesting, gentlemen. If you don't think I can stay apart from agitation and turmoil, you're mistaken. Nothing—*nothing*, I say, can make me break this pledge I've sworn to myself: William Weyland Allyn can never again be involved in anything outside the boundaries of this plantation."

Chapter Four

[1]

WHEN ELIZABETH knelt beside Edward Dedshall in the little Elm Creek Ford chapel and listened to Rector Micklejohn recite the words that would make her Edward's wife, the one hope that sustained her was that Edward really wanted the marriage.

He had assured her that he did, time after time, swearing by everything holy that no one had forced him into this.

"Can'st believe I truly love you, after all this time?" he had pleaded. " 'Od's blood, it's been almost two years since first I declared my love for you."

Actually, their wedding day was three months short of being the second anniversary of Edward's strange declaration of love. Indeed, every aspect of this love affair had been passing strange, not at all what Elizabeth had dreamed when she had been a little girl, playing with her dolls at Middlebend. Where were her lover's swooning glances, the palpitations she should feel with every glimpse of him, the passionate declarations of eternal love, the little jealousies, the lovers' quarrels, the tearful reconciliations?

Even the priest who was joining her in this union was not what she expected. Micklejohn was an Anglican and that was another strange thing, that Father should have insisted on an Anglican to perform the marriage. He was from Hillsboro, which had been Childsborough until a month ago, and his appearance was far better suited for a funeral than a wedding.

She did not know how many marriages Rector Micklejohn might have performed in what must have been fifty years of service but one would have thought he wouldn't have to read the words so timidly from the Prayer Book. At this pace the ceremony would go on till midnight. Elizabeth was sure her knees would never last. She wondered what would happen if she broke in on Rector Micklejohn's mumbling and asked if it would be all right to stand.

She supposed that wouldn't do at all. She had to get through it without giving the gossips any more to talk about. God knew that half of Orange County and *all* of the Alamance section must have chewed the whole affair to shreds before this.

It was a good thing that she was kneeling with her head bowed so that nobody in the chapel could read the expressions on her face, as she recalled the past months.

The two Quakers who had told of Edward's arrival in the area were somewhere among the wedding guests. Their appearance had surprised both Philip who had insisted on inviting them, and Father who maintained that the invitations might prove an embarrassment to them, his understanding being that Quakers did not hold with such popish ceremonies as weddings.

"I heard somewhere that when Quakers marry, the couple sits in their meetinghouse at Cane Creek Ford, facing each other with a few of their close relatives there, nobody saying a word. After several hours of this dumbshow, they get up and walk out hand-in-hand, supposedly having been silently united by the Holy Spirit."

At the time, Elizabeth had wanted to say that such a wedding would be just fine with her, but of course she hadn't. All her life she had looked forward to her wedding day but the closer the time came, the less heart she had had for it. It wasn't just Edward—*it was not Edward's fault at all, not a whit!*—it was just that . . . well . . . it suddenly seemed as though everybody in the colony would come running to peer at the plain, gawky Allyn girl when she snagged herself a husband. Oh, the whispers, the nudges, the winks, and the sidelong glances that must be being passed around behind her as she knelt there.

Well, it's not my fault, either, she told herself sturdily. *I was perfectly willing to let Edward stay in Childsborough forever without sending me a word, if that was what he wanted.*

She had been willing, too, but hardly had Robert Hosban and his father paddled their pirogue around the bend than George was bellowing for the hostler to saddle up his stallion, Boreas, and telling Yulee to pack his saddlebags.

"Ye're not goin' to ride up there, all helter-skelter, without findin' out what's what, are ye?" Becky had cried.

"I'll find out what's what, all right," her brother muttered. "If I have to beat it out of him, I'll get the truth soon enough and stuff his lies down his skinny gullet if he tries—"

"Now hold right there," William Weyland Allyn had exclaimed. "You'll not go riding blindly off to stir up dust that will attract the attention of everybody in the western hundreds—I'll not have it."

"Who cares who knows him fr a faithless dog?" George snarled. "The more, the better."

"Is this the way you'd repay your sister for her tireless work?" Father asked, "by throwing her to the gossips? I thought you loved her—I've heard you say you did often enough."

"I do, I do, and that's why I needs must ride up there and show this trothless knave he can't play his stinkin' games with my dear sister, not and stay healthy, he can't."

"You'd show him that, would you?" Elizabeth said to her own astonishment. "And what' that supposed to prove when you're done? That rather than marry me, Edward would sooner take a whipping or even have his neck broke by a man who's twice as big and strong as he is? Oh, George, you can't do it—you can't?"

She had felt Becky's arm about her shoulder and had turned to let the tears flow free. She had not intended it, but her tears had served to stop her half brother's headlong dash to Childsborough.

Her face buried in Rebecca's soft shoulder, she heard George cross the room to put a hand on her arm. "Don't weep,

Betsy," he said in a husky undertone. "Hurtin' ye's the last thing I'd do, baby sister."

She had turned and clung to him then, smelling the rum and tobacco and horse that somehow blended to give him a cleaner aroma than precious scented soap. "I know you'd never mean to, brother," she choked, "but—oh, I don't want them to laugh at me and that's what they'd do."

"They'd better not," George rumbled. But as he held her close she felt the rage flow out of him and when at last she stopped her sniffling and drew free, he turned to his father and said resignedly,

"All right, then, what's y'r plan, sir? Surely ye mean to do somethin', don't ye? Or does what ye told old Hosban about never mindin' anything that happens outside this plantation hold true here?"

William Allyn replied in a level voice. "You know I mean to deal with this. But carefully, son, as befits intelligent men."

"I don't want anyone to deal with anything," Elizabeth cried softly, the tears threatening again, but she might as well not have spoken.

"I'll send young Langhorn up to Childsborough with a letter for Philip," her father explained. "I'll instruct your brother to tell us what he knows, either by return letter or in person." He shook his handsome head slowly and added, "I'm sure there's a good explanation for this, George. Philip's not one to scamp his family duties."

"Lawyers," George had grunted. "He's prob'ly pokin' through his law books to see what proper action he c'n take, Thingumbob versus What-d'ye-callem, King's Bench Archives, Fourteen Fifty-two. Whilst that beanpole struts about as big as life."

Elizabeth remembered the horrid giggle that had risen in her throat at George's mimicking of Philip.

But now she brought herself back to the present, back to the Elm Creek Chapel. Rector Micklejohn was still stumbling on at a snail's pace. This would go on till dark unless somebody yelled Fire!

Elizabeth returned to her own thoughts. Henry, she remembered, had ridden off that morning, glad to escape his gardening assignment, and although Father had strictly warned him against overtaxing his horse, he must have known that Henry would ride straight through to Childsborough if he could. As it happened, a rainstorm had forced him to camp for a couple of hours but according to Philip, it was lacking an hour of dawn when he was brought springing out of bed by Henry's pounding at Squire Davis' door.

"Frightened the old gentleman half out of his wits," Philip told them when he rode back to Part-of-Providence with young Langhorn. "Me, too, I must confess. Since Tryon became governor, things have been edgy in Childsborough—and in every other town in the colony, I trow—and being awakened at four in the morning's a frightening thing."

He was with his father and brother in the little office that had been added to the manor house at the end of the lower hall. The room had scarcely been roofed over before Elizabeth discovered that it was even easier to overhear the conversation that took place there than the office at Middlebend.

"Never mind about that," George had rumbled. "S'pose ye explain why ye didn't let us know the Dedshalls were in town the minute ye saw them."

"Well—damme, George, tell me what you would have done. I heard some time ago that the family of eastern gentry staying at Bartram's Forge had another name than the one they called themselves. Rumor had it that the head of the family was one of Dobbs' or Granville's assessors who was fleeing William Tryon's wrath."

"Didn't ye go see f'r y'rself?"

"No, I didn't. This country is fair crawling with Tryon's enemies who are running for cover. I had no idea 'twas Ben Dedshall. As for going out of my way to find out who this particular man of mystery was, if I did that with all these refugees I'd be sure to find that half of them were old friends and then I'd feel obliged to help them. Which, if you recall, I'm forbidden to do under the restrictions of that damned fealty oath that Tryon forced on us."

"I can see your painful position and I commend you for your prudence," Father said.

But George muttered, "Ye can't tell me that Ben Dedshall could keep his mouth shut f'r longer than it'd take to boast that he was Lord Granville's bailiff at Edenton. Not unless he's changed a heap since I last saw the little windbag."

Philip said drily, "I imagine that a man changes considerably when William Tryon's baying at his heels."

Father asked, "When did you first know that it was, indeed, Benjamin Dedshall?"

"About a fortnight ago."

"A fortnight ago!" George exploded. "And we had to get the news from a couple of passing strangers?"

"Now, hold a moment while I explain. When first I heard that the people at Bartram's Ford were the Dedshalls of Edenton, my first impulse was to ride down there and greet them, of course. But then I told myself that this might be dangerous. If the family were not in dire straits they surely would have got word to me. But on the other hand, I was under Fanning's eye so their wiser move would have been to send a message to you, here on the Alamance. For all I knew, Edward might be here and everybody concerned might be keeping silent for fear I'd unwittingly give Tryon's hounds the scent again."

"There's a lawyer fr ye," George said. "If it'd been me, I'd ha' snaked darlin' Edward out of his hidey-hole as soon as I heard he was there and dragged him here by the scruff of his neck."

I don't want him, Elizabeth had told herself fiercely, crouched in her hiding place. *Let him stay in Bartram's Forge forever.*

"And I suppose Betsy would have covered you with grateful kisses," Philip had drawled acidly. "For Christ's sake, brother, think of her pride! That sweet child hurt by the likes of Edward Dedshall? Never! She's an Allyn—since when has a man been dragged up by the scruff of his neck to marry an Allyn?"

"Well—ah, go on, go on. What happened?"

There had been a long pause that had made Elizabeth squirm with impatience until Philip finally spoke.

"What happened next? Why, I was called on by that little redheaded minx, Mistress Millie Dedshall, if you can believe it."

"Millie?" Father asked. "She was alone?"

"And as much at ease as a duchess, I'll be bound." A laugh. "I was hard at work in the squire's office one bright morning when in she walked, bold as brass, and told old Jonathan, the porter, that she must see Mister Philip Allyn on a matter of great importance."

"She was always a forward child," Father said. "But bright as a new sovereign."

The only true friend I have, Elizabeth had added silently. *Willing to brave Tryon's soldiers to . . .* to what? She had pressed her ear even closer to the thin partition.

"I confess I didn't recognize her at first, she'd grown so tall since I last saw her," Philip was saying. "Then, when I came near calling out her name she warned me with a finger to her lips. She whispered that she had a secret message from her brother and then proceeded to recite the damnedest fairy story I've heard since Cinderella."

Yes, Elizabeth had had to agree, *Millie always did love to embroider the dull stuff of truth.*

"It seems that her brother Edward would have made his way to Betsy long before had he not been continually engaged in mortal combat, with the Indians, with Tryon's minions, with outlaw bands that had beleaguered them ever since they had fled into the wilderness—enemies too numerous to count. Heroically, he had subdued his feverish yearnings to see his beloved so he could stay with his family and fight off these assorted villains—although not without suffering grievous wounds from which he had finally recovered, at least enough to send this message to me."

William Allyn had made a sound that was almost a chuckle but George burst out, " 'Od's blood, Philip, do we have to listen to this child's prattle forever? What about Edward Dedshall?"

"I'm coming to it," Philip said. "I have to tell it to you as it happened so you'll understand my position."

"Get on with it, then. If ye won't let me go after Dedshall, I have work to do."

Elizabeth broke off her reveries long enough to hear that a new sound was now punctuating the droning words of the gaunt Anglican priest. Rain? Why, of course. What else for Elizabeth Allyn on her wedding day? She supposed she should feel grateful that it wasn't snow. Not that it couldn't turn out to be next winter's first snowstorm before this priest got through with his sermon.

Better to retreat into memory than to dwell on the agony in her knees—or the moment when she would be alone with Edward Dedshall as his wife.

"When I gave Mistress Pert to understand that I didn't

believe a word of what she'd told me, she allowed herself two seconds of high dudgeon," Phil had continued. "Then she cheerfully admitted she had stretched the truth a bit—although not much—and finally I got her to confess that neither Edward nor her father knew she was calling on me. She said her father had come to town to talk to Edmund Fanning and she had coaxed him into letting her come, too. Edward stayed behind at Bartram's Forge."

"Where else?" George had growled.

"It took some doing but I finally got it out of her that neither Edward nor his father had sent word to you here at Part-of-Providence, that they'd been afraid to make a move until Ben was sure of Fanning's friendship—which must mean that Dedshall met Fanning's price." There was a pause and then Philip went on earnestly,

"Mayhap you'd have to live in Childsborough to understand this, but I could and easily enough. Since Tryon, everybody's suspicious; a man says 'Good morrow' to you and you wonder what he really means by it, you find yourself speaking in whispers and looking over your shoulder even though you've nothing at all to hide."

"I've known times like that," Father said. "Virginia under Gooch was near as bad."

Having no patience for such explanations, George had broken in, "Well, now that ye knew 'twas Edward Dedshall hidin' in Bartram's Forge, did ye ride down to face the man?"

"Aye, but not at once. I asked Mistress Millie to tell her father I must see him as soon as he could call without risking his position. Don't bow your neck and paw sand at me, George. I tell you 'twas the only conscionable thing to do."

"The devil take conscionable things! Why didn't ye—"

"Now, George," Father had interrupted sharply. "Hear your brother out." Turning to Philip, he asked, "Did Dedshall make reply?"

"The same day. He came to the office, muffled to the ears like a spy, and we adjourned to the Grey Goose—that's a tavern on the edge of town where conspirators go when they hope not to be noticed. Of course, there are so many whisperers and plotters in the place that it's hard to find space for your tankard but, Dedshall wanted it that way, so I agreed."

"Damme," George had complained, "it all sounds like play-actin'. Muffled to the ears, conspiratin' in an alehouse jammed with conspirators—ye're all playin' children's games, I vow."

"George, I beseech you," his father remonstrated. "Go on, Philip."

"I've already told you the gist of what Ben said. He feared to make a move until Fanning agreed to serve as his protector. Now that it was set, he intended to see that Edward carried out his obligations."

Obligations! What a horrid word to attach to a love affair!

"He asked me not to send word to you until Fanning wrote to the Governor and got certain assurances. I balked at that. If Dedshall was trying to put us off, he could drag out such an arrangement for months."

" 'Twould be like the little bastard," his brother muttered.

"Well, I must confess he's changed mightily from the man we knew in Edenton," Philip said. "Running for his life, as he must've done when Arthur Dobbs died, has deflated his spirits and his belly, too," he paused. "And I imagine the change from Queen Street to Bartram's Forge must have been irksome to dear Ethelind and she'd hardly be one to bear any setbacks cheerfully, d'you think?"

"By God, I'd forgotten about Ethelind," George exclaimed. "Now that she's out here mayhap we c'n arrange that prize match, after all. That'd make the place complete, Edward in one house with Betsy and Ethelind in another, as Phil's blushin' bride."

"I always thought she gave you a moister eye than she ever threw my way, dear brother. I think you're the bucko who can tame that shrew," Philip said calmly.

"And I think both of you would do well to stop bandying a young lady's name about so carelessly," William Allyn said. "Philip, keep on with your account. You protested Dedshall's proposed delay—what then?"

"Why, the bailiff—or the former bailiff, rather—was in no humor to argue, Father. I was to send off a message to the Alamance and he would wait on your advice, sir."

"But you did not inform us. Why not?" There was a brief silence, and then Philip said slowly, "I put it off because of Betsy. Suddenly it came to me that it was as if we were bargaining for a horse rather than my little sister's happiness. You know how I've always felt about Edward Dedshall, except for that one time when he nearly drowned himself in the river, coming to Betsy's rescue. You, too, George—you've never had any great love for him. As for Elizabeth—well, I've never understood her liking for the man but I've never understood women, anyway, so mayhap her affection's real enough.

"But my anger over the Dedshalls' strange backing and filling was all family pride. So's your resolve to make Edward come out of hiding and present himself to Betsy as he swore he would last Fall. But what about Elizabeth, herself? Would I be really serving her best interests by smoking Edward out or would she be a thousand times better off if I let him renege on his pledge, if that was what he intended to do?"

"She would be sorely wounded if he did have the temerity to put her off, Philip," William Allyn said. "But on the other hand, you're right; if Ben Dedshall and I *forced* Edward to —ah, 'tisn't an easy question to answer offhand, is it, George?"

"No," George said glumly. "But one thing is sure; whatever we decide, Betsy must never hear a word about darlin' Edward's craven ways."

"Amen to that," Philip said fervently.

Elizabeth's memories were suddenly broken off by the appalling realization that Rector Micklejohn had stopped talking and that an accusing silence lay over the chapel. She raised her eyes to meet the priest's stare, then glanced sideways at Edward who was looking at her strangely, perhaps even fearfully.

Unsure of what was expected of her, she mumbled a low sound that might have been taken for clearing her throat. Whatever it was they were waiting for apparently was satisfied because the gaunt Anglican priest uttered his next words in ringing tones:

"Therefore, I do pronounce thee, Edward, joined in holy wedlock to thee, Elizabeth, to have and to hold from this day forward, for better or for worse, for richer for poorer, in sickness and in health, to love and to cherish, till death do thee part."

[2]

Elizabeth had feared and dreamed of that night for as long as she could remember. As the wedding day drew closer she had been grateful to have Rebecca to reassure her and advise her. Without her half sister beside her she would have gone to the marriage bed a trembling wretch. But with Rebecca's moral support she managed to walk up the steep steps to the bedroom of the new little house that George had built for them. Unaided she got out of the splendid wedding dress that Becky had stitched for her and the beautiful smalls that Millie had helped sew and into the nightrail that she herself had made.

Now as she lay there, wondering whether to snuff the candle or leave it lit, she found herself breathing a prayer. Not a proper prayer, of course, because she was not down on her knees and her eyes were wide open, but a prayer, just the same. *Don't let me disappoint him. Don't let me be a failure.*

She knew what was expected of her. She knew what Edward would do and what she must do. It was proper that these things be done. There was no shame attached to any of it. God had fashioned men and women to do this thing in this way and according to Becky, it would not be nearly as awkward or difficult as it sounded.

Millie Dedshall had also reassured her. "When the time comes ye'll go gallopin' off with him like ye'd never done anything else in y'r born days," Millie had predicted. Her advice on the ways of man and wife, filled Becky with laughter.

"Where did ye get so much weighty wisdom, anyway?" Becky asked with a chuckle. "Ye scurse look old enough to have had an old granny-woman's experience in such things."

"Well, I ain't," Millie confessed, "but I've seen enough and heard enough just by keepin' my eyes and ears open."

"Ye've been peepin' and listenin' in the wrong places, then, ye sly puss. Better wait till ye get a husband of y'r own before ye tell others how it's done." Rebecca shook her head. "Some of the things ye said—I vow, I'd give my hope of heav'n, almost to see poor Betsy try to follow y'r instructions."

Millie had come to Part-of-Providence the week before the

wedding, along with Ethelind and her two young randipole brothers, David and Francis. Edward and his father had stayed behind in Hillsboro (as Governor William Tryon had decreed that old Childsborough be called in honor of Wills Hill, Marquis of Downshire, and Earl of Hillsborough, and George III's secretary of state for the colonies—and a close relative of Dame Tryon) until three days before the marriage.

Of course Elizabeth had been overjoyed to see Millie again but she wished that the other Dedshalls had stayed behind with Edward and his father. Their descent upon Part-of-Providence had created additional strain and doubling up.

George, working his crew from dawn until after dark to get Elizabeth's house finished in time, had done his best to be polite to Ethelind and the Dedshall boys but Ethel's fawning and the boys' deviltry soon exploded his patience.

"One more wrong move out of either of ye and I'll grind up y'r bones to make mortar," he had warned the boys and they obviously had believed him. After that, although they continued dogging his every step, they regarded him with something approaching awe. George, it developed, was the one man in the New World who could make the two hellions behave.

In dealing with Ethelind, George had used a different, though scarcely less blunt tactic. When her syrupy attentions got too much for him, he arranged for her to "accidentally" stumble on him and Yulee together, not in any outright embrace but in a situation that sent Edward's spinster sister scurrying.

("Ye drew it pretty fine, didn't ye?" Rebecca asked her brother after Ethelind's scandalized report was whispered into her amused ear. "If Father ever found out there'd be the devil to pay, ye know that.")

Elizabeth had marveled at Rebecca's graciousness toward Ethelind and Millie also had been amazed by Becky's even temper. "Why don't y'r sister tell Ethel to keep her long nose out of everything?" Millie had complained. "I was listenin' to 'em yesterday when they thought I was sommers else and I vow, Ethel did everythin' but ask Becky how many times a night Harry Tarbell used to swive her."

"How many times he what?"

"Oh, Elizabeth, *you* know! Swived her, rogered her, boarded her, covered her, mounted her—why pretend ye don't know what it means, and you about to be marrit in a few days?"

"Well, I didn't—I hadn't heard that word," Elizabeth said feebly. "Every time you say anything about it—every time you use a different word."

The two girls were sewing in a downstairs room of the new house. Saws and mallets rang in the upper storey so they were sure of not being overheard even by Francis or David. Millie grinned as she held a needle and thread up to the light. "They all mean the same thing, don't they? I swear, there must be more ways of sayin' that than there are anything else. I know at least a dozen diff'rent ones. There's—"

"*Never mind!* Mildred, honestly!"

"Ho, ye'd better not be so nicey-nice when it comes your turn, Elizabeth. Edward ain't no rollickin' lover, I grant ye, but 'twould vex even him if ye froze him when he tried to cuddle ye."

"Oh, Mildred," Elizabeth wailed, "do you think I'm good enough for your brother?"

"Good enough f'r Edward?" The redhead's eyes popped.

"I mean—well, does he truly want to marry me? 'Twas you, not him, that called on Philip and told us of your whereabouts. If you hadn't, do you think he'd ever have—"

"Of course he would. Elizabeth, believe me, he w'ld have made his way to ye in spite of everythin' if it hadn't been f'r the—the Tryon spies and the Injuns and—and—ye've no ideer how we was beset by enemies at the Forge."

"Oh, Millie, you know that's not so."

A brief silence and then the other girl said reproachfully, "Ye promised to call me Mildred, like I always call ye Elizabeth, 'stead of Betsy. You must know how I hate Millie."

"I'm sorry,—but—Mildred, you know there were no Indians, or Tryon spies, either. If he'd wanted to, he could have got some word to me. All that time and he didn't try to—"

"I tell ye he did! Pa forbade him, was what happened. Pa was so skeered of bein' found out before he paid old Fanning to give us sanctuary that he wouldn't even let us tell anybody our right name." She snorted. "Greeber was the name he give us. If he had to pick a name why couldn't he ha' picked summen like Percy or Norfolk, summen with some *style* to it?"

"I tell ye ye've got it all wrong, Elizabeth," she said, returning to the main subject. "Why, 'twas Edward made me promise to seek out y'r brother in Childsborough and tell him where we was and that he was pinin' f'r a glimpse of you. Honest, he did! He—he gave me the task cuz he figgered I'd be able to go where Pa durst not and that's how it worked out, didn't it?"

Elizabeth shook her head woefully. "I don't know," she said in a low voice. "I listened to Father and Philip and George that day Philip came down from town, and it seemed that the last thing your father or Edward or anybody wanted—save yourself—was for Edward to rejoin me. All they talked about was my pride and—and horsewhipping—that was George, of course—and what was the right way to work it so the Allyn name wouldn't be besmirched or I wouldn't be heartbroke."

"Well, ye know what store y'r folks put on y'r name. Ye couldn't expect y'r pa to take a single step without first considerin' everything on all sides and up and down too, to make sure the fambly name wouldn't get a single spot on it."

Elizabeth nodded. "Oh, yes, I know. Sometimes I think the name's more important than anything else. If it wasn't for the need to keep the Allyn name snow white I'm sure Father would have sued to make Mother's brothers turn her loose. But seeing that would cause a scandal, he never made a move and now I'm to be married without my own mother being here or even knowing it."

"Shh, shh, don't cry, Elizabeth. When ye're marrit, mebbe Edward c'n do summen to get y'r ma back. I know I laugh at him, most times, but he did win more times than not in the Edenton courts before old Tryon sent us all packin'."

Elizabeth had tried to imagine Edward beating down all the church and crown officers and bearding Mother's brothers in their den but somehow she couldn't see it clearly. Still, perhaps she could persuade him to *try*. If he truly loved her, he might risk his neck for her again as he once had on the Chowan River in a leaky skiff.

And certainly he had been persuasive when he renewed his suit, riding down to Part-of-Providence every chance he got. He had even overcome his timidity and kissed her, first her hand and wrist and finally her lips. It was an extraordinary achievement for one who had been such an irresolute lover in earlier stages of his courtship. She only hoped she had not been too brazen in inviting him to taste her kiss so that they would both have some idea of what it would be like.

Perhaps surprisingly, it had been exceeding fine. Although she might have day dreamed about a bold, reckless lover who would swoop her up in his arms and crush her in a near-savage assault, she had found that Edward's gentle, hesitant, almost *respectful* caress was infinitely better. Her only question was whether Edward might be more impulsive and less—dutiful in his courting, without two touchy brothers standing over his shoulder.

Lying on her bridal bed, Elizabeth reminded herself that she had given him plenty of chances to withdraw, but he had not chosen to do so. Finally she had told him that they would be married if he truly wished it and she would do her best to make him a good wife.

She had thought that they would be married as soon as she accepted and that she would go to live with him while he finished his studies. But in making such simple plans she had reckoned without her family. George insisted that he would build a house for them on Part-of-Providence and there she would stay, there at least until Edward became a full-fledged lawyer. She would not, he explained, be that far from her husband and in view of the total lack of decent living quarters in the county seat and Edward's need of uninterrupted study time during the vital last weeks before his examination, the couple would be much better off with the temporary arrangements that he proposed.

"If ye need a clincher, Betsy," George had told her, "just imagine y'self tryin' to start y'r married life in the same house with Ethelind Dedshall."

Perhaps if Becky had voiced her thoughts one way or another she would feel better about it now as she lay waiting for Edward to come upstairs. But when she had asked her half sister what she thought of the plan, Becky had only shrugged and told her that it was her new husband, her new life, and her decision to make.

"I can only remind ye that I went against the family wishes," she had added grudgingly when Elizabeth had persisted, "and ye can see what it got me." So perhaps that had been Rebecca's way of warning her that she must not rebel.

But if only . . .

Her thoughts fled as she heard Edward's footsteps on the stairs. A hand clutched her heart for an instant, then relaxed its cold grip. It was going to be all right. She would help him if he needed help and—yes, she knew it now—he would help her and no matter what they might have been or not been before, they would be complete and right together.

And so by some miracle, they proved to be. Hesitantly, but tenderly, they found each other in the deep warm bed. The upwelling of affection made her pain trivial and his absurd exclamations not absurd at all. She lost herself so completely in his embrace that never for one fleeting moment did doubt impinge on her recurrent ecstasy.

When dawn crept over the windowsill and across the floor to the bed to waken her and she found herself nestled spoon fashion against her husband, she did not waste a moment wondering who she was and how she had gotten there. It was still right and proper and always would be, God wot, so long as they lived.

Dame Elizabeth Allyn Dedshall. Goodwife Dedshall. Aye, the names had a nice ring to them.

[3]

Their wedding night was in the last week of February, 1766. Early the following August, Elizabeth knew she was with child.

"And about time," Rebecca said with a laugh. "I was beginnin' to think ye needed some more of y'r friend Millie's expert advice." Sobering, she leaned forward to kiss her half sister's flushed cheek. "Bless ye, baby," she murmured, and then asked, "Did ye tell Edward before he rode off this mornin'?"

"No, I meant to but—well, he's got a most important case to argue next week and I didn't want him to be distracted." It sounded lame in her own ears so she added, "Besides, I wasn't truly sure."

"So ye somehow found out f'r sure in the short time 'twixt his leavin' and now," Becky said, nodding solemnly. "Amazin'."

"Well, if you must know, I wanted to tell you first," Elizabeth blurted. "I'd want Mother to know first, were she here, and you're almost as close to me."

Rebecca was silent for a moment before she said huskily,

"Ye don't know how I'm touched by that, sister. I wish—but there's no good wishin' f'r the moon, is there? I ought to know that by now." She paused and then added, "Ye mustn't despair because y'r letter to y'r mother went unanswered."

"I don't but—well, it's been two months, nearly three."

"Write her another, now that ye have this grand news f'r her. Mayhap the other was lost or her answer went astray. Ye know what Phil says, only one letter in three gets to where it's goin' in anything like respectable time."

Elizabeth nodded without much enthusiasm. "I'll write another, then."

"Have ye told old Lis?" Rebecca asked.

"No, I'm going down there now. I should have looked in on her days ago but Edward was here and there were so many things to do around the house and time just slipped away. How is she, have you heard?"

"Ella says she's failin' pretty bad. Y'r good news sh'ld brighten her up but I wouldn't put off tellin' her, were I you."

She found Lis' cabin dark and filled with the bitter smell of sickness. One of Lis' granddaughters, a girl named Lolie, dozed on a stool beside the dying slave woman's pallet, her flyswitch on the floor beside her dangling hand. As Elizabeth entered, the girl got to her feet and dropped a curtsey, then yawned widely.

"Scusin' me, Mist'ess," she said, "but I been settin' all night. Jidder, she 'spose come set this dawnin' but she ain't and I lak t'starve. Ain' nuthin to eat 'cause Gramma, dey sendin' huh mush f'm de kitchen, all she kin take and she ain't hol' at down, nuthuh."

Elizabeth looked down at the wasted figure on the pallet. Lis lay with her toothless mouth agape, her eyes not quite shut, her bony hands folded over her chest atop a starched white bedgown. Poor Lis; how had she crumbled away so completely in these past eighteen months? When they come out to the Alamance, Lis had been as active as any of them, stronger than most, and now she was an empty, withered husk. For the past four months, keeping Lis alive and clean had been two wenches' only task and sometimes Elizabeth had found herself wondering if Lis would have permitted this when she had charge of the Allyn household.

She thought not. She could almost hear Lis sniffing and saying, "Ain' de Lawd's intention dat de time gits put off an' put off aftuh He sound de call. Ain' propuh dem gals waste all 'at time 'tendin' somebody that's ready to go."

"I'll sit with her while you find whoever was supposed to spell you," she told Lolie.

"Yazzum." The girl started for the doorway with a rush.

"Leave the flyswitch," Elizabeth ordered. "And have the girl bring some more sweet fern and pine needles for the fire."

"Yazzum, but dey don' he'p none," Lolie replied. "Mama say it de grave breff, kain't smoke it out."

"Hush your nonsense. Your grandmother's a long way from the grave. Now be off with you."

She took the stool as the wench scurried off. She wondered why dying was so undignified, the stench, the helplessness, the shameful exasperation it roused in even the most loving hearts at times. But then she told herself that Lis was the first old dying person she had ever watched over. Her little brother, Jeremy, had been sick most of the time but Mother and Lis had watched over him and, besides, death had not been inevitable in Jeremy's case.

Perhaps it was not always this way, even with old people. Maybe some old folks died gracefully, letting those who tended them feel nothing but gentle sorrow.

She saw the withered black lips move and bent over Lis. There was no sound so she said, "It's Elizabeth, Lis. I've come to visit with you. Is there aught you want that I can get for you?"

No response. She swatted at another fly, then leaned over the old woman when the lips moved again.

"Yo' chile," Lis whispered. "Li'l boy."

The last time she had seen Lis she had not been sure that her old nurse knew she was married. From the few words she had mumbled on that occasion, Elizabeth suspected that Lis thought she was back in Middlebend and that she, Elizabeth, was still a baby just off the teat. Perhaps she was wandering again but she said, "Yes, I just found out. Isn't that fair wonderful? You're the very first one I've told, Lis."

The old woman's lips twitched in what might have been an attempt to smile. "Marse Edward," Lis said, quite clearly.

"No, I've not told him yet. I had to tell you before anyone else." Well, who could blame her for that little lie?

The slave's eyelids rose a bit and she whispered, "Ain' mean him. De chile . . . li'l marstuh . . . you name 'im Edward, y'hear?"

She expected she would have a girl but she nodded to the dying woman and said, "I will, Lis. Edward George Philip Dedshall, how's that for a name?"

Lis rolled her eyes toward her without moving her head and now Elizabeth saw that the corner of her mouth was curved in a tiny half smile. She wasn't wandering, then; somehow she had known about the baby and by the same mysterious means, she knew it was going to be a boy.

Still, she said, "And if it's a girl we'll name her—what shall we name her, Lis, Rebecca?" The woman shook her head. Not Rebecca, most certainly not! She should have known better than to suggest that. "Well, Mary, then, after Mother." Another headshake; no, Lis had never forgiven Mother for abandoning her in Norfolk. "Louisa, then? You've always admired Marse Weyland's lady."

There was no response to that, although the suggestion of a smile came back. She supposed that Lis thought it was a waste of time finding a name for a girl when the baby was so certain to be a boy who would be named Edward. Strange that she had suggested Edward instead of William. But right, too. George and Phil could give Father grandsons named William, Edward deserved a namesake because he was the finest; kindest, most considerate husband in the North Carolina colony and she loved him a little more every minute of the day.

To think that she had ever wondered if she would be able to love him, really love him, instead of—well, making the best of a bad bargain. She should be ashamed of herself. There never was a finer man, nor one who was more handsome in spirit—and visage, too, when a child grew into a woman who knew enough to look for qualities beyond mere prettiness.

Old Lis was struggling to say something more so she bent close again.

"Mizz 'Becca . . . don' let huh . . . " She labored to go on but could not find the strength. Don't let Becky do what? No matter; poor Becky had made Lis her enemy simply by coming back to the family and no matter how kind her half sister had been or how understanding, Lis had somehow gotten it through her old head that she, Elizabeth, had been robbed of her rightful place in the family and would never forgive Rebecca for it. Hadn't Becky warned her that the crone would speak against her, even though she must know that it was on Becky's orders that she was being tended so carefully.

"Watuh," Lis managed to gasp and Elizabeth bent to soak a clean cloth in a bowl of water on the floor, putting the twisted end in Lis' mouth to suck. She repeated this half a dozen times before Lis signified she had enough. "Is there anything else?" Elizabeth asked. "Do you think you could eat something?"

"No, missy." The words were surprisingly clear. "Ain' nothin' Ah wants 'ceptin t'see y'r li'l boy-baby an' Ah'll be long gone afore den." Elizabeth started to demur but the dying woman kept on stubbornly. "Knows yuh don' lissen to anything Ah says no mo' but . . . but don' let Mizz 'Becca do nothin' to 'at chile. Or you. Don' let huh . . . " The brief spurt of energy dwindled and Lis fought for breath.

Fighting her fear Elizabeth leaned down to put her hand on the bony shoulder. "Now, now, don't worry yourself, Lis. Rest, go back to sleep. All's well and you've no need to imagine things. Whatever you say, I'll do, so you must not fret."

But Lis still fought to say what she had on her mind. The gasping grew even louder. Lis' eyes started from her head, her jaw dropped, and the knobby-knuckled hands twitched at the coverlet.

"Lie still," Elizabeth hissed in panic. "Lie still, d'you hear? Be quiet or I'll leave and never come back—I mean it! Oh, Lis, be good and do stop frightening me. I won't have it. You've no right. You—you're being impudent, Lis, you know you are."

Where was that wench who was supposed to relieve Lolie? If she didn't come in the next minute she was just going to walk out of there. Why not? Her being there only made Lis worse, she was actually doing the old woman harm, causing her to babble her nonsense about Becky. It wouldn't matter a whit if she were left alone for a minute or two.

"I'm going, Lis," she said sharply. "Unless you stop, I'm going to leave you."

The heaving gasps, the rolling eyes, the arching back. Elizabeth thought she must be having a fit. She had better call George or Langhorn or *somebody* who knew what to do. She whirled and started for the low doorway, then stopped as a slight figure crossed the threshold.

"Ah ain' t'blame, Mist'ess," the girl whined. "Lolie, she nevvuh tole me I was s'pose t'be heah, I don' care whut she say. I brung yuh some sweet fern lak she say but I coon' fin' no—"

"Never mind that," Elizabeth interrupted. "Run and find Marse George or Marse Langhorn. Tell them Lis is having some sort of seizure. Hurry."

The girl looked past her at the laboring figure on the pallet. " 'Scusin' me, ma'am," she said, "but 'at ain' no seizuah. She gits 'ataway all de time. Ain' nuthin' t'be skeered of, mist'ess."

"I am not scared," Elizabeth said icily.

"No'm, Ah din' mean t'sound uppity. Oney ole Lis, she git de heaves ever' so often. Mama say it's de li'l angels trompin' on huh chest so's she kain't breathe right. Dey tellin' huh to huyy up, she long pas' huh time, is all."

"Well, you tell your mama I never heard anything so cruel. You tell her if she feeds you any more such rubbish I'll have her—what's your name, girl?"

The wench seemed faintly astonished. "I'm Ella's Jidder, ma'am. Yo' fo'gits ah wukks in de laundry and de kitchen sometimes, Mizz 'Lizabeth?"

Did she mean to say that she was Ella's daughter, Drusilla? Impossible! Drusilla couldn't be old enough to—but closer examination in the dim light proved that it was indeed she. But, laws, how she had grown; a slip of a flat-chested child one minute and this half-grown wench with pointed breasts under the shift the next.

"Of course," she managed. "But Jidder—why do you use that ugly name when your proper name's so much nicer?"

The girl shrugged. "Don' know, mist'ess. Dey always done call me Jidder, 'ceptin' you an' de othuh quality, sometimes."

"My Mother suggested it when you were first born," Elizabeth said. "Ella asked her for a name that was different from all the others and Mother said Drusilla."

"Yazzum." Indifferently, for what had it gained a plantation pickanin to have been given a young lady's prettied-up name? "Yo' still want me to fetch Marse Gawge, Mizz 'Lizabeth?"

She looked at the pallet. The wrenching gasps had quieted and Lis' eyelids had dropped.

"No," Elizabeth told the young Jidder. "She seems to be

resting again. But if these seizures grow too bad you must come for me at once, do you understand?"

"Yazzum, I runs quick to fetch yuh, mist'ess, Ah do be suah."

Perhaps Jidder would have come for Elizabeth if she had been at Lis's bedside but the attendant was Lolie when the old woman died four days later. Nobody had told Lolie to fetch Mizz 'Lizabeth and so it was not until the next morning when she heard the keening from the quarters that the girl knew Lis was dead.

She wept a little but not much, because she had been prepared. And when Becky said, 'twould be neither fitting nor good for the baby for her to attend the laying-out before the burial, she protested hardly at all. Presumably, Lis died of nothing more than the old-age miseries but still she could not risk catching something by mixing with a crowd of slaves who did not expect her and probably would feel more free in their mourning if she were not there. All that mattered now was the safety of the child within her—Lis would be the first to agree to that.

Elizabeth did attend the burial with George and Father and Becky and said her own prayer for Lis' soul when Father read the service over the grave.

She wondered if Lis would discover that the blacks' great hope was true and that in heaven they were all white and lived a life of ease. She prayed that this would be so, although she had trouble imagining Lis spending Eternity with her idle hands folded in her lap.

[4]

Edward was almost the last to know that he would be a father some time the following February. Although Rebecca urged her to send her husband a note, telling him the news, Elizabeth insisted that she tell him in person. As luck would have it, he was tied up in Hillsboro for over a fortnight with a controversial case; the case involved a big landowner in the northern part of the county who was appealing the heavy assessments laid on him by order of Governor Tryon.

Philip's sponsor, Squire Davis, was engaged in a similar

case but the Allyn twin managed to ride down for an over-night stay to consult with his father on some matter.

"Your Edward's fighting a losing battle, just as Squire Davis and I are," her half brother told her over the supper table. "But he's putting up a stout fight, I'll give him that."

"D'ye mean to say he's a better lawyer than you?" George asked.

Phil shrugged his slender shoulders. "Let's say he's more reckless than the Squire lets me be."

"Edward, *reckless?*" Becky asked.

"Aye, you'd be surprised to hear some of the broadsides he fires when he's before the bench. I know *I* was the first time he let loose, all hot shot and grapnel. Whilst I, when it came my turn to speak, had to be content with a feeble squib."

Elizabeth glowed. Praise from Philip was worth a wagon-load of Edward's own opinions of himself. Not, she hastened to remind herself, that Edward was overly boastful: if a man couldn't speak frankly with his wife about his own qualities, with whom could he be honest? She had known ever since February that Edward was the best lawyer in the colony but it was good to know that even a carping critic like Philip was coming around to her side.

"If Squire Davis let you go all out I'm sure you'd do almost as well, Philip," she said generously.

Her half brother looked down the table at her with a smile. "Thankee, baby sister. I'll remember that kind remark when I get too close to despair."

"Ho, we'll have to stop callin' her baby sister now that she has a loaf in the oven," George said with a laugh.

"And I'll not have you calling her anything if you can't give your sister more respect, young man," William Allyn snapped. "Her condition will not be mentioned in words you'd use for a field wench, George. We're both waiting for your apology."

George looked crushed. "I do 'pologize, Betsy, have I offended ye. Ye know I wouldn't slight ye f'r all the gold in Cathay."

"I know," she replied. "You're forgiven, brother." She turned to Philip. "And remember, I have your pledge not to tell Edward."

Phil nodded. "Nor any of the Dedshalls, although that's one crime I'll not be easily forgiven by your great admirer,

Mistress Millie. You'd best make arrangements for her to be at your side when the great moment arrives, else she'll be desolated, I vow."

"She'll be welcome if she leaves the others behind," Rebecca said and they all laughed—except Father who seemed to find the whole subject unsuitable for table conversation.

"These cases that are being argued," he asked, "do they all stem from the same special tax you spoke about?"

Philip nodded gloomily. "Tryon's special assessment is to build him a new palace in New Berne Town. Even some of his strongest supporters are raising their hackles over this latest gouge."

"What of Baron Granville? Can't these protests be addressed to him?"

Philip shrugged. "The new Lord Carteret, Sir Robert, shows no signs of his father's fiber. He seems content to give Tryon a free hand even though his income from this colony must be cut to nothing."

"If ye lose at Hillsboro, who d'ye appeal to next?" George asked.

"The high court in New Berne, I suppose, for whatever good it'll do us. But that will be a drawn-out, costly thing, and I don't think the little complainants have any stomach for it."

"What then?" Father asked.

Philip frowned as he reached for his winecup. "Why, unless their temper changes, I wouldn't be surprised in the least to see them try to take matters into their own hands. They've done it before, you know."

"But surely they must see the folly of such action," William Allyn exclaimed. "Manhandling the officers as they did last time can only bring Tryon's fist down on them."

" 'Tis easy for us to counsel cool heads," Phil said slowly, "because for some reason we weren't burthened with this special tax and even if we were, we could pay it without its hurting us too much. But to some of these people, the assessment might mean the difference twixt survival and ruination, twixt going to bed hungry or fed."

"You must exaggerate," Father said in a shocked voice.

"Not by much, sir. I'm a lawyer who's supposed to have cold water in my veins instead of hot blood but I tell you, sometimes I'd like to forget who I am and throttle Fanning's toplofty little men with my bare hands. Their total disregard of the public good is enough to make a strong man retch at times."

William Weyland Allyn motioned to the serving wench, Hauny, to fill his cup and changed the subject again. "Is Benjamin Dedshall's new house finished?" he asked.

"Almost, and it will be as big as Edmund Fanning's when it's done. That man amazes me, Father. You'd think that after his narrow squeak at Edenton he'd lie low for a time. But hardly had Fanning fixed it with Tryon to let friend Ben stay in Hillsboro than he set about building a mansion. To do this in the face of the unrest up there took more gall than I think I'd be able to find without looking real hard."

"That's somethin' Ben Dedshall never found lackin'," George said. "As f'r me, I say more power to him. Compared to some of the faint-hearted gentry in Edenton, he was re- freshin' as a cold drink on a hot day." He grinned at Eliza- beth. "Let's hope y'r son has some of his grandfather's mettle and none of his looks, eh?"

Elizabeth was shocked to see how wan and drained Edward looked when he finally returned to Part-of-Providence. She told herself that she should have sent word of the baby, the news would have sustained him when he needed it most and she had been selfish keeping it from him.

"No, no, I'll be all right," he protested, with a sagging voice, when she tried to coddle him with soft orders to rest. "'Twas a most toilsome court session and I'm downhearted over our prospects but 'tis part of the calling, I suppose." He lay back in the big wing chair, his long legs thrust out in front of him, looking up at the ceiling. "All the way down here I wondered if I had erred on this point or mayhap scamped another, if 'twould have been better had I done thus and so or left off arguing in such and such a direction." He heaved a deep sigh. "You've no idea how different it is, the law as it's set down in the books and as it's debated before the bench."

"Philip says you're quite the ablest counselor in Hillsboro," she told him.

He nodded in agreement. "But it seems there's more needed than ability in these times. What does it gain a man to present his case well if the justice's decision has already been de- termined by orders from New Berne? Or if the justice is so full of rum that he can't possibly understand the point you're proving by law?"

He shook his head slowly. "Sometimes I'm tempted to advise my clients that they'd be better off slipping Edmund Fanning an expression of esteem under the table and getting their assessment lifted forthwith."

"Edward, you could never condone that."

"No, I couldn't, for some reason, and so you might find yourself with a permanent law clerk for a husband instead of an accredited lawyer."

"Do you mean Mister Fanning would thwart your admission to the bar?"

"Not openly, but he can throw obstacles in the way of neophyte lawyers whom he suspects of opposing him. Of course the examiners are all his men else they'd not be examiners."

"Then that means Philip will have trouble, too."

She thought she detected the slightest hesitation before her husband said, "P'raps not so much as me, dear Elizabeth. For Squire Davis is most cautious in his opposition to Fanning's despotism and so, of course, your brother must be, too. My sponsor, Squire Longman, spends most of his time in the tavern so he cares little what I say or do so long as the clients are satisfied well enough to pay their fees." He attempted a laugh. "'Tis indication of the state of affairs in this province when a lawyer can speak out only if his sponsor's always in his cups."

"But enough of my troubles," he said briskly, straightening in his chair. "What's happened here since I've been gone? You must be fair bursting with news, I've been so long away."

Now that it was time to make the glorious announcement, Elizabeth felt a strange reluctance. What if he did not want another worry added to all the cares that weighed on him so heavily? What if he upbraided her for keeping it a secret from him when everybody else on the plantation knew of it? What if . . .

"There's one bit of news," she began. "I—uh—you—"

All the flowery speeches, the tender hints, the joyous superlatives suddenly deserted her.

"I'm going to have a baby, come February," she blurted. He stared at her, his faintly protuberant eyes gazing at her uncomprehendingly for a moment before they took on a shine that melted her heart. "Elizabeth, do you mean it?" She nodded, unable to speak. "In February?" Another nod. "Oh, dear wife—my dear wife!"

He sprang from the chair and enfolded her in his long arms. As she nestled there, content, complete, she felt his heart thudding against her breast. A strong heart in a strong man, soon to be the father of a strong child. God had indeed blessed her far beyond her just deserts.

Chapter Five

[1]

"*N*AY, ROBERT," Rebecca said in a low, husky voice, "ye don't know what ye're sayin'."

The big, yellow-haired man reached out to push aside a low branch that hung over the creekbank path. "I know well enough, Becky. The question is, dost thee know the answer that's in thy heart? Really know it, I mean, beyond the objections thee raised when thee realized a lowly Quaker dared ask for thy hand."

"Lowly?" She gave a laugh under her breath. "Ye demean y'rself, Robert. I'm the lowly one of this unlikely pair, I vow."

"Because thee lived in the mountains with thy husband and had to do without white sugar for a time?"

The memories crowded in on her for an instant and she shuddered, then forced a brazen laugh. "A bit more than that, my friend. And I hold ye to y'r pledge not to burthen me with y'r urgin', remember?"

The late September heat still lingered in the brakes although she could hear the first evening winds sighing far overhead in the tall pines. The doves were sounding their vespers, and the mournful sound contributed a certain feeling of peace even though she was being pressed for an answer she could not possibly give to the big, decent man beside her. Marry Robert Hosban? Nay, for although she had few scruples

left in her tattered morality, she could never betray his in-
nocence to that degree.

They reached their favorite trysting place—for Rebecca
thought of it as such despite her brave resolve to cool Robert's
ardor by any means, excepting an honest confession of the
kind of woman she had been. She dreaded doing that although
she must have known secretly that this would be the only
way to turn him away from her. But not yet. Let her hold
this bit of happiness for awhile longer.

She moved to a fallen tree that lay beside a tiny greensward
that was set in a thick tangle of brush and briars, and faced
a deep pool. Towering oaks marched down to the shore on
the opposite side, and amid the massive trunks there was a
luxurious growth of dogwood, flowerless now but heavy with
the waxen red berries that were almost as beautiful as the
white blooms. To Becky, this spot was especially lovely at
eventide when the martins swooped across the purpling sky
and the fish rose to the evening catch with an occasional
splash.

Far off in the deep woods an owl was sounding its first
low whoops and from still further away there came the cry
of a wildcat. The night frogs were beginning to tune up their
shrill pipes and from somewhere down the creek came the
solemn chant of a big bullfrog, *Jugarum, jugarum.*

Ah, could this but last forever. . . . But she knew it could
not. Robert Hosban was a man and although he was a kind
and gentle man, he could not be satisfied forever with peace
and beauty. No more, she added honestly, than she. She
might indulge herself in these virginal pleasantries for a while
but there would come a day or night when her own blood
would run hot again, demanding surcease.

She had been without a man for—how long?—two years,
lacking a week or so. That was a century for a woman like
Rebecca Allyn. When she had fled Red MacLynn's cabin she
had sworn that never again would she let a man touch her in
love—or what had passed for love in the men she had known.
Battered and bruised, her beauty all but beaten out of her by
the fists of anger and of lust, she had vowed that she would
never need another lover.

When she had first made her torturous way back to her
people, the fresh memories of Red MacLynn writhing on his
cabin floor had been enough to cool any surges of longing

that stirred within her. When she awakened in the night with empty arms she had only to cast back to MacLynn—and the others—to thank God that she lay alone on her bed, without a big, smelly male beside her.

MacLynn, she thought now, *may he roar his way through hell and back till the end of time!*

Brute! Savage! Heartless rapist!

"But ye wouldna have it any other way," he had growled when he had picked her up, bleeding, black-eyed, and tossed her on the bunk. "Ye have na feelin' f'r the finickies, ye slut. Na, ye must be beat proper before ye'll gie y'rsel' in love. See? See how ye twitch f'r it?"

Then his booming laugh. Because she had twitched for it, so avidly that the memory of it flooded her with shame after all this time. She had twitched for it and begged for it and practiced every wanton wile to rouse Red MacLynn out of his drunken stupors and into his lusty rages. She shrieked and cringed when he came at her with his big fists and feet, she snarled her fishwife curses and vowed to kill him someday, but after the brawling was finished and she was on the bed, whimpering, wanting to die, he needed only to brandish himself before her to make her join him as brazenly as the lowest whore.

If she closed her eyes even now, she knew she would put herself back in time to that dull, foggy October morning when Red had ridden back to the tumbledown cabin where she awaited him. He had left her with only a few scraps of food but a full jug of white whiskey when he had ridden off to sell his furs. After the food was gone she had drunk whiskey, day after blurred day. When MacLynn's shout finally announced his return, she had staggered to her feet, brushed back the greasy hair that fell over her puffed face, and peered out the door.

A slight woman stood beside him.

". . . so drag y'r stinkin' carcass out o' here," he snarled. "I've a proper woman now, a wee bonny lass 'stead of a worn-out cow. Come meet her, bitch, and see what a prime piece she is."

She remembered that she had leaned to steady herself on the table, staring at this—this usurper. A baby, a child who stood beside the door with one hand to her mouth as though wondering how she found herself in this fix.

"Bring us drinks," Red had ordered her brusquely. Obediently, she went to the nearly empty jug and tilted it over two dirty cups while MacLynn dragged his new prize to the stinking bed. With shaking hands, she had carried the cups over to them, and *waited*, bovine and uncomplaining, while he had smothered the woman's feeble protests and had taken his will of her. *She had stood there*, the only thought in her fogged brain the hope that somehow he would find the new girl lacking and not throw her out, after all.

For she had no place to go, nobody to take her in. Nobody in the valley would open a door to her. The few times MacLynn had taken her to the trading post, the roughest, most uncouth men had turned their backs on her and even the Indians had shown their contempt. If he cast her out she would starve, for she had sunk too low for any other man in the Noglichucky to want her.

"Are ye still here?" MacLynn snarled when he was finished, then saw the cups in her hand and reached up to take one from her. She looked at his throat under the red beard as he threw back his head to gulp down the whiskey and the idea stirred deep in her drunken brain. If she was doomed to die, then so was he.

But first she would try to convince him to keep her. "I'm better than her, MacLynn." She whined. "Ye know f'r a fact that she don't know how to pleasure ye half as good as I do."

The woman on the bunk whispered, "I ain't—I dunno how it happened, ma'am. I didn't want to come."

Red slammed his big fist into the girl's face to silence her. Then he looked up and took the second cup from Becky. After swigging down the drink, he handed it back to her and yawned. "Get ye gone," he told her. "If ye're still here when I wake I'll kick y'r head in."

She moistened her dry, cracked lips. "Why don't ye keep both of us? I c'ld do the cookin' and she—"

"Get ye gone!" This last came drowsily as MacLynn rolled away from the girl and snuggled his big, shaggy head in the crook of his arm.

She remembered making her way back to the jug and pouring herself a drink. She sipped it, eyeing the pair on the pallet. When Red awakened he would kill her if she was still there. He had given her warning and she knew he meant it. Without him there would be no roof over her head or food for her belly or drink to make her forget who she once had been. As Red MacLynn's outcast mopsy she was as good as dead. So before she died she had to take her revenge on this beast who had dragged her down to this shameful state.

Tiptoeing across the dirt floor, she eyed the sharp knife he wore on his belt. The new woman watched her uncomprehendingly. In two swift motions, she slipped the bright blade out of its sheath and stabbed it deep into Red MacLynn's guts, just under his ribs.

As soon as she drove the blade home she knew she had made a mistake. She should have stuck the knife in his throat. It would have been easy to slice his gullet and let him cough out his black soul. But by knifing him lower down she had roused that great hulk out of his sleep, bringing him towering to his feet with his hands fluttering at the knife handle that jutted from him.

His bright eyes blazing, he cursed her as he struggled to remove the knife and then crumpled in a heap.

He thrashed furiously for awhile, his booted feet drumming on the dirt floor. Then he got to his hands and knees, his head low between his shoulders, and stared at the floor.

"I'll find ye, ye know," he told her quietly. "Ye can run to the ends of the earth but the MacLynn will find ye."

"Die, ye turd-eatin' dog," she spat at him. "Die and remember all through hell the things ye did to me."

"Ah, girl, girl, ye know I always . . ."

Slowly he rolled over on his back. She watched as his life drifted away. Finally, he lay still, his eyes studying the smoke-blackened eaves.

She started for the door and felt a hand clutching her skirt. "Please, ma'am, take me with you," the new girl whimpered.

Becky struck the girl's hand away. "Ye got here without any help from me," she snarled. "Make y'r own way out of here, if ye can."

[2]

Then flight, out of the Noglichucky Valley, laboring through the laurel hills of the Wautuga Range, painfully struggling over the mountains, shunning the easier way through McKinney's Gap because the soldiers would surely be there, and finally finding herself still alive on the eastern slopes, in sight of civilization.

She still couldn't remember many parts of her incredible escape but one shining fact would never be dimmed: she had been shown compassion by all the settlers she was so sure despised her. She had been thrown out by one of the most hated and feared man in that wild country. For all her benefactors knew, Red MacLynn might have been hot on her heels. Yet they had fed her out of their meager larders and replaced her rags with others, little better but clean and darned, and had shown her the secret trails that led east. Somebody had even provided her with a horse, a spavined nag but a precious possession among those people who had so little.

She had tried hard to remember who had given her the horse and under what circumstances, but somehow it eluded her. Sometimes she was almost sure she had stayed at one cabin longer than at any of the others and while there she had let a man make love to her—or had it been Red Mac-Lynn possessing her again in her feverish dreams? This man, she was almost sure, lived alone and he had begged her to stay with him. When she would not, he had given her his horse, a love gift that rivaled a king's jewels—if it had really happened.

There were other fragments of memory that almost convinced her that there really had been a sick old couple whom she had helped after she stumbled on their cabin in the hills. These were the old people she had mentioned in the fanciful tale she had told her family on the night of her return. Perhaps the lie had some basis in fact, or, perhaps the old people were merely products of her crippled mind. If they had been real, the old man might have given her the horse in gratitude for what she had done for them.

Somehow she knew she must forget the whole dreary story. Memory could only lead to grief and danger. She must simply pray that no one from that shadowy past ever walked into her life.

Nor should she let herself worry about what she might have said while she was delirious from the fever that had finally laid her low in the Hoags' cabin at Cedar Valley. When she had come back to reality, the kindly Scots had told her only that she had been ill, so ill that they had sent for their Presbyterian preacherman, for what purpose she had never asked. Perhaps to shrive a babbling madwoman of the sin of murder?

Later, she had talked to this strange priest, this Ian Mac-Cutcheon and she had done her best to coax the nature of her ravings out of him but to no avail.

"Aye, ye rambled a bit, lass, but it meant nothing to me save y'r mention of Middlebend and y'r people, the Allyns whom ye'll soon be wi' again, prrrraise God."

"If they'll have me," she muttered. "There's been many a long day and unlikely happenin' since I ran away from Middlebend, Rev'rend."

"Ah, with them, too, but I pledge ye they'll receive ye back wi' open arrms and an overflowin' hearrt, all the past forgi'en and forrgotten on both sides. Ye'll see,"

MacCutcheon was a good man. Even if she had told the whole story of Red MacLynn, he would keep her secret. Certainly he would. She prayed to God he would.

". . . can't let thy past misfortunes put an end to thy life now, Becky. Thou art too young and full of life to let that happen to thee. Why, thee cannot be more than . . . I mean, thou art so young and pretty that thou cannot shroud thyself in widow's weeds, not now."

She threw back her head and laughed, glad to be wrenched out of her black memories. "Young and pretty, am I? Come, Robert, ye know full well I'm old enough to be y'r mother, in experience if not in years."

"Hush your nonsense, I won't listen."

"How old d'ye think I am? I'll make ye a wager that ye'll guess wrong by years, no matter how kind ye try to be.

"What kind of wager?"

"Ye can name it, but keep it small, do. Part-of-Providence may be growin' into a grand plantation but I've scurse one copper to rub against the other since I came home.

"Not," she added quickly, "that I've any use f'r coin—ye've seen how they've heaped everything on me till I had to cry stop. This cloth that Philip brought down the last time he came, d'ye fancy it, Rob?"

He nodded. "Thee called for a wager. A kiss 'gainst—let's see—this hinged Sheffield knife thy brother admires so. Thee can give it him for his birthday if thee win."

"Ho, and bring thunder and lightning down on my head, too. More suspicious than a dotard husband is our George.

But done and done, the wager's set. I'll use the knife myself when I win it. 'Twill come in handy f'r cuttin' flowers and sharpenin' quills."

"Thee said I couldn't guess within years—how about two years, one way or the other?"

"Aye," she said smilingly, "but if ye guess ten years too high, I'll box y'r ears."

"Well, then, I guess you've just turned twenty-one. But by only a few days—I remember thy sister mentioning thy birthday and I cursed myself for not having a gift."

She laughed, warmed by his guess, just two years under her actual age. Although she knew he was being polite, still she *had* lost most of her wrinkles and her hair *had* regained some of its shine despite the gray, and her body *had* firmed up in all the right places. Too much in some places; she'd have to rein herself in at table or she'd soon have as big a belly as poor Betsy. "I thought you Quakers were against such fanciful things as birthday gifts and Christmas feasts, as well as slaves and dancin' and pretty gowns and a hundredscore other things I love so."

"Never mind about us benighted Quakers—do I win my wager?"

"Na, na, of course not. Ye missed by—well, I won't tell ye but ye were off by a bosseyed surveyor's mile."

His honest face fell but rallied instantly. "Then I owe thee my knife," he said, and offered it to her, resting on his wide, clean palm.

She looked down at it, then up at him, her mouth curved. "Oh, Rob, I'd not take y'r prize blade. Keep y'r knife and come claim y'r wager."

She thrust her face up toward his, her eyes dancing, a laugh bubbling in her throat. Such a girlish game for an old, used-up woman. If Robert Hosban but knew . . . but he did not know. He never would know, God willing.

His face came closer and she lowered her long-lashed lids, parted her lips. It was still a game—of course it was—and no matter what this big man made of it, 'twas merely a bit of play beside the river on a warm September evening. His lips touched hers and then his arms were around her, straining her to him so that she felt his heat flow through her unbound breasts, into her very center, feeding her starving womanhood, sending the half forgotten waves of desire flushing through her body.

For a moment, she forgot all her stern resolves, and clung to him, her mouth opening, her thighs parting langorously— and then, just before she would have thrown herself upon him shamelessly, she heard the echo of Red MacLynn's jeering laugh.

With utmost control, she managed to keep from wrenching herself out of his arms and rudely thrusting him away. He didn't deserve that and, besides, there was a cleverer way to end this before it went any further.

She took her lips away and drew out of his arms, then deliberately smacked her palm against her own cheek. "These pesty flies," she complained. "Ain't they bitin' ye, too?"

He drew back, his hurt visible even in the dim light. "I've not felt or heard any, not a single one," he said stiffly. "I thought . . ."

"That I was so swoonin' I'd not feel 'em when they were eatin' me alive?" She laughed. "Why, Robert, if I didn't know ye better I'd think ye was boastin'." She got to her feet and shook out her skirts. "We'd best go back."

"But we just got here."

"The bugs just got here, too, and as f'r me, they c'n have my seat on the log and welcome to it. If ye want to stay and dish 'em up a banquet, that's y'r privilege."

She turned and hurried up the path, making waving motions in the darkness to give credence to her lie. Within, her heart mourned its loss. Perhaps she should have stayed in his arms. She was no heroine; 'twas not her duty to protect a man 'gainst his honest love. Perhaps it was meant that she be given this great chance for a new love, a new life, the happiness of which she had been robbed so many years before when she had run off with Harry Tarbell.

Ah, what a prize, dear Harry! But it had all been her doing. She had known where she was heading the first time she had "surrendered" to Tarbell's feverish entreaties, that night under the pines at the edge of Middlebend's sweeping lawn. It had been no surrender at all, of course; she had brought Harry Tarbell to that uncontrollable pitch as deftly as she had ever spurred a jumper over a fence. Her sense of triumph had been even greater than her passion that wild night.

If she had only given half an ear to all those who truly

loved her and sought to protect her, if she had had the wisdom
to realize that Father's preachments were delivered more out
of love than a desire to rule his family's lives, if she had
only . . .

She remonstrated with herself for her self-pitying thought.
After all, she had known what she was doing and she had
declared herself willing to pay the cost for having her own
way.

She would survive without Robert Hosban, without any
man, without the real happiness that came from birthing
babies. She had survived starvation and cruel beatings, the
whiskey horrors, unnumbered days and night wandering in a
wilderness. She had whored for darlin' Harry and knifed a
brute who had tried to cast her off; she had broken all the
commandments and according to the priests she should be
dead and burning in Hell. But she was *alive*, her heart thudding steadily in her breast, while good, chaste women lay
under the ground, dead and forgotten.

She was strong, indestructible. Evil but alive. She would
keep on living, eating, drinking, lying in a warm bed. All she
had to do was to deny the weak, womanish longings that came
over her, as they had a moment before in Robert's arms, and
remember that survival was the only thing that mattered.

"Thee needn't hurry so," Robert Hosban murmured behind
her. " 'Twas only that one wager and it's been collected. I'd
not try to claim more unless thou wished it."

"Oh, Rob, did'st think I fled our little arbor out o' fear ye'd
forget y'r Quakerish ways and manhandle me? Nay, one
thing I c'n say about you Quakers, ye might be on the dull
side but ye'd never savage a poor defenseless widder, now,
would ye?"

His voice when he answered was quizzical. "Defenseless,
Becky? Methinks thou art better at disarming a man than one
of Tryon's musketeers. A couple of words, a slap at a mos-
quito, and he's reduced to rummage."

She laughed. "I told ye I was experienced enough to be
y'r mother, didn't I? Now there's the house; I beg ye, don't
let George suspect we might ha' shared a kiss. He'd not believe 'twas only a joke and there's no more spleenish a man
on God's green earth than George when he thinks an Allyn
woman's been treated lightly, even his old widowed sister."

"George is my friend," Hosban said gravely. "I can't think he'd suspect me of anything dishonorable."

"Ye don't know him. He was my husband's dear friend, too, but when poor Harry spoke to him before he approached my father, George all but called him out f'r it. If Philip hadn't been handy, God knows what w'ld ha' happened—they might ha' fought a duel and I'd ha' been widdered before I was wed."

Where do these lies come from? Do I get pleasure from imagining Harry properly approaching Father with an honorable plea for my lily white hand?

"What was your husband like, Becky? Or does it pain thee too much to speak of him?"

He was a dog—worse, 'cause even a cur would draw the line at some of Harry's delights.

"Nay, it don't pain me none, hardly at all, it's been so long ago. What d'ye want to know about him? He was the prettiest man God ever fashioned and brave, in a quiet, modest manner. If he had a fault, 'twas that he was too unassumin'—there were times when he vexed me by lettin' others claim the credit f'r what he done." She paused. "Ye know how he died, don't ye?"

"George said he was killed by the Indians."

"A pack of Catawba devils he'd befriended all winter when they'd ha' starved if it hadn't been f'r him. But as I know Harry, he died forgivin' 'em, prob'ly explainin' to God that they didn't know better, bein' savages."

Whoa-up, you're making him such a saint that even Robert can't swallow it.

"Oh, he had his faults, too," she went on with a wry laugh. "Always seekin' out adventure, goin' places that cautious men warned him 'gainst. And so overly generous that sometimes we went hungry 'cause he'd given away what he sh'ld ha' kept f'r his family. And he was—"

Revulsion gripped her suddenly and she broke off her lies. "I find it does grieve me, after all, so let's talk no more of Harry Tarbell." She felt a sudden surge of anger. "Why d'ye want to know about him, anyway? Just curious about the kind of man who'd throw himself away on a woman like me, perchance?"

"Nay, Becky, thou know'st 'tis not idle curiosity, girl," he said soberly. "If I've offended thee, I beg forgiveness. 'Twas only that—ah, let it go, let it go."

She detected a curious tone in his voice and turned around to try to read his eyes in the darkness. "What is it?" she demanded. "Ye're keepin' somethin' from me—I know ye are!"

He shook his head, the long hair brushing his shoulders. "Not so, I swear it. I've stirred thee up with my clumsy questions and I'm truly sorry." He looked away from her searching gaze, nodding toward the house. "Am I to be asked in for a cup before I start for Cane Creek?"

She shook her head. "Not tonight, Rob. I find I'm overweary and as sure as you come in, you and George will get to talkin' and it'll be hours before ye'll remember the clock. Ye do forgive me, don't ye?"

He nodded and turned toward the shed where he had tethered his horse. "Goodnight then, Becky. And don't bother thy head about aught I said. I vow I'm keeping naught from thee."

"I know—'tis only my weariness, no more," she said. "Goodnight, Robert, and I wish ye a safe ride home."

Quakers, she thought, as she mounted the steps to the porch, made damned poor liars.

[3]

Benjamin Dedshall sat down behind his fine Queen Anne period walnut desk and waved a stubby hand at the upholstered chair opposite. "Sit down, sit down," he said irritably. "Ye must give me a bit o' time, Edward, I care not how busy ye say ye are."

Elizabeth's husband folded his lean length slowly, his eyes on his father. He noted the troubled, shadowed face, the sagging eye pouches, and the shrunken neck that disappeared into the too loose collar. His father stoutly claimed that he was as robust as he'd ever been but Edward knew that something was gravely wrong, something other than Orange County politics.

Even Millie had noticed, and when she took time from her own madcap caprices to see that something was amiss the situation must be bad, indeed.

"He ain't eatin' hardly anything, Edward," his sister had

confided just the previous day. "And I've heard him pukin' out in the privy many a time after meals."

"Has he seen a doctor?" he had asked.

"He says he has but I don't think so, not really. Ye know what I think? I think he's skeered to."

"Nonsense," he'd told her. "You're imagining things." But he had known that Millie was not embroidering on the facts this time.

He wanted to talk to his father about seeing a physician, but decided to put it off, perhaps out of his own fear. He had a good excuse; Squire Longman was expecting him in the ale-house, to discuss a forthcoming case, there was a deal of study to be done on some points of law concerning another piece of litigation, Judge Lesmythe had ordered him to call at his chambers before the next session opened, and . . . oh, there were plenty of reasons why he couldn't sit down for a heart-to-heart talk with Pa right now.

A heart-to-heart talk? When have we ever really discussed anything, man-to-man? If he's not been angry about something I've done or failed to do, he's been tongue-tied by his own strange sense of inferiority, as though his lack of schooling and the dirty things he had to do as Granville's bailiff made him unworthy to discuss anything with me on an equal footing.

If only we could have just a little of the close feeling that joins Philip and even George to their father despite William Weyland Allyn's cold offishness. If I could but reach out and clasp his hand and have him unburden himself of his troubles, tell me about this vomiting. . . .

Instead, he complained, " 'Od's blood, Pa, will you get on with it, whatever it is? You must know how full my calendar is. I'm trying desperately to clear it so's I can ride down to Part-of-Providence to see Elizabeth."

"I know, Edward, but this can't wait. How is y'r dear wife doin'?"

Edward shrugged. "Fine, or at least that's what Rebecca tells me."

"Don't ye think she'd be better off up here in Hillsboro? They say there's some of the best midwives in the colony here."

"She won't hear of it. Rebecca has taken charge of every-thing, it seems, and she insists that their slave midwife has a marvelous touch. And Elizabeth says she wants to stay at home, so that's that."

Ben nodded, rubbing his chin. "I s'pose," he said. "When's it due—this month, ain't it?"

"Heavens, no, not till sometime in February if they've counted right. Today's November twenty-one so that's two months to wait, at least." He took a snuffbox out of his waistcoat pocket and offered it to his father, wincing inwardly when Ben shook his head reluctantly. He dipped snuff, sneezed, and blew his nose on a fine lawn kerchief.

"Now, then, what did you want to see me about, Pa?"

His father frowned down at his hands which were clasped loosely on the desktop. He seemed to cast about for the proper language then said, "It's come to my ears that ye've been approached lately by a damned rebeller, one of them fire-eatin' Regulators, who asked ye to defend him when he's brought to justice in the comin' court term. Am I right?"

Edward's face tightened. "You must know that even if a client told me he belonged to that secret society—and I ain't saying that any did—I couldn't betray his trust."

Ben made an impatient gesture. "Pish-tush, don't play the lofty lawyer with me. Ye'd be breakin' no trust, f'r God's sake—we know the man's name and how many times he's been to a Regulators' meetin' and the treasonable things he's said there."

Edward grimaced. "Aye, being Edmund Fanning's lieutenant, you must give ear to all the feeble lies his trothless spies give him."

"Feeble lies, eh? Ye'll find out how feeble they are when they stretch y'r friend's neck—unless ye accept a generous proposal I've been told to offer ye."

Edward laughed. "I can imagine how generous it must be if it comes from Fanning."

"Edward, Edward, when are ye ever goin' to get it through y'r head that when the big dog barks, the little dog had better listen or get his gullet chewed out? No, now wait, hear me out!

"Ye know that the Register rules this county with Will'm Tryon's full backin'. Ye know that as long as he does rule, them what opposes him c'n only bring trouble down on their own heads. I've got as much respect as anybody f'r a man who'll fight against long odds if there's a chance of winnin'—

oh, yes, I do, no matter what ye think of me. But a man who'll keep buttin' his head against a wall when he knows he can't loosen a single brick is a fool."

Edward said scornfully, "If every man in history had believed that, there'd never have been a tyrant overthrown."

Ben Dedshall fastened his eyes on his hands again. "I don't know much about hist'ry, as ye know, but from what I've heard, most tyrants were overthrowed by other tyrants who wanted their throne and the gold that went with it, not by young backwoods lawyers with lofty ideers."

"That's the way it has been, till now," Edward admitted. "But there's a new age dawning wherein the little man's voice will be louder than a tyrant's cannon."

"P'raps ye're right, and p'raps there'll be a day when big fish won't gobble up little fish and lords won't levy taxes, but we won't live to see it, son. Meanwhile, we must look out f'r ourselves as best we can under today's order."

"Do you mean we must become usurers and embezzlers, too, so that petty tyrant in the courthouse will be assured that we're of the same breed? Is that it?"

"There's a nicer way of puttin' it, ye know," Ben said in a low voice. "I've heerd it spoke of as swimmin' with the current 'stead of drownin' in an upstream effort that leads nowhere."

"But, Pa, don't you see—"

"No, I don't see," Dedshall cut in, his voice harsh. "I've learned lately that what ye think ye see and what I see plain as day are two diff'rent things. I hoped that when ye marrit Elizabeth Allyn ye'd go back to bein' the sensible man ye were in Edenton, highly regarded by the substantial men of the colony."

"Oh, aye, they admired me to my eyes for my bootlicking, I'll be bound. You saw how they all came to my aid when Tryon ran us out of town like a pack of tinkers."

"Is that what changed ye, then?" He sighed. "I s'pose I sh'ld ha' spelled things out f'r ye at the time, told ye what to expect. Ye must've thought it was the end of the world when all it was, was a bad spell that w'ld improve as soon as I made certain—ah—improvements to the situation."

"Paid bribes, you mean," Edward muttered.

"Bribes, expressions of gratitude, call 'em what ye like. 'Tis the way things are done, Edward, and always have been. As f'r those substantial gentlemen in Edenton failin' ye, men who had any position to protect have always shied away from them that got in trouble no matter how much they might secretly approve of 'em.

"Ye spake of hist'ry just now—mayhap ye c'n remember what happened to kings and princes what let their hearts overrule their heads and flung themselves into a doomed cause f'r friendship's sake or even 'cause the doomed man was a brother or an uncle. I tell ye, son, when the axe swings it's likely to take off the heads of them close to the intended mark so it's best to draw off as far away as ye can."

Edward stirred restlessly in his chair. He knew that he could debate this thing until the following summer and his father still would not understand a word, any more than he could now accept the cynical thoughts of his father. If called upon to explain the reasons for the recent changes in his thinking he doubted he could present a lucid argument, at least not one that would be understood by anyone in his own family or among the Allyns. Dear Elizabeth would blindly accept anything he might say as unarguable truth but if he tried to explain to her just why he knew that there were worldshaking events in the making that would bring justice to the meanest borderer in North Carolina, the poor girl would be utterly confused.

As for his father-in-law, William Weyland Allyn, he would be shocked out of his chilly politeness by the merest hint of what Edward Dedshall believed was coming. The old gentleman took refuge in the fealty oath that William Tryon had forced him to take that evening at Middlebend but Edward was almost certain that even if he had not been dragooned into swearing that obnoxious oath, William Allyn would still stand clear of any rebellion against the old established order.

As for Philip—where was the stormy rebel of Edenton's Green Ribbon Club now? Another year or so and Philip would be a solid member of the Fanning gang, his purse as swollen with gold as his belly was getting from those four-hour dinners at the Three Plovers Inn, the Fanning toadies' gathering place.

"If ye won't think of y'rself, ye'd best think of y'r wife and the babe that's soon to be born," his father was saying. "For I warn ye, Edward, do ye not listen to reason now and nothin' I c'n do c'n stave off the disaster that's headin' y'r way—a disaster that'll carry y'r Betsy as low as it'll carry you."

Edward said haughtily, "Elizabeth would be the first to tell me not to worry about any of Edmund Fanning's machinations."

"I dunno what the word means but I agree, Betsy w'ld gladly trip down the path to Hell itself if she thought that's what ye wanted. She depends on ye to perteck her—and her fam'ly, too—so she'd never dream ye'd recklessly sacrifice her and the babe out of y'r own pride."

"Pride? Do you call it pride to refuse to deliberately throw a case after swearing to defend the man's life and liberty?"

"Who said anything about losin' the case? Nay, 'tis just the opposite, man."

Edward stared. "The opposite—what d'you mean?"

Ben Dedshall hunched over the desk and dropped his voice to a conspiratorial whisper. "Why, I've been given the word to pledge ye that ye'll win this certain case, against all odds, and y'r client will go free as a bird." His father went on in hushed eagerness. "Ye've been told that Justice Lesmythe wants t'see ye, ain't that so?" When Edward nodded, Ben grinned. "Ye see? The judge wants t'instruct ye on what he'll want ye to say and what he don't want ye to say in y'r speeches f'r the defense, so's his verdict will sound reasonable to all the carping doubters in the county. 'Twill come as the biggest surprise in many a fortnight but the verdict's as sure as taxes and think what a feather that'll be in y'r cap, Edward. Why, ye'll be the most sought-after barrister in Orange County, amongst the Regulators and their friends."

"But—but—ah, I'm beginning to see."

"I knew ye w'ld, son," Ben crowed. "Trust my Edward to see what's what at a snap of his fingers, I told 'em."

"What you're saying is that Edmund Fanning wants me to earn the Regulators' trust so's I can serve as his spy amongst them, is that it?" There was disgust and something approaching sorrow in the young man's voice. *My own father, holding out thirty pieces of silver to me. How can he?*

"Stop fastenin' on the word 'spy'," Ben said irritably. "Loyal subject of the king sounds better, good husband and father, better yet. Pertecter of the innocents, how's that?" As Edward started to struggle out of his chair, his father held up his hand and his voice changed abruptly.

"Hear me out, I tell ye. 'Cause if ye don't say yes to this, ye'll ruin y'rself and all chance of happiness. The Allyns will suffer and y'r own family—I don't s'pose none of us means nothin' to ye but unless ye agree to this, y'r sisters and brothers will find themselves out on the street and y'r old father— aw, ye care naught what happens to me so why bother to tell ye?"

Edward settled back in his chair. "You—you're making empty threats."

"I wish I was, boy. But I ain't, not a bit of it. Why d'ye s'pose Edmund Fanning's been lettin' ye spout all y'r wild talk in court? Why d'ye think Squire Longman's been settin' in the alehouse, never interferin' with y'r recklessness? D'ye think Fanning's gone blind and deaf? Nay, not him. He needed somebody f'r the rebels to trust and ye suited his purpose exactly."

Edward spluttered, "But—but—ye must be wrong! I've been warned by the judges and every other court officer time and again. They've told me to temper my arguments or—"

"Hah, the better to build ye up as a champion of the malcontents, ye dolt. There wasn't a minute when they couldn't ha' put ye in gaol f'r flagrant disrespect—and would have, had not the Register bade them let ye rant and rave."

"Ye knew this and never said a word to me?"

"Would ye have listened? Nay, I'm an old fool who don't know nothin' about these new days, ye've all but told me so to my face." Ben's eyes fell under his son's accusing stare. "I c'ld have told ye but I knew 'twould do no good and, besides, I had myself and my fam'ly to look out f'r. If I'd warned ye before Fanning told me to set ye straight, 'twould have meant the end of all I've spent so much arrangin' here. If it's any comfort to ye, he's got me under his thumb, too, ye know. I do what he says and I prosper. If I tried to slip the leash, I'd go down to a ruin that'd be final, this time."

Edward gnawed his lip, then asked, "And if I refuse to play this stinking game—or say I will and then apostasize?"

"If that means betray Fanning and the Governor, why then we'll all go down, you, me, y'r wife and babe, the high 'n' mighty Allyns and the lowly Dedshalls, all in a common heap. That's it in a nutshell, boy, and no matter how ye scowl at it or who ye blame f'r it, there's no escapin' it."

Ben sighed. "If 'twere only me who'd suffer, I'd tell ye to go y'r noble way and damn Edmund Fanning. I really would,

Edward, though I know ye find that hard to believe. I wouldn't care overmuch 'cause 'twixt us two, I don't think I've much more time left to worry about whether I spend it bein' rich or poor, in prison or walkin' the streets with an ivory-headed cane."

"Now, Pa, you don't mean that. Why, a proper medicine and you'll be as good as new."

"P'raps, but I don't think so. In any case, it's you and y'r goodwife and poor Ethelind and the boys I'm thinkin' of. And ye must, too, Edward, else ye'll hate y'rself f'r lettin' y'r dauncey heroics cast them on times so hard 'twould make the Devil weep."

[4]

Edmund Fanning, Register for Orange County in the North Carolina Colony, looked over the throng that crowded his grand house and decided that his Christmas rout was a success. Not that he had ever doubted it would be. Fanning demanded success in all his affairs, social as well as political and financial, and if he did not achieve it he knew the reason why. If the jollity of his Christmas party was not sustained, his lieutenants knew they would suffer for it, so at least a dozen clever men were kept busy making certain that nothing did go wrong.

The fiddles squeaked and the clavichord jangled for the dancing. The conversation grew louder and freer, as the level of the great punch bowl sank and rose again under the ministrations of the slaves. The table holding the festive meats and pastries was plundered, replenished, and plundered again. Some eyes grew brighter with excitement and wine, others were dulled by too much rum and too much food or by the languor that followed visits to the pergola at the far end of the garden on this mild December night.

Those that drank, danced, and even made love on this Christmas night, 1766, had earned their pleasure. For being a friend of Edmund Fanning was not quite the bed of roses that those carping outsiders supposed. They might have money and all the creature comforts that the western outpost could offer but they lived under the constant threat of bodily harm, even the lowest clerk's youngest child. There was no telling when a rock might come sailing through their front window at night or a volley of mud balls be thrown at their backs in broad daylight. Coach wheels had a strange way of falling off when the rider was a Fanning man, and more than one of the group that danced, swigged, laughed, and flirted on this Christmas night had been flogged, stoned, or otherwise mistreated by those treasonous bastards who called themselves the Alamance Regulators.

As for the ladies, they were constantly subjected to indignities by the townspeople. They affected to be amused by this treatment but Edmund Fanning was a keen judge of human nature and knew that their tender sensibilities were bruised by the jeers and name calling.

The Register looked down at the little man beside him and remarked, "They seem to be enjoying themselves, eh, Dedshall?"

Ben turned, raised his haggard eyes, and attempted a wan smile. "Aye, y'r honor, they do and well they should. A more bountiful celebration I've never seen anywhere, not in Edenton or New Berne or even Lunnon."

I'll wager the only celebrations you ever saw in London were public hangings, Fanning thought to himself. Aloud, he said indulgently, " 'Tis kind of you to say so. Your daughters look exceptionally beautiful tonight. Let's see, the elder's named Millicent, is that right?"

"No, y'r honor, that's Ethelind, the tall one in blue. Millie's the one with red hair, just a bud unfoldin', as the poet says."

More of a pepper plant than a rose, I'll be bound. The other one's the gawkiest crow that's ever graced my hall. "Do you suppose Mistress Millie would think me a forward old man if I asked her for the next Minuèt, Dedshall?"

"Forward old man? How c'n ye say that, sir? She'd be most honored—'twould quite overwhelm the child."

Yon "child" has a nice pair of tits, he thought. "Then will'st convey my plea, friend Dedshall? I fear I'd frighten her by presenting this great hulk without warning."

He watched as Dedshall scurried off to do his bidding, then sipped from the wineglass in his beringed hand. He made a handsome, imposing figure and he knew it. A bit fleshy perhaps, but nicely balanced, with a pair of the best-turned legs in Orange County, bar none. His looking glass showed him that his features might be too heavy to suit some of the more effete standards, but even at fifty-seven it was still a strong-nosed, firm-chinned, heavy-browed face. There might be other men in the room who were prettier but none, by God, whose features show such strength of character, indomitable purpose, and—if she knew what to look for—promise of excitement for a venturesome lady.

His elegant suit of dark green satin with the daring orange inserts had been tailored in Sackville Street. His prized legs were encased in the finest silk and his silver shoe buckles were almost as big as saucers.

Without succumbing to the least immodesty, Fanning knew he had the most brilliant brain in the colonies, the shrewdest perception when it came to choosing his underlings and un-masking his enemies, and an almost mystical gift for predicting and making adjustments to future events.

The matter of Tryon's ascension to the governor's chair was a case in point. Edmund Fanning had somehow guessed that Tryon would be the next royal governor of the colony almost as soon as he had set foot in North Carolina. A few discreet inquiries made of friends in England had brought him a full dossier on Tryon, including the fact that the gentle-man was connected with the Marquis of Downshire through his lady. It had then been easy for him to deduce that Dobbs was on his way out and Tryon was on his way in.

While other colonial officers had treated the newcomer cavalierly, he had made it his business to offer Tryon his full cooperation. When he first met Tryon in person, it had taken the Register only a minute or two to correctly evaluate the next governor's principles or lack thereof and by a few oblique inferences, assure himself that as long as he shared in the boodle, William Tryon could easily look the other way where it concerned Fanning's lucrative management of Orange County.

So, while the other colonial and proprietary officers in North Carolina had scurried about in confusion after Dobbs' death Fanning had found himself in his usual unshakeable position.

That position would remain inviolate, come Dobbs, Tryon, the next Governor, whoever he might be, come Scots, Quakers, protestors, agitators, or the Alamance Regulators. Edmund Fanning was ready, especially for the Regulators now that he had young Dedshall firmly fixed in their confidence. And anything else they might do to embarrass him would be repaid a hundredfold by Governor William Tryon with an army at his back.

"You have my word that should these miscreants dare to rise in any outright rebellion you can't contain, I'll come west myself, with men and horses and cannon, and put a stop to their complaining forever," the governor had promised him. And although Fanning did not believe this would ever be necessary, it was a comforting thought whenever the going got difficult in Hillsboro.

"Y'r honor, may I present my daughter, Millie, Mistress Mildred Dedshall. Millie, ye know this is the Register, Mister Fanning, and he wants ye f'r his partner in the next dance."

Returning to the present, Fanning bowed to the young redhaired girl. As Millie curtsied deeply, the Register noted her remarkable breasts. She was no beauty, he thought, but still there was a certain charm in her green eyes, and in the way she held herself, as full of life as a racing filly.

"Mistress Mildred," he murmured, looking deep into her eyes. "Would'st do me the honor?"

"If ye like," she chirped. "But I warn ye, ye'll prob'ly find me the worst dancer in the hall."

"Now, Millie," her father fussed. "Ye mustn't talk down y'r dancin'. Ye know ye're as lightfooted as any of 'em."

"I don't know how I could be," the girl said frankly. "Nobody ever asked me to dance in Edenton—I never even got *invited* to a single ball back there. Here, we do better but I still ain't seen any great rush to get me f'r a partner. Savin' a few gentlemen that had somethin' besides dancin' on their mind, ye can be sure."

Fanning threw back his leonine head and roared with laughter. This girl was as refreshing as a cool breeze on a muggy day, her honesty as uncommon as it was delightful. He spent half his time listening to his hangers-on boasting of how important they had been someplace else and to have somebody, even a slip of a green-eyed miss, admit that she was something less than the Quean of Love and Beautie where she came from was a wonderful surprise.

"Now, now, Mistress Mildred," he chuckled. "I vow you malign yourself fair cruelly." He had only to raise a magisterial hand to stop the fiddles. As the figures on the dance floor disintegrated to await their host's direction, Fanning bowed to Millie again and asked, "Will'st give me the pleasure of exposing that libel in a Sarabande? Or would a Minuet be more to your liking?"

The girl curtsied again, fully conscious of the Register's dark eyes on her bosom, and said shyly, "Why, if ye like, I guess my Gavotte's the best of a poor lot."

Fanning restrained a wince—the Gavotte was meant for younger legs and slimmer bodies—but his smile and voice were smooth as silk. " 'Twould be excellent but I fear my fiddlers know no Gavotte tunes. Perhaps we'd best settle for a Minuet."

"As Y'r Lordship pleases," Millie murmured and a moment later they were tracing the steps that even in this frontier town of Hillsboro were becoming so stiff and stylized that the dancers resembled actors going through the motions of a slow, dull play. With such rigidly controlled movements, almost any girl could pass as a dancer, but still the redhead managed to impart a vivacity to her steps that the others lacked. She was actually an excellent dancer although what she had told Fanning about the Dedshalls' ostracism in Edenton was true enough. What she had failed to mention was that she had practiced the intricate figures on her own—and added refinements that made her quite the most delightful partner Fanning could remember having in quite some time.

When the dance was over, the County Register reverted to the outmoded ending of the Minuet by planting a hearty kiss on his young partner's cheek. "Extremely well done, Mistress Dedshall," he breathed. "I was sure you stretched the truth when you said you were a poor dancer but I didn't dream how far." He took her captive hand and tucked it in the crook of his arm.

"Now will you indulge me further by joining me for a stroll in the garden?" he asked. "I've been told it's like spring outside and till now I've been unable to leave my host's duties."

"Most pleased," Millie murmured and left the ballroom with Fanning, basking in the envious looks from the ladies who had not been asked to stroll in the garden with their host. *I knew I could dazzle any buck who'd take a chance with me,* she exulted, *but I didn't know I'd be all that good. Fair swooning, the old man was when we finished.*

She stepped onto the gravel path, looking down the aisle of yew and boxwood. *And now what's up with him? He*

*wouldn't dare play the rake here, behind his own house full
of people. Would he?*

If she felt any timidity, it was soon gone. Imagine being
set upon by Edmund Fanning, the richest, most powerful man
in the county. How she could high-nose it over all those
beautiful women back there if he did try to make free with
her. Plain Millie Dedshall stealing their prize right out from
under their noses.

But then her inner caution raised a voice. To let him have
his way with her first crack out of the box would be to brand
herself a cheap and easy conquest, a young trollop of whom
little more could be expected, her being a member of the
Dedshall tribe, not quality at all.

So when Fanning reached the secluded pergola, drew her
down on the seat beside him, and made as if to clasp her in
his arms, she planted both hands against his befrilled chest
and said, "Oh, no, milord, 'taint right ye sh'ld overpower me
with y'r charms so suddenlike."

"Sooner or later, what matters it?" he muttered. Her lithe
youth excited him. "Haven't you heard, *Gather ye rosebuds
whilst ye may, Old Time is still a-flying?*"

"I know it by heart," Millie said tartly. "I vow, 'tis the one
scrap of verse that's spouted by every cock in the colonies
with brash ideers. My ma told me one from the Bible; it says
sommen about a virtuous woman bein' worth a bushel measure
of rubies."

"The Bible," he scoffed. " 'Strooth, I didn't expect to find
a little Puritan here." He pulled her to him again and this
time Millie did not resist too much. *A kiss or two, who can it
hurt, and it might please the old man. Maybe enough for him
to . . .*

But being kissed by Edmund Fanning, she discovered, was
far different than being smacked by other boys or even being
dandled by Midshipman Edgar Kent, that night so long ago
in Edenton. She struggled out from under his possessive
mouth and pushed away the hand that explored her bodice.
"Milord," she managed, "ye make my head spin. Ye—ye
must be gentle else I'll have to leave ye."

"No chance," he growled. "I'll not let you go. God, it's
been too long since . . . come here, fresh little flower."

"Which is goin' to have a sprained stem if ye don't go
easier," she complained. "Na, na, ye mustn't tear my gown.

What'll Pa say, or—or Dame Fanning? Ye mustn't shame me before all the others, sir, not here, not now."

"Then when?" he panted.

"Why, almost any time 'cept now. They all watched us come out here and they'll be lookin' sharp to see if I'm flushed or disarranged. I ain't schooled in this, Y'r Lordship; I'd be sure to give us both away and ye wouldn't want that, w'ld ye? Not at Christmas time. Why, I wouldn't be able to show me face again if everybody knowed and Pa—I dunno what he'd do to me."

"Don't worry about your father," he said, but he drew away a little, frowning down at the girl in his arms. "No matter what happened to you, I'd assuage your hurts so you'd never mind, I pledge you."

She peered up at him. "By doin' me a great favor mayhap?"

"Anything," he said heavily. He might have known. The little minx wanted pledges made before she gave in. Now she would name her price, as they all did sooner or later.

"I might ask ye f'r more than ye're ready to give," she warned.

"Try me, Millie, but for Christ's sake let's put an end to this fencing. I have to get back to the hall before too long."

She said slowly, "All right, then, here's what I want. Ye must promise to let my brother Edward off as y'r spy 'mongst the Regulators."

Anger squelched Fanning's desire. He dropped his arms and sprang to his feet.

"What nonsense is this?" he boomed. "Who filled ye with any such stuff as that?"

" 'Taint stuff," she replied calmly as she stood up beside him. "Nobody told me—I mean they didn't know I was anywhere about when Pa talked to Edward, so don't blame them. Y'see, I been listenin' to everything's been happenin' in Pa's office, here and back in Edenton, and not much gets past me."

"Let's get back to the hall," he blustered as he started up the path. "I've no time to listen to schoolgirl twittering."

"Ye didn't think I was such a silly schoolgirl a minute ago," Millie said reproachfully as she trotted behind him. "Ye promised me ye'd do me a great favor if—if I listened to y'r poetry 'stead of rememberin' Ma's. I might ha' knowed."

He stopped and turned back. "You might have known what?"

"That ye'd break y'r word. They all say ye can't be depended on but I thought they lied, makin' ye the Devil in all things, even denyin' y'r sacred word."

"Who told you I wasn't to be trusted? Name him and I'll make him swallow his lies in front of you."

She hunched her thin shoulders. "Ye'd have to haul a hull comp'ny up before ye to get a tenth of 'em. But never mind, Y'r Lordship, one more won't make no diff'rence, 'specially when she's a twitterin' schoolgirl."

He glared down at her in the darkness. This little chit had said it for him; what difference did it make if Ben Dedshall's brat joined all the others who called him trothless? But—but she had been a sweet morsel in his arms and she'd be even sweeter if . . .

" 'Twould make a difference to me, Mistress Mildred," he said in a softer voice. "When I pledged you I'd grant what you asked, I had no idea 'twould be mixed up with politics, for God's sake. As for your brother, I know naught of any spying. If your father said I fixed any such arrangement, he lied—p'raps to cure you of listening when you shouldn't."

Millie heaved a sigh. She should have known the grand Edmund Fanning could not be trapped by the likes of her. At least she still had her maidenhead all in one piece, for what that was worth.

"One thing more, Mistress Mildred," the Register said as she started up the path again. "You'd be making a grave mistake if you even whispered such a lie about spying. Baseless though it be, should it reach the ears of the mongrel Regulators, your brother's life wouldn't be worth a pinch of snuff, I warn you."

Millie nodded. "I know that full well, sir. But even if I keep quiet and he keeps on spyin' f'r ye, they'll find out sometime—they're bound to. Then Edward will be kilt and Elizabeth will be a widder, her new babe will have no father, and all 'cause ye didn't find me comely enough to make good y'r pledge."

Suddenly, overwhelmed by the horrid prospect, she burst into tears. Even while the aghast Fanning tried to quiet her, her sobs grew louder, then mounted into piercing howls. Millie was not a delicate weeper.

"Hush, ye little devil," he hissed as he clamped a meaty

hand over her mouth. "Would'st rouse the whole town? They'll think I tried to rape ye."

A shriek escaped between his fingers. His hand was soaked by a new freshet of tears. He damned himself for being witless enough to have gotten entangled with this green-eyed witch in the first place. With all the amiable ladies present at his Christmas rout, why in Christ's name had he been such an idiot as to make a pitch for this hoyden, Millie Dedshall?

"Will ye behave?" he asked. "If I let you go will'st be still?"

She shook her head furiously. No, by God, Edward was doomed and she had failed Elizabeth and the unborn babe and nobody was going to make her hush.

"I'll say ye're daft," he threatened. "I'll tell them ye drank too much. I'll tell them ye—ye took advantage of me and tried to squeeze money out of me by threatenin' to raise a pudder. I vow I'll tell them—"

He checked himself as he imagined the look on his underlings' faces when he cried out that he had been victimized by a child young enough to be his granddaughter. He groaned. "All right, all right. I'll release your precious brother from his obligations. Only for the sake of the gentle Jesus, stop your screaming. Stop it instanter or I'll change my mind and turn your brother in to the Regulators, to boot."

Magically, the girl stopped weeping as suddenly as though someone had righted a tilted bucket. Fanning loosened his grip, then muttered something under his breath as the light from the nearest window revealed Millie's beatific smile.

"Thankee, y'sweet man," she said sunnily. "And I'll be most happy to live up to my end of the bargain any time ye can fix it."

He recoiled as though she were a deadly serpent.

"D'you think me totally mad?" he cried in a stricken voice. "Nay, I beg of you, forget what happened back there—forget we ever danced a minuet. Ye'd please me mightily if you forgot you'd ever laid eyes on me, Mistress Mildred Dedshall!"

When Ben Dedshall told his son that Edmund Fanning had changed his mind for reasons never explained and required no more secret reports on the activities of the Alamance Regulators, Edward's response was singularly disappointing.

"Did ye hear me aright?" the little man asked after vainly waiting for a gleeful outburst.

"I heard you, Pa."

"Then where's y'r gratitude? I thought ye'd dance f'r joy. God knows ye've been gloomin' about y'r loyal duties enough ever since ye were put to the task."

"Loyal duties? A pretty name for betrayal, I'll be bound. When I'm found out I'll send for you so you can explain to the Regulators just how honorable these loyal duties were."

"Found out? Why sh'ld ye be found out now? They never got a sniff of y'r real stand whilst ye were doin' the Register's biddin' so why sh'ld they discover ye now, lad?"

But Edward would not be appeased. "You can't dismiss their suspicions by telling me to stop spying," he said. "It's not that easy. They've come near finding me out half a dozen times and one day they're going to be sure. They're not dolts, you know, especially Herman Hosban—he's kept an unwinking eye on me from the start."

"How c'n they find out when not a single one of 'em's been caught up by anything ye ever reported on?"

"True, but there'll come a day when Fanning will use all that information 'gainst them and then they'll know where he got it, never fear."

Dedshall attempted a laugh. "There's no need to worry, my boy. I know how ye feel—God knows I've spent many a sleepless night thinkin' about just such an undoin'—but I tell ye it's all over and done with and nobody hurt."

Edward said, "I hope you're right, Pa. I hope to God you're right."

Chapter Six

[1]

ELIZABETH'S BABY, a straight-limbed, deep-lunged boy, just as Lis had predicted, was born at ten o'clock in the morning on Wednesday, the seventeenth of February, 1767.

Becky, the midwife, and Dame Aliceanne Burnett, their

new neighbor, all said she had an easy time of it for a first baby but if she had been asked for her opinion, Elizabeth would not have called eleven hours of labor exactly easy. Of course all memories of pain vanished the first time she suckled Little Edward at her full breast.

"You were a brave girl," Dame Burnett said over and over. "With Jaimie, my first, I nearly shrieked the shingles off our house in Richmond but never a whimper did I hear from you, young lady."

The Burnetts were Virginians and rich ones, too, judging from the manor house they had built on the acreage adjoining Part-of-Providence, the previous fall. Burnett's family had always been in tobacco, he had explained to William Weyland Allyn, and he had decided to move because his land on the James River was exhausted and because he was apprehensive about the dangerous direction taken by the Virginia House of Burgesses.

"Especially this hothead, Henry—Patrick Henry, or whatever his full name is," Elizabeth had heard James Burnett say. "A back country lawyer just lately elected to the Burgesses who has most savagely attacked the church and spoken all but treasonably in his speeches. If many more are allowed to spout as seditiously as Henry did 'gainst the Stamp Act, then they'll have an outright rebellion on their hands, mark my words."

She had sat silent at table during this tirade, but she could have told Mister Burnett that William Weyland Allyn would approve of any man who "most savagely attacked the church" in Virginia, no matter what other vices he might have. She had prayed that her father would keep quiet about his own bitterness against the Virginia Church and Crown officers and he had. The Burnetts were too welcome as new friends and neighbors to have political or church differences intervene at the start.

Aliceanne Burnett proved a godsend at the lying-in. She had birthed ten children, all but three of whom had lived, and her brisk efficiency reassured Elizabeth the moment she walked into the bedchamber. Tall and straight despite her middle age, her brown hair neatly coiled and capped atop her head, she knew just what to do and did it herself, when the slave midwife proved too slow to her liking.

Without Aliceanne Burnett, Elizabeth would have been

terrified even though Rebecca never left her and surely would have known what to do, having had two babies of her own.

Now she looked down at the red-fuzzed child at her breast and whispered, "He's got his father's hair. His eyes, too, I think, and his mouth."

Her half sister said dryly, "Oh, aye, he looks ready to go plead a case in Hillsboro tomorrow, or the day after, f'r sure."

Aliceanne asked, "Mister Dedshaw's not here?" She insisted on calling it "Dedshaw," just as she called George, James, and Philip, Fred or Francis. She had a comic failing with all names, even her own family's on occasion.

Becky answered for Elizabeth. "No, we thought this stranger was at least a week away and Betsy's husband is arguin' a case at the capital. A message has been sent and we c'n expect a downpourin' of Dedshalls any minute."

"Downpouring of Dedshalls?"

"Oh, my sister's pleased to make jokes about my husband's family," Elizabeth said with new found maturity. "They're really fine people, Dame Burnett, and—"

"I bade you call me Aliceanne, remember?"

"Aye, but it sounds impertinent, still."

"Do you mean my hoary head deserves more respect?" The neighbor's laugh was that of a young girl's, much like her mother's had been.

"Nay, anything but that—ah—Aliceanne. You're the youngest woman in the house, I'll be bound. As for me, I feel a thousand years old after the long time I took birthing this young scamp." She looked down at the baby again, then up at the two beside the bed. "Don't you think his head's most perfectly shaped? And just look at his hands! Little marvels, aren't they?"

The Burnett woman nodded. "Aye. Now, do you feel up to receiving guests, madam? Your father and your brother have all but worn a trench in the parlor floor below, each assuring the other that nothing could possibly go wrong and sweating like a pair of draft horses in their anxiety." She laughed again. "Mayhap it's well that Mister Ded—did you say Dedshall?—couldn't be here. If there'd been three of them they'd have surely walked their way through to the cellar."

Becky added, "And after them, there's the Langhorns and then the servants at the big house and—I vow, Betsy, ye'll be bathed in adoration till dawn tomorrow if we let 'em all in."

"But they must all be let," Elizabeth said firmly. "To tell the truth, I do feel like a queen and Little Edward's my prince. So have them up—but first, is my hair respectable? Do I need some powder to cover up my blotches?"

"Ye look like ye'd just been bathed and preened f'r a ball. Here's y'r glass if ye don't believe me."

Studying herself in her looking glass was something that Elizabeth seldom did, never having found anything particularly encouraging in the reflection, but when she saw the new mother's face looking back at her she could not repress her approving smile. Motherhood had made her almost beautiful, she'd be bound and flogged if it hadn't! When Edward came down from Hillsboro he'd find a new and comely wife instead of the unsightly, scatterbrained Allyn girl he had left when he had ridden off. It had been all his doing, too. Pure magic!

She wondered if her father noticed the change when he gravely bent over her and kissed her forehead. His austere face showed nothing but the hinted tremolo in his voice gave him away as he said, "God bless you, daughter. You've given me quite the finest grandson a man could ever claim."

"And Edward's got the best grandfather any child could claim, too," she offered. It may have sounded mawkish but it was heartfelt. In the past, Father might have seemed cold and distant when she wished he could be warm and loving but no finer gentleman ever lived. If only Mother . . .

"D'ye mean this is all ye've come up with after all that time?" George cried. "I thought 'twas twins, at least, more prob'ly triplets by the time ye took."

She smiled up at him. "I thought about having twins but then I remembered that one of a pair is always a mannerless heddy-doddy so I settled for one perfect boy."

George staggered back, his big hands clutching his middle, and groaned, "Right in the shot locker, not that I didn't have it comin'." He advanced to the bedside again, leaned over and kissed her beside the mouth. "Well done, Elizabeth," he said in a low voice. "I wish ye both all the joy that's due ye— nobody c'ld want more."

"His full name's to be Edward George Philip William Dedshall," she assured him. Her eyes moved to her father. "I knew you'd understand, Father, the first son. . . ."

"Of course," he said, smiling warmly. "And as a small measure of esteem, your brothers and I have set aside a few

acres for young Edward, where he can build his house when
it comes time."

"Born, married and a landholder, all in one mornin',"
George crowed. "Slow up, Father, or ye'll make him a dodderer before his time."

After her father and half brother came the others, John
Langhorn, all shined up for the occasion, with Martha Langhorn, beaming her delight and outwardly, at least, not miffed
a bit by her exclusion from the lying-in; Nappy Langhorn,
fatter than ever and almost a stranger now although she had
been Elizabeth's playmate back at Middlebend, and finally
Henry, the only man besides Edward she had ever kissed.

He obviously came on his father's order. If it had been left
to him, Elizabeth knew that he would have been able to
forego the pleasure of greeting Edward Dedshall's son. Or
was she deluding herself? Did Henry remember those first
kisses beside the tidewater creek?

She looked up at him as he stood beside her, trying to keep
his eyes from straying toward the ceiling. "Hello, Henry,"
she said, too soberly. "My thanks to you for coming to see my
baby."

" 'Tain't nothin',", he mumbled. His hands seemed to have
taken on a life of their own, as they moved first to his hips
then fell like stones at the end of his lanky arms. "I mean, I
wanted to. He—he's a buster f'r certain, ain't he?"

Perspiration leaked from the edge of his straw-colored hair.
"He sure is a fine baby, Mistress Eliz—ma'am." He gulped.
"I'm glad ye didn't—I mean, I'm glad everything's all right.
He sure is pretty." With which he mumbled something about
an unfinished task and fled from the room.

And that was the boy she had once romanticized, just as
she had romanticized the Presbyterian minister, Ian Mac-
Cutcheon, out of gratitude for his appearance at Jeremy's
burial when all the Anglican priests had turned their backs.
Ah, what a giddypate she had been as a girl. It seemed impossible to believe that she had been so goosy, and *only three
years ago!*

"A penny," Rebecca said gently and she caught herself
with a start.

" 'Tis nothing," she said hastily, then saw they were alone.
"Well, it is, too, to be honest. I was thinking of what a little
noddy I was just a few years ago and how everything's dif-

ferent now. Is that how it was with you and Harry Tarbell?
I mean, did you suddenly find yourself so much older and
wiser with your first baby?"

She watched her half sister's eyes, suddenly afraid that
mention of those ill-starred children might wound her, but
Rebecca nodded, a reminiscent smile on her lips.

"Indeed I did, Betsy. 'Twas as though I stepped into another world." She paused. "Art weary, sister? The others can
wait till another time if ye're overtaxed."

"Well, the house servants, at least, and I'll see how I feel
when they're through. Do I have anything to give them from
the little master?"

"That's all been fixed. They tell me that y'r babe scurse
let out his first bawl before George was scatterin' birthday
presents over half the county. I vow, ye'd think he had somethin' to do with the whole thing, he's so puffed up about it."

Then came the house slaves (Elizabeth's own three, Poppy,
Nell, and Lucy had assisted at the lying-in, of course) led
by Yulee who lost her tawny-eyed insolence in a burst of
genuine delight when she first saw the baby, followed by Ella
and Hauny and the others, and finally Jidder who goggled
at the child in Elizabeth's arms and asked in a hushed voice,

"All 'at li'l boy-baby come outta *you*, Mist'ess?"

When they stopped laughing, Elizabeth told Rebecca that
the others would have to wait; she was weary and aching.
"But not so bad that I can't sleep for a month, sister," she
added hastily. "Nell, be sure to wake me when the baby
needs feeding."

"Don't worry, he'll wake ye himself when he's ready,"
Becky said with a laugh. She picked up the baby and handed
him to a delighted Nell whose six-month age advantage over
Poppy had won her the nursemaid's post, then turned back
to Elizabeth. "Before ye sleep I'll send over somethin' f'r ye
to eat y'rself. All dishes that'll make y'r milk flow in a fountain,
I pledge ye."

Elizabeth glanced down her front and said, "I'm glad I'm
well fixed there. I was afraid I'd be like Mother and have to
give my baby to a wet nurse."

"I c'ld have relieved y'r worries, had ye asked. Ye were put
together with an eye to nursin' babies."

"Oh, Becky, I hope I have an army of 'em."

The older woman laughed. "What, ye've just birthed one

and ye're eager to go through it again so soon? Mayhap y'r husband'll have somethin' to say about that."

Elizabeth's elation faded a bit. "When do you suppose Edward will get here?" she asked.

"The earliest minute he can, ye know that."

"I know, and I hope it won't be too inconvenient." At Rebecca's exclamation, Elizabeth hurried on. "I mean, he's seemed so worried lately and sometimes I think it's not all because of his father's illness. That's bad enough, poor little man, but—mayhap I shouldn't tell you this but the last time he was home he had such awful dreams. Hardly a night but he shouted and struggled in his sleep and each time it seemed he was beset by some monster."

Rebecca had taken full note of Edward's preoccupation, his deep silences, and his disinclination to expound on the political theories that he had once been so ready to debate with Phil, George, or Father, but she said, "Too much good food after the miserable fare he must be gettin' in Hillsboro, prob'ly, no more than that."

"I hope that's all but sometimes I fear—"

"And I say ye must stop worryin' about nothin' else ye'll sour all that lovely milk," Rebecca broke in briskly. "Now lay back and think pretty thoughts of y'r new son whilst I see about gettin' ye some of that good food I just boasted about."

[2]

While Rus, the black messenger from Part-of-Providence, rode toward Hillsboro with the news that Edward Dedshall was the father of a son, Elizabeth's husband was sitting beside Ben Dedshall's bed waiting for the clock to tick the last moments in his father's life. The doctor had just left after forcing another huge draught of laudanum down Ben's gullet to relieve the pain, the only ministration left to him.

"I doubt he'll live till nightfall," the physician had told Edward. "To be truthful, I'm fair amazed that he's held on this long. I gave him up over a month ago."

Edward had known that his father was deathly sick but had never found the courage to speak of it although there had been times when he thought that Ben Dedshall was silently begging him to do so. The rest of the family had kept their silence, too, all except Millie. She told Edward that she had pleaded with her father to travel back to Edenton where Dr. Benson could treat him proper, but Ben would not listen.

"He says 'tis only somethin' he et, and all the time he's wastin' away to nothin', Edward. Cans't beg him to go to Dr. Benson? He'll heed you, no matter what ye tell him to do."

"I've tried to talk him into such a journey but he won't hear of it," he had lied. "I'll speak to him again."

Now he asked himself why he had never brought himself to it. Was he such a coward that he could not face the fact that his father's illness was caused by something a great deal more serious than "somethin' he et?"

He did not know. He did not suppose he would ever know. One thing sure, he would be eternally damned for his cowardice. He was, he told himself, the only man in the world who loved his own father so little that he would not share a confrontation at the end.

He had always been an unworthy son. As a boy, he had been ashamed of his father's Ramsgate speech, his overloud laugh, his pretentions, and the manner in which he had built his fortune. The luxuries his father had heaped on him had done nothing to raise the father in the son's regard. All his life he had been conscious of the sneering whispers behind his back because he was Ben Dedshall's son. All his life he had doubted that his accomplishments had been truly of his own making. Even his marriage to Elizabeth had been arranged betwixt Ben Dedshall and William Weyland Allyn, the patrician Allyn agreeing to the match in return for what? Had Pa really called off Tryon's dogs in the Rector Maule situation in return for Allyn's acceptance? It was hard to imagine Allyn sacrificing his daughter, no matter what danger he might be in, but, then, the past few years had taught Edward that lofty principles had a way of disappearing under greed or fear, at least in the North Carolina colony.

He looked up from his deep study of the carpet as Millie slipped into the room, gently closing the door behind her. He started to tell her there was no need to tiptoe, Pa was dead to the world, but he did not speak.

"How is he?" she breathed as she came up beside him.

He shrugged and nodded toward the pathetic little heap under the bedclothes. Millie looked at her father, her eyes showing her pain, then back at Edward. "Ye've got to leave him f'r awhile," she murmured. "Old Fanning's sent f'r ye."

"I can't. I mustn't leave here now."

His sister leaned closer, her lips at his ear as though the sick man was straining to listen. "Ye've got to, Edward. I told the man our pa's dyin' but he said 'twouldn't take long and it was most important. If ye don't come down he said he'd have to come up and get ye."

"Who is he?"

She hunched her shoulders. "One of Fanning's lieutenants, I forget his name. Big feller with bushy eyebrows. Mean lookin'."

"Jamieson. Didn't he say what the Register wants of me?"

"No, but when I said ye couldn't leave, no matter what, he said to tell ye Squire Longman's with Fanning. When that old sot leaves his tavern I figger it must be sommen like Judgment Day a-comin'."

"I'll talk to him and send him away. You stay with Pa."

She nodded and took his chair as he got up. "Don't worry, I'll take good care of him whilst ye're gone," she whispered.

Edward assumed a pose of serenity, even though there was a ball of fear in the pit of his stomach and his knees felt unsteady. Jamieson *was* mean looking and he was the one Fanning sent to bring in men who might decide to resist his order.

"What do you want?" he demanded when he reached the bottom step. Jamieson thrust his bulk up out of the hall chair. "Didn't my sister tell you my father's very ill?"

"And didn't she tell you that the Register's waiting for you?" the big man asked bluntly. "Squire Longman, too, if you need to be impressed with the importance of the matter. So get your coat and hat and hurry doing it. We haven't much time."

"Time for what?" Edward asked. He hoped his voice was not quavering. This was an outrage, this brute invading a house of sorrow this way. What he should have done, what he should do now . . .

"Mister Fanning will tell you in good time," Jamieson grunted. "Right now, he's waiting for you in his office and the Register don't like to be kept waiting."

"But my father—"

"Ben Dedshall's been dying for a week—he'll wait another

few minutes till you take care of this matter. Get your coat.
And hurry!"

*Dog. Scurvy dog. Someday Fanning's black-hearted gang
will see the people rise up against them and then . . .*

"I am hurrying, ain't I?" Edward Dedshall whined.

"I've been warned that Hosban plans to lead the rascally
Regulators in a raid on my office this very day, probably
within the hour," Edmund Fanning told him, his words flat,
stripped of all inflection. "You must head them off."

"Head them off?" Edward asked stupidly.

"That's what I said. Convince Hosban and the other leaders of this mad pack that this violence would be sheer folly.
Tell them that if they persist in this rebellious misadventure,
I'm prepared to defend myself and my people with bullets.
If that don't stop them, tell them Governor Tryon has already
been advised of this treasonable situation and I've asked him
to send troops."

"Ye wouldn't," Edward exclaimed. "Ye wouldn't bring
soldiers here to trample down your own neighbors, man."

"Say 'sir' when you speak to me, Dedshall," Fanning said
icily. "And as far as my calling on the governor for protection from this lawless rabble, I'd turn cannon on these dogs
and take a pinch of snuff whilst they fired." His bleak eyes
held Edward's in a chilling stare. "D'ye think I wouldn't?"

"N-no, sir, but—"

"We have no time for discussion of this point, Dedshall,
even if I were so disposed." The Register waved a hand at
the purple-faced man in rumpled black who sprawled in a
nearby chair. "Squire Longman agrees that it's your duty to
do your utmost to stop these rebels."

"Fullest agreement," Longman burbled. "Damned riffraff."

"But, sir," Edward protested, "they won't heed me."

"You'd better make 'em," Fanning grated. "If ye can't I
fear you must pay for the poor quality of your persuasion."

"What d'you mean? Sir?"

"Why, any lawyer who can't talk a dirty peasant rebeller
into seeing reason is hardly qualified to argue before the
colonial bar, d'you think? So if you fail here, we'll be forced
to take steps to right an obvious misqualification." The Register's heavy mouth curled. "D'you understand the nice legal
wordage or shall I give it to you straight? Plainly put, I mean
you'll be disbarred."

Edward's mind whirled. He knew it was wasted breath to attempt to appeal to Fanning's compassion but he was grasping at straws. "Mister Fanning, you must know my father, your trusted aide, is lying at death's door. I just left him, and Dr. Smallwood says he won't last—"

"Then if the physician says there's no hope, you'll be doing him no good by sitting beside him, wringing your hands, will you? Life's for the living, Dedshall. Let the dead bury their dead. Holy Writ. And I must remind you, you're wasting valuable time hemming and hawing. You'd best seek out Hosban and his dogs and begin your argument."

He raised a hand and Jamieson grasped Edward's bony arm in a rude grip. "This way," he said gruffly. "The latest word was the Regulators were meeting in Drury's Grove on the Nutbush Road."

"Oh, he knows their meeting place full well," Fanning threw after them. "My man has attended near as many of their rebellious conclaves as old Hosban, himself, haven't you, Dedshall?"

He paused.

"A fact the Regulators would no doubt like to know—that he's my man."

With the threat still ringing in his ears, Edward was led—virtually dragged—out of the courthouse and down the steps to a hitching rack where stood half a dozen saddle horses, the cold making their breath come in steamy puffs. "You can use the mare at the far end," Jamieson told him. "If you lose her it won't be no great loss."

He lent a knee to the lanky lawyer and Edward found himself in the worn saddle, gripping the mare between his knees, groping for the reins that the other man tossed up to him. He was a poor rider—just as poor as he was at everything else, he told himself dismally. His only forte was spouting high-flown rhetoric and that was about as important as a trickle of piss in a millrace, when it came to improving man's lot in Orange County, North Carolina. *Poor Elizabeth*, he cried inwardly. *Why did she have to be inflicted with a husband like me? And the babe . . .*

Well if nothing else, perhaps he could prove himself a credit to his unborn son by this day's work. Perhaps the strength given him by the knowledge that he was about to sire a son (for he had never considered the possibility of a daughter) would give him powers of persuasion that would stop that old firebrand, Herman Hosban, and make Hosban's Regulators see the enormity of the odds against them. Perhaps in years to come they would marvel at the level-headed ease with which the father of the second Edward Dedshall had cooled the hot passions of a mob, thus warding off a blood bath. Perhaps there would be sermons preached and speeches made in the Legislature about this modest hero, Edward Dedshall. Perhaps . . .

"Are you going to sit there or are you going to do Mister Fanning's bidding?" Jamieson asked harshly. Edward came back to the present, dug his heels into the decrepit mare's flanks, and set her off down the wide street.

As he jolted in the saddle, trying not to look wholly ridiculous, Edward became aware of the eerie silence, the empty streets. There was nobody in the courthouse square, which was the heart of the county's business and political life. Shutters had been drawn on most of the dwellings he passed. The town barber had closed his shop early and so had the candlemaker, the saddler, the wigmaker, and the—the whole town was shut down, in hiding, expecting the worst. Those Hillsboroites who were not secret members of the Regulators had been given the word to stay indoors or be identified as Fanning's henchmen. When the Regulators struck they would not take the time to question the politics of anyone found abroad. They were through with temporizing. The hotheads in their ranks were demanding action. Even Herman Hosban's Quaker sentiments had been destroyed, by Fanning's lies and contemptuous tyranny. Now Hosband, the elder, was as rabid as the shortest-tempered rebel in the ranks.

Edward hoped that *Robert* Hosban was among the Regulators when he reached Drury's Grove. At least, then, he stood a chance of claiming one ally. The younger Hosban was at best a fringe member of his father's band and more often a reluctant fellow traveler. Since Robert had fallen in love with Rebecca Tarbell he had become a backslider in the Regulators' movement. Edward had heard Herman complain more than once about his son's interest in the woman he called "a member of a monied family, tobacco aristocracy from the East, deliberately set down amongst us to help fashion William Tryon's yoke for our yeomen's necks."

Still, despite the breach Rebecca had driven twixt father

and son, Edward knew that Herman had a deep love for his son and even, rarely, a respect for Robert's advice. If Robert was at the Grove and if he could get Robert to stand beside him in a plea for reason, mayhap he could . . .

Reason? Whose reason? Edmund Fanning's kind? And by whom was this appeal for reason to be made? By Edward Dedshall, son of the corrupt father who lay dying in the mansion built with gold stolen from the little people when he was Lord Granville's agent in Chowan County. The same Edward Dedshall who would appeal to these honest, hardworking, persecuted yeomen and small planters, tradesmen and trappers only because his own worthless neck was at stake, not out of any real love of justice. For if he did not succeed now, he'd be a lawyer no longer; he'd be disgraced, exposed as a Fanning spy. His wife and unborn child would be taken from him by her family, the haughty Allyns of Alamance who could allow no failures in their midst.

"Oh, Jesus," he mumbled, "let Robert be there and let him aid me. Give ear this once and I pledge Thee I'll mend my ways. Somehow, I'll take Elizabeth to a place where they don't know the name of Dedshall. I'll . . ."

At the sound of shouting voices, Edward gathered in his reins, and, peered down the Nutbush Road. Herman Hosban was leading his Alamance Regulators around a bend ahead.

He dismounted, whereupon his mare jerked up her head, snorted, and went galloping back down the road in her first show of spirit. He looked after the disappearing nag and wished he had stayed in the saddle. Being aboard a runaway horse was better than standing there in the road, one man against thousands.

Well, maybe not thousands, but Hosban must have called out all his rebels for this attack. To Edward's panicked eye the thick column of enraged farmers and small tradesmen seemed to stretch back out of sight. Every man Jack of them carried a club and here and there a fowling piece or an old bell-muzzled musket.

And he was expected to halt this mob with his lawyer's tricks? Impossible? He would be wise to turn and run.

But he could not. This was madness but he had to at least try, for Elizabeth, for his unborn son.

He flung up a long arm as the column bore down on him

and yelled, "Halt!" The word squeaked from his dry throat. He wet his lips and tried again.

"Stop!" he cried, and was gratified to hear his command emerge in a passable baritone. "Stop before ye bring ruination down on all of us!"

They kept on coming as though he had not spoken, Hosban stubbing along on his bowed legs, scowling fiercely, shaking what appeared to be part of a wagon tongue.

"I beg of ye, listen to reason," Edward bawled. "Ye'll gain nothing but Tryon's bayonets if ye go through—"

"Get out of the way, Dedshall," Herman spat at the lanky lawyer. "Get out of the way afore ye get hurt."

"You must heed me, sir," Edward begged. "Fanning has sent to New Berne for troops. If you don't turn back, you'll be massacred."

A roar from the crowd drowned out his next words. "Turn back? Not us, not this time! . . . Tell Fanning he can send to London for soldiers, he won't stop us! . . . Get out of the way, tubman, afore we trample ye! . . . Tell y'r master we're through listenin' to his pet spaniels' yappin'."

Edward flung both arms wide. "This is Edward Dedshall— you all know me!" His voice cracked disastrously but he kept on. "Haven't I always served your best interests? Haven't I? I wouldn't advise you except 'twas for your own good. Hearken to me, do!"

"Stand aside," Herman Hosban growled. "We ain't got the time to talk about what we've just heard, that ye're Fanning's spy and always have been. Not now—we'll deal with that later. Right now we have business with the Register that can't wait."

"Sp-spy?" Edward stammered. "How dare ye call me that, friend Hosban? After all the times I've pleaded your followers' cases in court, you'd call me a spy? For shame!"

Hosban hesitated, some of the fury leaving his red face. "I said Jacob could be wrong," he admitted, "but they say—"

Impatient curses from the halted column made him stop and turn to his men. "I'm in command here," he barked. "I'll have no foul talk fr'm ye or threats to this young man who's—"

"Get him outta the way," somebody yelled from the rear. "We're givin' Fanning time to run fer it, standin' here listenin' to a lawyer's mumbo-jumbo. On to Hillsboro!"

"*Aye, on to Hillsboro! We want Fanning!*" The cry swept

through the crowd. Those in the rear began pushing forward, forcing the front ranks to stumble ahead or be overrun. Herman Hosban was shoved into Edward, although the little man tried to dig in his heels. "I'm in command and I say ye must be orderly!" he yelled, spreading his arms.

They refused to heed him. Cursing, yelling, laughing, bawling *On to Hillsboro!* and *Death to the Fanning tyrant!* they pressed toward town. Hosban, infuriated, turned to confront his men. In scrambling frantically to regain his balance, he flung out the hand that was clutching the club. He said later that he had no intention of hitting young Dedshall but as he failed to keep his footing, the club inadvertently caught Edward on the point of his long angular chin.

Edward saw it coming and he raised a hand to ward off the blow but he was too late. There was a stunning crack on his jaw, then for a moment everything was blotted out. Then clarity returned and with it, fearful pain.

Confused, hurt, scared, Edward tried to get to the side of the road. Let them pass. Let them go to Hillsboro and complete this madness. He was wounded, clubbed by the madmen's leader, and all he could do now was get out of these wild devils' way so he would not be hurt again. He was no hero.

Someone blocked his way to the roadside ditch. Blindly, he tried to thrust the man aside.

"Outta the way, you turd," he managed, and struck out awkwardly at the man who kept him from the safety of the ditch.

"Who're ye callin' a turd?" That was all he heard before there was a smashing blow on the back of his head and Edward Dedshall pitched forward into the black void that opened at his feet.

[3]

"Believe me, friend Philip, I've spent many a prayerful hour trying to decide what would be the wisest course before coming to thee with this painful puzzle."

Philip, standing at the window, ran a hand over his dark, queue, then pulled at his lower lip, scowling blackly. "You say you're the only one who knows of this?" he asked after a long pause.

"Of course my father knows," Robert Hosban said quietly, "but there's no danger that he'd tell anyone, even if he still remembers. He's so bound up in—other concerns that he pays little heed to aught else these days."

Philip turned from the window and walked slowly back to his desk. He stood there, frowning down at the creased, thumbworn sheet of foolscap that Hosban had given him to read. "Even did this wild story hold a scrap of truth, he never wrote this. As I remember him, he was barely able to scrawl his own name."

Robert gestured toward the letter. "Thee will note somewhere in it that he speaks of having it writ for him. Is that his signature?"

The black-haired lawyer shrugged, then dropped into the desk chair with a muttered exclamation. "I can't say. I was never that close to Tarbell." He picked up the letter again, turned it over as though some explanation might be written on its back. " 'Strooth, it looks as if you've been carrying it about for months."

Hosban nodded. "I told thee I've been studying on it for a long time, mayhap too long a time."

"And you've said naught about it to my sister?"

Robert hesitated, then said, "Just once a long time ago I tried to speak to her about it. She became so discomfitted by my mention of her husband that I—well, to be honest, I lied and told her I asked about him out of mere idle curiosity, no more."

Philip flung himself back in his chair, his hands behind his head. "Once more, how did this come about? From the beginning, prithee. I still can't understand how—but tell it to me again."

Patiently, his voice as toneless as if he were reciting a dreary lesson, Hosban said,

"It all began when my father wrote his sister in Philadelphia, Dame Patience Wellborn. He seldom writes a letter but when he does he fills pages with his observations, speculations, predictions, recriminations, and so forth. Perchance thee can imagine how wound up he becomes when his quill starts running away with him?"

Philip nodded. He could, indeed.

"Well, his letter to my aunt, my father mentioned that I was wooing the Widow Tarbell, daughter of William Weyland Allyn of Part-of-Providence. I suppose you know he disapproves of my suit, not out of any disesteem of Rebecca but because he fears the difference twixt the Allyns' and the Hosbans' stations is too great."

The handsome Quaker's mouth twisted. "For all his talk of equality, my father pays more heed to the differences of wealth and family than most men. So I suppose he complained to my aunt about my courtship, set twixt diatribes 'gainst Fanning and Tryon, no doubt.

"Now, my aunt is a fine old lady but she's a gossip. Not a malicious one, but she has long made it her business to know everything about everybody in Philadelphia. So back came a letter saying that if this Widow Tarbell was married to Harry Tarbell of Chowan County in North Carolina Colony, then she was no widow at all. Her husband, she wrote, was alive and would prove his existence by writing me himself."

"Where did your aunt say she met this man?"

"She never has explained it, Philip. When Father showed me her letter, I sat down to write her, telling her to keep her hands off my affairs, but I was too late. This letter came to me the day after I sent off my plea to Philadelphia."

Allyn asked, "Do you mean you'd run the risk of becoming a bigamist if Becky said yea to you?"

"I believed Rebecca," Hosban said firmly. "I still do. I'm certain there's a mixup of identity here or this man's an outright liar who hopes he'll be paid for his silence."

"But if you have full faith in Becky, why didn't you throw this stinking scrap in the fire?"

The Quaker's blue eyes held Philip's. "Could'st thou?"

The lawyer started to assent, then paused. "I suppose not," he finally admitted. "Or if I did I'd curse myself for burning the evidence I might need to set this dog to dancing at the end of a rope."

"Could he be hanged for this?" Hosban's voice sounded shocked.

"Aye, blackmail's been called 'moral murder' by the highest courts since sixteen hundred. Blackmailers once were drawn and quartered, now they're merely hanged. But even Tryon's judges would take pleasure in handing down the heaviest penalty to such a bit of human filth." He thumbed his chin again. "As far as I know, there's never been a case of black-mail in this colony. Before this."

The Quaker plainly showed his distress. "I'd not like to send a man to the gallows, Philip."

"But I would, and I mean to, if I can."

"But how. I mean, this man's in Pennsylvania and wouldn't the great distance thwart thee? And do the Pennsylvania courts hold it to be so foul a crime? And—and, well thee can see the difficulties ahead, friend Allyn."

Philip's voice was cold. "What I see most clearly is that you fear this scurvy dog might prove to be Rebecca's husband, after all. You're afraid Becky's story of Tarbell's murder by the Catawbas could've been made up out of whole cloth—am I right?"

He expected fierce denial but Hosban pursed his lips and nodded reluctantly. "I suppose so," he said in a low voice. "Forgive me if you can, but I love thy sister so much that if 'twere possible I'd say let sleeping dogs lie."

"And if Becky married you, you'd spend the rest of your life fearing that Harry Tarbell would someday come knocking at your door." Philip waited, then went ahead, almost briskly. "I commend your honesty, friend, but this pustule must be lanced. And never fear about my sister's name being besmirched. As I remember my law, a blackmailer can be brought to justice by an anonymous plaintiff, so her name need never be revealed. We'll get a good man in New Berne to take the case and—"

He broke off as the distant grumble he had vaguely thought sounded like unseasonable thunder grew louder, punctuated by sharp cries. Puzzled, he swung his head toward the window, then sprang to his feet.

"By God, the rumors must have been true," he exclaimed. "I heard your father's Regulators were going to raid Fanning's office today but I didn't believe it—they've always struck without warning before this." He ran to the window, followed by the big Quaker. "Did you know this was going to happen?" he threw over his shoulder.

"Nay, at least not for certain. My father and I have fallen out lately of the Regulators' mood for violence."

"Mood for violence is good," Philip said grimly, staring out at the courthouse square. "Just look at 'em. This time Fanning will be lucky to get off with as few bruises as he did the last time they paid him a visit."

Hosban stood beside Allyn, his broad face anguished. "I must go down there and try to stop them. I can't stand here, doing nothing, whilst my father puts his neck in a noose."

Philip said sharply, "You'll stay right where you are. There's naught you can do with that crowd except get your head cracked. He paused. "Besides, I don't see your father anywhere. Mayhap he's finally come to his senses and has let these Toms o' Bedlam dance their way to the gibbet without him."

Robert crowded Philip at the window, peering down on the wild scene. "Thou'rt right, he's not there, praise God! What d'ye suppose happened to him? Could Fanning's bullies have already cast him in irons?"

"No chance, all the Register's mastiffs are rallied on the courthouse steps to protect their keeper." He laughed shortly. "And not a one but wishes he were twenty leagues away, I'll be bound."

They watched as the mob swirled toward the courthouse. Two Fanning guards lost their courage and fled as the first stones sailed through the air. They scurried down the steps and around a corner of the building, a screaming knot of pursuers after them. The main body of Regulators rushed the courthouse steps and both men at the window involuntarily grunted as they saw Fanning's lackeys buried by a human avalanche. Clubs rose and fell. Feet thudded savagely into the prostrated men. Screams cut through the eddying roar. A Fanning deputy staggered out of the melee, his clothes in rags, his face a bloody mask. The others disappeared and neither Philip nor Robert could tell whether they escaped or were carried off. The mob flowed into the courthouse, thirsting to get at Edmund Fanning.

They were out in the square again in a trice, it seemed, most of them carrying fistfuls of legal papers, tax records, court dockets and the like, which they put to the torch that flared in the hand of one of the rioters. There was no sign of Fanning.

"I've watched three such kettledrums," Philip mused, "and one thing struck me each time—notice how there's never a pane of glass broke, nor a chair smashed, nor any other damage done the courthouse. Can you think why?"

"I ought to be able to," Hosban replied wryly. "I've heard my father remind them often enough that their taxes bought these things so they'd be destroying their own property." He laughed but without humor. "Oh, aye, he's drawn up a fancy set of rules for them to follow whilst they break every law in the colony."

"Whatever the rules, they missed their quarry this time. Their bird has flown the coop."

"Aye, they're buzzing about like bees around a bear's head," Robert chuckled. "And twice as venomous, too. I can't say I'm sorry the Register got away; 'tis bad enough they manhandled his—but what's happening?"

A wildly excited Regulator burst out of the courthouse, shouting wildly and stabbing his hand in the direction of the building that housed Philip's office, and beyond. The crowd stilled so that the two men by the window could make out the agitated announcement.

"Fanning's hidin' in Ben Dedshall's place! He is! I beat it out of Jamieson!"

The mob answered with a howl and turned toward the street that led off the square, past Philip's office and up the hill to Benjamin Dedshall's mansion.

"Christ's thorns!" Philip cried. "They're going to attack Ben's place and I know for a fact the old man lies dying. We've got to stop them."

The big Quaker did not hesitate. "Can we beat them there?"

"Out the back way and down the alley, thence through the back yards—we can beat 'em if we leg it."

They bolted out of the office, down the stairs, through the hall to the back door and out onto the muddy alley. Neither one stopped to think how two men could keep that raging mob from breaking into Ben Dedshall's house; they only knew the rioters had to be turned back before they spent their blind rage on Elizabeth's dying father-in-law. And Edward, too, for if that poor gawk roused the courage to try to defend his family instead of taking to his heels, they'd murder him when they found they had been duped. It was clear to Philip, at least, that Fanning's lieutenant, Jamieson, had set the mob off on a false scent that would bring disaster to Fanning's "friend," Ben Dedshall, in a plan schemed up by the Register. As he ran for the house, Philip figured out the reason for this treachery. Dedshall was close to death, his usefulness to Fanning was finished; *ergo* he would throw the old man to the Regulators, and have a weighty complaint with which to summon William Tryon's soldiers from New Berne.

"Scurvy bastard," he panted aloud. "Someday his perfidy will land him on the gallows, and I'll help spring the trap, myself."

They crossed another back yard, never pausing as an old man hobbled out of the back door and yelled something at them. *'Tis too early to plant a garden*, Philip told himself as he ran on, his lungs aching. *I wonder what that granther's so wrought up about?*

They came in sight of the imposing Dedshall mansion and saw they had been outdistanced by one runner, a small boy who stood at the front door, pounding the brass knocker as he looked over his shoulder down the hill. When the lad saw the two men he dropped the knocker and started to take off, then recognized Philip and checked himself. The two men came panting up the steps and the youngster gasped,

"Mister Allyn, they're comin' to kill Millie's pa. They think old Fanning's in there."

"We know," Allyn puffed. "Get going, boy. We'll take over here. Godspeed, whoever you are—ye've done well."

His hand was reaching for the knocker when the door opened and a blazing-eyed Millie cried, "Hush y'r racket, Tommy! Don't ye know my father's—oh, Philip!"

Refusing her apologies, Philip pushed her inside the house, and bolted the big door behind them, top and bottom.

"What's amiss?" the girl demanded. "Where's Edward? Fanning sent f'r him but he said he'd be right back and— what's that row down the hill?"

Philip's voice was as steady as his heavy breathing permitted. "Millie, listen. Get Ethelind and your young brothers and get out of here, fast. Don't even stop for a cloak."

"What is it, Philip?"

"The Regulators. They raided Fanning's office and one of his men told him Fanning was hiding here."

"He lied. There ain't nobody here but—"

"We know, we know, but those madmen out there think their fox has gone to ground here. Hosban and I can keep them off but not if you or the others get in our way."

"Run from them knaves?" the redhead cried. "Not on y'r

life. Ethel and the boys c'n run if they want to but not me.
Where's Edward? Why ain't he here to help us?"

Robert Hosban said, "We don't know—we hope he's safe.
But what friend Allyn said is true; thee'd only make it harder
for us by staying. Trust us to keep thy father from harm."

Millie squinted up at the Quaker. "Ain't ye old Herman's
son, the one Becky's fair mad about?" When Robert nodded,
she cried, "Why did ye let y'r father sic his crazy men at us?
If ye're Becky's darlin', why didn't ye—"

At that moment there was a thunderous pounding on the
door. Somebody yelled, "Open up—we know Fanning's hidin'
his worthless carcass in there."

"Aye, surrender him or we'll smoke ye all out," another
bawled.

"Smoke 'em out, anyway. 'Twould de me good to burn this
fine house paid for with the gold the old bastard stole from
honest men."

"He didn't!" Millie yelled back before the others could stop
her. "He never stole a penny of yours. He worked hard 'stead
of settin' on his fat behind complainin', ye rebel dog."

There was an answering flurry of angry voices. A parlor
window broke with a crash and a rock thudded on the floor
of the adjoining room.

"Millie, Millie, they're goin' to kill us!" Ethelind screamed
from somewhere in the rear of the house. "Bid 'em begone!"

"Come out here and help us stand 'em off," the redhead
called back. "Bring Pa's pistol and the fowlin' piece in—"

"Ethel, take the boys and run for it," Philip cried. "Out the
back way and head for St. Matthews—Rector Micklejohn will
take you in."

"Injuns," whooped one of the Dedshall boys, as he came
dashing down the stairs from the second floor. "A massacree!
Wa-wa-wa-wa!" As Allyn turned he saw to his horror that the
boy toted an ancient snaphaunce musket, the lid off the powder pan and the hammer at full cock. "*Where in Jesus' name
did you get* that?"

"Give me that musket," Robert shouted. "Be careful, lad,
or thee'll—"

Too late. Either by accident or intent, young Dedshall
pulled the trigger. The hammer fell, striking the flint and a
shower of sparks fell into the pan, igniting the powder. Mir-
aculously, none of the people milling about in the hallway

were in the line of fire. The ball crashed into the front door, gouging out a long splinter and causing the glass to shiver in the fanlight overhead.

When he found his voice, Philip snapped, "Millie, get upstairs to your father—no, I insist! Take Ethel and this young hellion with you. Bundle your father in the bedclothes and carry him down the back stairs. The three of you ought to be able to lift him."

The redhead nodded gravely, still jarred by the explosion. "I c'n carry him myself, he's that shrunk," she told the lawyer.

"Lay him on a kitchen table and wait till I tell you to leave," Philip went on. "Mayhap your brother's shot has scared them off but I doubt it."

As if to confirm his doubt, the crowd outside began hurling more rocks through the front windows.

"Git a battering ram," somebody yelled.

"Throw a torch through the winders," somebody else said.

Allyn turned to Hosban and said, "I'm going out there. You and Millie get Ben downstairs by the back door. I've got to stop them before some fool throws a firebrand."

"They'd stone ye to death, friend," the Quaker protested. "Let me go—after all, my father's one of their leaders. They'll listen to me."

"We'll both go, then. I got you into this and—"

"Lemme load this thing again—I know how," the Dedshall boy suggested. "One more volley and they'll—"

"Give me that god-damned gun," Philip gritted. He wrenched the old musket out of the boy's grip and flung it to the floor. To Millie, he said, "We're depending on you to get your father downstairs, remember."

"It'll kill him," the girl said mournfully.

"We must chance it." He turned back to Hosban. "You draw the top bolt and I'll take the lower. One, two, three . . ." They flung open the door and slipped out onto the porch, into the middle of the jostling, ugly-tempered mob.

One man swung a club at Philip but his arm was checked by somebody behind him. "Hold," a deep voice bellowed. "That's young Robert, Herman's son."

The tall, fair-haired Quaker called out in a high, clear voice, "You all know me—will'st take my pledge that Edmund Fanning's not inside?"

A giant of a black-bearded man in buckskins, his thick hair

hanging to his shoulders, snorted, "No? Then why's his black-guards shootin' at us, if not to defend him?"

"'Twas an accident, a frightened boy," Robert explained.

"Ah, that's likely," the bearded man sneered. He obviously was leader of the mob in Herman Hosban's absence. "What're ye doin' on the side of rich tyrants, Robert? Did Ben Dedshall buy ye off?"

"Where's my father?" Hosban demanded.

The buckskinned man hunched his shoulders. "He stayed behind to nurse that scurvy spy, young Dedshall—or bury him, I dinna ken which."

"Do you mean you've killed Edward?" Philip put in.

Another shrug. "I hope we did. 'Twould be little enough f'r a skunk that's been tellin' Edmund Fanning all our secrets whilst pretendin' to be our guid friend."

Philip heard Millie's screech and looked up to see her standing at the open second story window. "He never did, ye lyin' caitiff, Jock Hoag! If Fanning says he did, Fanning's big a liar as you are, ye cockeyed Scot!"

The eyes of the crowd swung upward and there were several whoops of laughter among the surly threats.

"Ye've met y'r match now, Jock," a voice called from the rear of the crowd. "Don't tangle with that little wildcat else ye'll be sorry."

"I'll wildcat you, Bill Remeger," Millie spat back. "What d'ye mean stonin' a house where an old man lays dyin'?"

Philip saw the man named Remeger actually touch his cap with a forefinger. Then he shouted, "We don't mean to harm y'r pa, Millie. We just want Fanning, is all. Hand him over and we'll be on our way."

"He ain't here. Didn't ye hear Mister Hosban tell ye he ain't? He ain't never been here. Ye dolts, Fanning sent ye here on a wild goose chase whilst he slipped away in the other direction."

There was a clamor of disbelief and Millie cried, "Ain't that the way he does things, siccin' an army on a poor sick man that's s'posed to be his good friend whilst he takes off f'r some hidey-hole, laughin' at ye fit t'burst his sides? Can't ye see him doin' it?"

Quiet fell over them. Then the curses mounted again but now they were mostly directed at the fools who had let themselves be duped. Hoag, the leader, ground out an oath and craned to look at the redhead in the upstairs window.

"Will ye gie me y'r word that lobscosel's not hidin' in y'r hoose, Millie?" he asked.

How in God's name does she know all these men? Philip Allyn asked himself. *But bless her for knowing them—she's worth a company of Royal Fusiliers.*

"Ye can come in and see f'r y'rself, but just ye alone," Millie called down.

"And walk into a trap?" Jock sneered.

The redhead's laugh sounded almost carefree. "Oh, aye, I've got me little brothers here to overpower ye and my sister, Ethel's hidin' sommers with the nigras 'cause I ain't seen her. So there's three of us bullies waitin' to spring the trap, Jock. Mebbe ye'd best bring y'r regiment in with ye to perteck ye."

The buckskinned giant scratched the side of his bushy face for a moment and then shook his head. "I'll take y'r worrrd f'r it," he said. "But if ye're cozenin' me, I'll come back and throw up y'r skirts and blister y'r bum f'r ye."

"See here," Philip began, "you can't talk that way—" He stopped as Robert Hosban clutched his arm.

Millie's laugh pealed again. "From wot they tell me, that's all ye're any good at when ye're under a leddy's skirts," she jeered.

There was a whoop of laughter. The crowd began to turn away, their savage mood vanished, dispersed by a green-eyed girl with a saucy tongue. As the Regulators drifted off, Robert Hosban tightened his grip on Philip's arm and hauled him inside the house again. "Best get out of sight before their mood changes," he explained. "If we say another word we might spoil everything."

Philip nodded and let out a long sigh. Now that the danger was over, he felt his knees tremble and his heart pound jarringly. He stepped over to a hall chair and fell into it, conscious for the first time that he was soaked with sweat.

Well, I did better than I ever thought I could. I'm proud of myself, even though without Millie, I might have cried craven —or if Hosban hadn't been with me when I faced the choice of doing something or pretending I knew naught of any need to act.

His head swung toward the stairs as a thin wail came down from the sick room on the second floor.

"Oh, Pa," Millie cried in a choked voice. "Pa!"

So, Philip thought, Ben Dedshall was dead, and probably Edward, too. While he sat there commending himself he had given no consideration at all to the knotty problems that lay ahead. Betsy was likely a widow and Harry Tarbell, his ghost or an imposter, was writing threatening letters from Philadelphia. The Dedshalls would have to be cared for somehow, now that they had no men to act for them, not even that earnest but ineffectual champion, Edward. Governor Tryon's troops doubtless would come marching into Orange County on the heels of this latest attack and more unrest, possibly outright warfare, lay in the future. Then there was the matter of Mary Hughes Allyn, Elizabeth's mother. Should he urge his father to get her back, or must the Allyns let the insult to their family name stand without redress?

And what was he, Philip Allyn, going to do in the dark times ahead? Would he be a bystander in the forthcoming upheaval? Would he act as a Fanning lickspittle in order to get the lucrative law practice that the Register could throw his way? Or did he have the courage to break the fealty oath that Tryon had forced upon him and uphold his own principles?

You say you did well? he asked himself. *You've done nothing, really. All the real doing lies ahead. God grant you have the mettle for it.*

Epilogue

EDWARD DEDSHALL did not die beside the Nutbush Road. For two days he lay in Herman Hosban's bedchamber, where he was carried by the old Quaker and two other remorseful Regulators, without recovering consciousness. Then he returned to a strange muddled world, a world peopled by men and women whose faces were first blurred, then sharp, then blurred again.

He groped for a way out of the fog in which he found himself, but those whom he petitioned for help could not seem to understand. His words rang clear in his own ears but these vague figures spoke a different language or perversely refused to listen. Instead of giving intelligent answers, they tried to quiet him with senseless mumblings and the idiotic petting that fatuous mothers inflicted on their children.

If they would only leave him alone. He knew he would be capable of dressing himself, feeding himself, going on with the life that had been broken off sometime long ago, he knew not how nor why. With increasing frequency, he was beset by a nightmare in which he was threatened by—whom? He never did see his enemies plainly enough to identify them but he knew they menaced him and everything he held dear. How else could they instill such terror?

Once in a great while he found himself with a soft woman who held him close and chattered away in her primitive tongue and laughed so gaily that she made him forget his nightmare. Then he smiled or even chuckled. Sometimes she wept, too, but not often or for very long. She left him when the tears came, a genteel conduct of which he approved and tried to so inform her, to no avail, of course. Poor confused female, she grew frightened of him once or twice when he had simply meant to show her that of all the shadowy forms surrounding him, she was the least feared.

All he had meant to do was . . . what? Well, whatever it was, she misunderstood and cried out for the others to come save her from this ogre. Ogre? Why, he could see it all quite plainly now. He was no ogre; he was . . .

They had even robbed him of his name!

"He'll get his senses back someday," Elizabeth said stoutly. "I know he will."

Millie and Rebecca nodded mechanically. Millie said, "He seemed to know me just the other day, I vow. He came that close to callin' me by name." But neither Millie nor Becky could meet Elizabeth's eyes. Edward's stare was as clouded as ever and—oh, God, how long must Elizabeth go on pretending? Why didn't she admit the truth to which everyone else had long since submitted, that Edward would have been better off to have died beside the Nutbush Road?

Becky bent to her sewing, wondering how much longer their lives were to be burdened by this pitiful creature who made horrid mewling sounds, wept for no reason, soiled himself and sometimes turned on Betsy with a fury that would

someday do her harm. For all these long years they had gone
on, day after uncertain day, and from the way things looked
it would go on forever.

Poor Betsy. But at least she had Little Edward to love, even
though she had never dared show the child to his father after
that one terrible experiment. What was God's purpose in
making a tiny baby seem a ravening dragon to a drooling
idiot?

Still, Elizabeth had her boy and she, Rebecca, had no one.
Not even darlin' Harry Tarbell who had risen from the dead
long enough to write that cursed note to Robert Hosban,
back in '66 and then disappeared again. For although she
had sworn by every oath that Harry had been killed by the
Indians in the Noglichucky Valley, her brother Philip, had
insisted on trying to track down the writer of that letter. After
almost a year during which she had suffered all the tortures
of the damned, word had finally come from New Berne that
the blackmailer had vanished without a trace and that further
search was useless.

Even if Robert Hosban's father had not contributed to
making a helpless loon out of Elizabeth's husband she could
never have married the big decent Quaker after finding out
about the letter. He might swear that he had never believed
a word but she knew men well enough to realize that no matter how much he might love her, there would come a time
when he would wonder, despite himself.

So poor Edward's misfortune had given her the means of
turning Robert away, at last. George had said it for her: "If
you or y'r trouble-makin' father ever set foot on Part-of-
Providence again, I'll shoot ye like I would a mad dog, I
swear it." And nothing Philip had said in Robert's defense
had budged George a hairsbreadth.

Millie stuck her finger with her needle and swore vividly
before she remembered the baby might be within earshot.
"I can't help it," she complained when the other two giggled
like schoolgirls. "Why can't Ethel run off and get marrit,
'stead of puttin' us to all this trouble, sewin' gowns f'r her
stylish weddin'?"

If anything could have shaken Edward out of his daze, it
would have been the knowledge of Ethelind Dedshall's forthcoming marriage to Rufus Jamieson, Edmund Fanning's righthand man. Becky knew, because Philip had told her privately,

that it was Jamieson who had sent the Regulators to the Dedshall house that black day, three years before, but even if Ethelind knew of his action, it hadn't mattered a whit. Ethelind, now thirty, had given up hope of finding a husband, and even Becky had to admit that the twice-widowed Jamieson was a fine figure of a man. He was also a bully who would use a heavy hand if Ethel didn't learn to keep her mouth shut.

If only he would take Ethelind's three brothers along with her and her money, Becky sighed inwardly. *But no, we're stuck with David and Francis and most of all, Edward, for the rest of time.*

Even though she wished that the Dedshall boys would be taken off their hands, she never felt that way about Millie. Elizabeth needed her too much. But if she knew the signs, Mainwaring Burnett would be taking the redheaded spitfire out of the Allyn family circle before too long. Becky sighed and nipped a thread. It would be a good match and God knew Millie deserved some happiness. As did Elizabeth. If Edward would only die, mayhap the oldest Burnett son, Jaimie, might . . .

"Did you say Ethelind wrote that Rector Micklejohn's going to marry her?" Elizabeth asked breaking into the busy silence.

"Aye, in St. Matthews Church," Millie replied. " 'Twill be the grandest affair since—what's that?"

The three women raised their heads, listening. There was a faint shout down by the indigo factory, a dog's urgent yelping, and then silence. "Prob'ly Langhorn talkin' politics to some tree," Millie said, after a pause. "Since George and Philip rode off to see about buyin' that land, Langhorn's been playin' lord o' the manor to the hilt, I'll be bound."

"Whilst Langhorn's son, Henry, has been moonin' after a certain red-haired miss so much he's been lettin' the nigras do everythin' wrong," Rebecca said.

Millie laughed. "Moonin', is he? Then I wisht he'd tell me what he's doin'—I thought he was colicky." She turned to Elizabeth. "Was he so strange-actin' when he had his heart set on you?" she asked. "I vow, I've done about everything except—"

"Oh, hush," Elizabeth broke in, her face turning crimson. Silently, she damned her weakness for blushing at the mention of the one time Henry Langhorn had kissed her. "If you don't stop, I'll tell Becky what I heard Main Burnett say last night when you thought I was asleep."

"Hmph, ye c'ld publish that in the Hillsboro *Gazette* and nobody'd be shocked," Millie said calmly. "There was a boy up in town that *really* said things. Why, d'ye know what he said to me one night? We was—"

She stopped again as more shouting sounded in the distance. Uneasily, Becky turned to Elizabeth and asked, "Who's with him, Rus?"

Elizabeth shook her head. "Nobody's with him. He was so quiet and—and agreeable I didn't think he needed anybody. Sometimes he almost seems to beg me to leave him alone and so I—"

Becky was on her feet, her sewing cast aside, and almost running down the hall toward the back bedchamber where Edward Dedshall lived his life. She slid back the outside bolt and flung open the door. She gasped and muttered a taut word under her breath as she saw the curtain flapping at the open window.

Behind her, Elizabeth uttered a choked cry. "But he was so *quiet!* Oh, Becky, where has he gone?"

"Don't worry," Millie said. "We'll find him before he gets far. I'll run blow the big horn and we'll get everybody lookin' f'r him."

Rebecca said, "No, not the horn—they'd hear it over at Burnett's and down at Grossman's and Father wouldn't like that. Millie, run tell Father what's happened whilst Betsy and I start callin' f'r him. He's prob'ly right around here sommers."

As Millie raced up the path to the big house, Rebecca and Elizabeth began calling Edward's name, knowing in their hearts that he would not answer if he heard, somehow knowing, too, that he had fled outside the range of their shrill voices.

William Weyland Allyn arrived on the scene at about the same time that John Langhorn came into view.

"Was that him we saw makin' out over the ridge?" Langhorn cried. "I yelled at him but he wouldn't stop. He was runnin' like a deer, sir. I took after him but he hit the woods like the Devil was after him."

William Allyn said in a quiet, steadying voice, "Have

Chanticleer saddled, Langhorn. I'll go after him and bring him back all safe and sound, I pledge you, daughter."

Elizabeth started to protest, then held her tongue. If there was anybody who could stop poor Edward's runaway attempt and bring him back, it was Father. Those terrible times when Edward had tried to—when his injuries had pained him too much to bear, it had been Father who had with a few soft words made Edward release her.

So, with her lips moving in prayer, she watched William Weyland Allyn ride off from Part-of-Providence. He rode purposefully, certain that he could deal with this misadventure quietly and swiftly, and without attracting the attention of anyone outside his family.

He was confident that he would find Edward somewhere along the Hillsboro Road. Twice before, his daft son-in-law had run away and each time he had been found blindly making his way to town. If he saw Chanticleer he was almost bound to come in. The animal seemed to hold a certain fascination for him in spite of the fact that Edward had cut a sorry figure in the saddle even when he had all of his senses.

Reaching a slight rise in the road, William Allyn reined in and stood in his stirrups to see if he could catch sight of the poor wretch. Nothing, except a cloud of dust some distance to the northeast in the direction of Hillsboro, a farmer taking a herd of cattle in to the town slaughterhouse, no doubt. He hoped the animals would not frighten Edward into hiding; cattle sometimes terrified him.

Perhaps, he thought, he should have brought a gang of slaves to fan out through the countryside but this would have attracted the attention of people who would spread the word that William Weyland Allyn's crazy son-in-law was on the loose again.

He knew that they gossiped about Edward, delighting in any misfortune that might befall the high 'n' mighty Allyns. Because he had refused to become involved with their petty embroilments, the ragtag-bobtail collection of little malcontents who called themselves the Alamance Regulators despised him; he knew this and it bothered him not at all.

He might have wished the situation were different if only to provide Part-of-Providence with more social life, but even if he did lower his standards and stand cheek-by-jowl with these yeomen, what then? Did anyone think he would permit

Rebecca or Elizabeth or even Millie Dedshall, now that she was his ward of sorts, to participate in any of the rude rustic turnouts that were the fashion in these parts? No, an occasional visit by the Burnetts and the Pardees, newly arrived from South Carolina, and the Youngs were quite enough for an old man. After he was gone, the boys and Rebecca could do what they liked about companionship but until he went, Part-of-Providence was under his stewardship.

The going would come sooner than his family suspected. Because it was an embarrassing, humiliating ailment—*though painful, Christ, how painful at times!*—he had visited no physician, taken neither George nor Philip and certainly not either of the girls, into his confidence. His body slave, Martin, was sworn to silence on threat of being sold and till now, at least, he had proved to be clever in keeping the bloody linens out of sight during their laundering or, in some instances, their burning.

He hoped that when this loathsome thing became too serious to hide, the end would come quickly. He had considered taking matters into his own hands only once when on a bleak night he had sat in his office, looking down at the pistol in the open top righthand drawer, and found himself overwhelmed by feelings of failure.

There was Mary's desertion, his flight from Virginia, his eviction from Middlebend—for that was what it had amounted to—the mistake he had made in giving his beloved daughter, Elizabeth, to the man who was now a mindless vegetable, and the coldness that had forced Rebecca into the arms of harebrained Harry Tarbell and had brought her all that misery. A catalog of his misdeeds and lacks seemed to add up to the fact that, nearing the end of his life, he was a very rich and very lonely old man.

Where were his friends? Dead or back on the Chowan that he should never have left, William Tryon and Daniel Maule be damned! William Sharpe, Foster Fentridge, Michael Singleton, Hugh Morton—he would never see them again.

Even the letters from Weyland, his eldest son, had been coming further and further apart, as though his son sought to sever all connection with his family.

William Allyn brought himself up sharply. Here he was deep in his own thoughts when he was supposed to be looking for poor Edward. And if Edward refused to come with him, what then? How could he struggle with a madman at his age when he was suffering from a fatal affliction?

His thoughts erratically returned again to the night he had almost used his pistol on himself to end the loneliness. It had been an odd experience, for when he had at last thrust away the temptation, snuffed the candle, and walked out of the office, he had almost collided with a figure in the hallway, a man so real that he had stepped back and begun an apology—then choked back his words as the figure faded before his eyes.

Who had it been, the ghost of the suicide, Horace Iglehart of Maple Hill on the Chowan, come to welcome him to the company of the damned, or a figment of his own desperate imagination? He had never told anyone of the incident and never would, but to his dying day he would believe that he had seen *something*.

He rounded a bend, then reined in as a man rose from the roadside weeds and held up a hand. "Ye can't go further," he told Allyn. "Turn back if ye know what's good f'r ye."

"You dare to give me orders, fellow? Stand aside before I use my crop on you."

The yeoman recognized him then and used a different tone. "Y'r pardon, Squire Allyn, but there's goin' to be bad trouble ahead in a minute. Ye can see for y'rself." He turned and gestured at the cleared fields in the valley below.

Allyn stared. The field nearest him was jammed with farmers, some with clubs, some with pitchforks and scythes, a few with weapons. Milling about uncertainly, they were talking loudly enough for him to hear. Obviously, they were trying to keep up their courage, and that of their fellows', with wild boasts of what they'd do when they met Bloody Guts Tryon and kicked his arse all the way back to New Berne and beyond.

"Regulators," the man explained needlessly. "I'm a sentry, like. And look there—here comes Tryon and the whole eastern hundreds militia, God damn their eyes."

As William Allyn watched, a line of horse troops topped the slight ridge on the opposite side of the road from the massed Regulators. A Grand Union flag flapped lazily from the staff carried by the horseman who stood next to the mounted officer in red tunic, cockaded hat, white vest, white breeches, glistening thigh-length black boots, and gold epaulets. William Weyland Allyn immediately recognized that officer. He was William Tryon, late lieutenant-colonel of His Majesty's First Foot, now Royal Governor of the Colony of North Carolina.

Allyn started to swing Chanticleer around. This was the long-awaited confrontation between the rebel rabble and the forces of authority and he must not be anywhere in the vicinity of the massacre that was about to start. He had taken a solemn oath of fealty to uphold the King and all his officers and oppose all instruments of rebellion. The search for Edward Dedshall would have to wait.

He nudged his stallion with a heel, then reined in again as the sentry grunted and cried, "Hully jeezes, what's that goddam fool tryin' to do?"

Even before he focused his old eyes on the tall, ill-clad figure who wobbled down the road between the two armies, he knew who it was.

"Halt!" came the cry from the mounted militia.

"Come back here, you fool!" somebody in the Regulators' ranks yelled.

Let him go, poor Edward. 'Tis the answer to the sad problem.

But his daughter loved this creature. He was a member of the family of William Weyland Allyn and therefore his responsibility. Madman or not, he had to be brought to safety and returned to his wife.

"Hold, ye can't—" he heard the Regulator squawk as he spurred past. He thumped Chanticleer with his crop, bent low over the stallion's neck, his eyes on the crazy scarecrow who ambled off the dusty road, jumped the ditch and started running up the rise toward William Tryon and his troops.

"Halt or I fire! One . . . two . . ."

Back up the road, the sentry winced as the volley smashed the sudden stillness. "The crazy old bastard," he muttered sullenly. "It ain't my fault. I tried to stop him, didn't I?"

I earnestly petition Yr Lordships to give no Credence to Certain Distorted Reports that may have reached Your ears concerning the so-called Battle of the Alamance. On my oath, the Five Thousand assembled Rebels (there were actually 2,000 Regulators) *were given Ample Opportunity to lay down*

*their Arms before the Four Hundred and Thirty Five gentle-
men Rankers under my Command (actually 1,200) were
forced to Defend themselves only after the rebels mounted
a Charge on our Position.*

*While it is true that a Gentleman, Squire W. Allyn of a
nearby Plantation & his Son in Law, E. Dedshall, both suffered Mortal Injuries through a Misunderstanding, all the
other Casualties were self-confessed Regulators. Proof of their
Rebellious Spirit can be found in the Fact that none of the six
Ringleaders hanged after the engagement expressed a Word
of Remorse or evidenced any Change of Heart.*

*Apart from the Regretable Deaths of Squire Allyn & D.,
this Encounter may be termed a Compleat Success. May it
please Yr Lordships to accept my assurances that the Spirit
of Rebellion has been Compleatly Crushed in the North Carolina Col. Word of the Battle of the Alamance will give Rebels
pause all through the other Colonies & assure Continued
Peace & Tranquility among His Majesty's Subjects in America.*

Yr Obt Svt.
Wm. Tryon, Gov.

New Berne, N.C.Col.
6 June 1771